THE QUESTION OF THE
MISSING HEAD

THE QUESTION OF THE
MISSING HEAD

AN ASPERGER'S MYSTERY

E. J. COPPERMAN

JEFF COHEN

MIDNIGHT INK
WOODBURY, MINNESOTA

Book design and format by Donna Burch-Brown
Cover design by Ellen Lawson
Cover Illustration: James Steinberg/Gerald and Cullen Rapp

Midnight Ink, an imprint of Llewellyn Worldwide Ltd.

ISBN 978-1-62953-303-2

Midnight Ink
Llewellyn Worldwide Ltd.
2143 Wooddale Drive
Woodbury, MN 55125-2989

Printed in the United States of America

DEDICATION

For everyone who is just a little bit different.
And you know who you are.

AUTHORS' NOTE

Collaboration on a writing project is never a simple thing, and this book is no exception. Writers have egos like everyone else, only more, and that means we had to compromise, each of us, from time to time in order to present Samuel's story in the best possible way. Working together is a learning experience, or so they tell us.

Nonetheless, this book couldn't have been written by just one of us. E.J. would like to thank Jeff for the cornier jokes we included, for the inside knowledge of living with an "Aspie," and for the mid-afternoon runs to Dunkin' Donuts for iced decaf, which sometimes even was. Jeff would like to thank E.J. for the adherence to a strong plot, the justifications for some of the more outrageous chapter endings, and for "Janet Washburn" especially, since her name had gone through about seven different permutations before hitting on the right sound.

The book you are (hopefully) about to read would never have reached your hands if not for the dogged determination of Josh Getzler at Hannigan Salky Getzler Agency. The authors probably would have given up about six times during the process, but Josh would not, and he found the series its very congenial home. Thanks also to Maddie Raffel and Danielle Burby, who at various times during the process had to deal with our lunacy and seemed not to mind.

Of course, the authors are in eternal debt to Terri Bischoff at Midnight Ink, who read Samuel's story and wanted you to have the same opportunity. That is a lovely thing for authors to experience, and we are thrilled that Terri responded so strongly to our story of a guy who isn't like most people.

Special thanks to Luci Hannson Zahray, known affectionately and respectfully throughout the crime fiction community as "The

Poison Lady." Luci is an absolutely essential resource to a writer who wants to kill someone, and when she shows up at a mystery book convention, no one ever lets her buy a drink. We're afraid to.

Thanks also to the indispensible D.P. Lyle, the crime doctor, who actually knows the boiling point of liquid nitrogen and such. We were both English majors, and so desperately need help when actual science is involved.

We believe we should also thank anyone who has ever met someone like Samuel—and we know a few ourselves—and seen the person, not the differences. It is Samuel's gift to use his own "quirks" to his advantage and that of others. If we all have a little bit more sensitivity to those who are demonstrably not like us, we might find that everyone benefits.

Thanks, finally, to you, because authors without readers are people screaming into a strong wind. We appreciate your looking up from your smartphone and choosing to take in a story the old-fashioned way, even if you're doing so electronically. We write because everybody can't fit around the campfire and, besides, there are bears in the woods. So keep doing what you're doing, and we'll try to keep our promises. How's that?

—E. J. Copperman and Jeff Cohen

ONE

THE TELEPHONE RANG.

It had probably rung two or three times before, but I hadn't noticed. It's not unusual for me to be consumed in thought and to ignore distractions, although others believe them to be important signals.

Personally, I don't understand why a ringing telephone should take precedence over a question I've been asked to answer, but there is a practicality to it—I do offer a service, and I won't find many new clients if I refrain from answering the phone. It is difficult, however, to train myself to notice such things when an intriguing issue is foremost in my mind.

I had been concentrating on the solution to a question that had occupied the better part of two hours. When I noticed the phone ringing, I noted the caller ID, which read *Taylor* with a phone number underneath, and reached for it.

"Questions Answered," I said into the mouthpiece. It goes against what I have trained myself to do: say "hello" whenever answering a phone. But for business purposes, it's necessary to reassure callers they have reached the entity they set out to find. It had only taken three weeks of trying for me to retrain myself, which I considered quite efficient. I was still working on the tone I used when speaking. Some people say my voice doesn't have much inflection on the phone. I don't hear a problem.

"Hello?" a woman's voice said. She didn't say anything else, which I thought was odd.

After a moment, I said, "Yes?"

"I have a question," she said.

"I assumed that." After all, the name of my agency is Questions Answered. I think some "typical" people overlook the obvious in favor of the distractions they think people like me miss.

"How much will the answer cost?"

"Is that your question?" I asked.

"No."

Again, for some reason, she said no more.

It occurred to me that she might want some encouragement. I wouldn't need any if I were calling an agency that offered to answer my questions, but I have come to understand that not everyone thinks in the way that I do. "What is your question?" I asked.

"Well, it's sort of complicated," the woman said. I checked the caller ID on the phone. According to her phone number's exchange, she was calling from Cranford, New Jersey, approximately seventeen miles from my office. "See, I was recently laid off from my job. I was a photographer at the *Home News-Tribune*, and they had to cut back on staff. So I spend a lot of time at home now, and I was sitting here doing the *New York Times* crossword puzzle."

I had stopped listening eight seconds earlier. "You are a photographer?" I asked. A photographer could be helpful in the work I'd been doing all morning.

The woman, whose voice put her in her early thirties, sounded surprised. "Yes," she said. "That's what I do. What will it cost to answer my question?"

"Your question will be answered with no charge," I told her, "if you come to our office at 735 Stelton Road in Piscataway." And I hung up the phone. Then it occurred to me that perhaps I should have said "good-bye" before I did that. Sometimes it slips my mind.

From Cranford would be a twenty-two-minute drive. There was nothing I could do but wait.

I had opened Questions Answered three months earlier and had provided service to only a handful of clients so far. I had done some advertising online, but the population on most social networking and service-sharing (classified ads) sites seemed interested in getting answers to questions about sex—questions I am not especially well qualified to answer. So a small advertisement on an inside page of the *New York Times* Arts section—which is less expensive than the news sections—had brought in three or four clients, but I was beginning to think that a local newspaper might be a better revenue generator.

Unfortunately, I read the *New York Times* and rely on no other offline news sources, so I'd have to ask my mother what other newspapers in our area might be appropriate.

Mother was supportive of the business, happy, I thought, to see me doing something other than Internet research in my attic apartment. I had to admit, answering other people's questions had provided me with more interesting avenues for my research.

I stood up, because I hadn't stood in twenty-three minutes, and I had resolved to do so three times per hour. The phone call had thrown me off my schedule. I walked around the office, flexing the muscles in my upper legs and raising my arms above my head as I went. It is important to periodically raise the heart rate and promote proper flow of blood through the system.

The room is relatively large, or at least appears so because it is almost entirely empty. I rented a former pizza restaurant named San Remo's when the owners had retired to that very region of Italy. Being retired, they had no need for most of the fixtures in the building, so there was still a large, unused pizza oven in the back of the room and a soda machine that I contracted to be stocked with green tea and spring water approximately once a week by a man named Les.

When I had finished six laps around the office, which constituted one-third of a mile, I reached into the change pocket of my gray pants to find five quarters, so I could buy a bottle of water from my drink machine. I would receive fifty cents back when Les came to collect the money.

I sat back down at the desk and looked at the time on the screen of my Mac Pro. Twenty-seven minutes since I had disconnected the phone.

The woman was late.

Distressed, I didn't pay attention to the rate of speed with which I drank the water, and I emptied the bottle in only four minutes. That was not good; I couldn't allow myself to get a new bottle for another twenty minutes, and I might have to use the bathroom sooner than I'd planned, which was a minor concern. Cranford was only a twenty-two-minute drive; there was no reason for her to be this long overdue.

Had there been a car accident? Had she failed to get proper directions? Perhaps I should have directed her here when we'd spoken. It had not occurred to me that someone might not know how to get to an office she'd called on the phone.

Perhaps she'd simply decided not to come. Should I call her back? I needed her to arrive soon.

I decided against dialing the number on the caller ID. It would have been my first choice in the past, but Mother had convinced me that people sometimes feel uncomfortable with those they don't know calling or visiting their residences. She called it "stalking." I had thought it was simply trying to establish communication.

My mother generally understands these things better than I do.

But another ten minutes crawled by, and my patience was thinning. Either this woman was rude, or I had done something to convince her not to come. I'd have to go back over the conversation mentally to determine if I'd said something that could be perceived as odd.

At 8:57, a blue Kia Spectra, six years old, parked in the painted space outside my storefront. The owners of the strip mall where my office sits had provided each business with four dedicated parking spaces, and there were the requisite number of spaces reserved for those with physical handicaps. But the businesses here were not attracting much traffic, so it was always easy to find an available space, Mother had told me when she dropped me off one morning.

A woman of about thirty-one got out of the Spectra and seemed to assess my storefront. I'd painted a sign on a large canvas reading QUESTIONS ANSWERED and hung it in the front window, because a larger sign over the door would have been much too expensive. I did not expect much walk-in business, so a professionally designed sign was a luxury that could wait for another time.

The woman turned to open the car door, but then looked like she was reconsidering. I wondered if I should go outside and ask her in, but that might be seen as "stalking." Besides, this might not be the woman who had called on the phone earlier. She did not appear to have a camera with her.

Finally, the bell over the front door rang, but she didn't so much enter as lean in. "Hello?" she asked. The woman's voice was the one I'd heard on the phone.

"It has been thirty-eight minutes since we spoke," I said. "It should take only twenty-two minutes to drive here from Cranford. You are late."

Her eyebrows rose, then fell. I've seen that expression before, and it seems to mean that I've said something confusing. "I took a shower," the woman said.

I didn't know her well enough to make a Beatles reference. Again, Mother has told me that some people find my interest in the band unusual, or "obsessive," where I merely like to accumulate information on topics that I find interesting. If I had known this woman better, I probably would have referenced "A Day in the Life," whose lyrics involve getting ready in the morning.

"You are Ms. Taylor?" I said.

The woman gave the door a glance, perhaps pondering whether to leave. "No. Taylor is my husband's name. This is Questions Answered?" she said.

It took me a moment to realize she was asking, and not stating. "Yes."

The woman took some time to think about that, but she eventually took a visible breath and said, "I'm Janet Washburn. How did you know I was coming from Cranford?"

"I have caller ID," I answered. "Your exchange gave me your location." I realized I wasn't making eye contact with her—I had been looking at my computer screen and the door—so I forced myself to do so now.

"You looked up my telephone exchange on the computer?" she asked. She was of average height, blond, and brown-eyed. I didn't think her hair was dyed, but it was possible.

I shook my head. "No. I memorize them."

"You remember every telephone exchange in the area code?" People often find that surprising. For me, it's a talent, like being able to juggle. I can't juggle, but I can memorize mathematical patterns when I try.

"No," I told her. "All the exchanges in the country. I'm working on some of the ones in Western Europe now."

Ms. Washburn seemed especially impressed by that; her mouth seemed to form words and then discard them before she could vocalize them. "Who ... *are* you?" she asked after the third try.

I knew how to do this—I put out my right hand and said, "Allow me to introduce myself. I am Samuel Hoenig."

She hesitated but took my hand. "Nice to meet you. Do they call you Sam?"

What did that mean? "Who?"

"I don't know. Your friends."

I shook my head. "I am Samuel." I did not feel it necessary to tell her I had very few friends.

Ms. Washburn nodded. "I have a question."

"You don't have a camera," I said. Had she been lying about being a photographer?

Again, the eyebrow movement, but quicker this time. "I left it in the car."

"It's not doing any good there," I told her. "Go get it."

She looked surprised, but she went out and retrieved a camera case from the trunk of the car. She came back into the office and stood a few feet from my desk, as if she were afraid I might pounce like a tiger.

Before I could explain what I wanted her to do, Ms. Washburn said, "Pardon me for asking, but do you have Asperger's Syndrome?"

Damn. She knew.

TWO

I AM NOT ASHAMED of my Asperger's Syndrome; why should I be? It is something that has given me aspects of my personality I find very useful. But I prefer to choose when to tell an acquaintance about it, if at all. And when someone confronts me with the question, as Janet Washburn had just done, I am momentarily unnerved.

Asperger's is a "disorder" (although I consider it merely a personality trait) on the autism spectrum. People who don't have it—and some who do—believe it to be a defect, a problem in communicating with or relating to others. They think, to be concise, that we are odd.

I consider most "typical" people odd, and believe that by contrast, I act quite rationally. But there aren't enough of us to constitute a majority, and we don't all behave the same way. Find six people with Asperger's Syndrome, and you will find six people who don't necessarily relate to each other any better than they do to strangers.

"I'm sorry," Ms. Washburn said when I didn't answer. "Did I embarrass you?"

That's an example of the kind of assumption I'm discussing. Because I'm not like her, Ms. Washburn believed I would somehow find my own personality objectionable, and so mentioning it would be an embarrassment.

"No," I told her. "You simply caught me by surprise. Yes, I have been diagnosed with Asperger's Syndrome. I'm surprised you could recognize it so quickly."

She appeared to be pleased, as if I had given her a compliment. "I used to be a substitute teacher," she said. "They gave us a course in autism spectrum disorders so we could recognize them and help the children in class."

I was given a diagnosis of Asperger's Syndrome when I was sixteen years old, so many of the therapies and techniques small children often receive today were not offered to me. My mother, however, did ask my high school for some support, and was roundly denied. She sent me to see Dr. Mancuso out of her own pocket. The legal battle with the school system went on for years, and in the end, Mother did not prevail.

"How fast is the shutter on your camera?" I asked Ms. Washburn, glad for a reason to change the subject. "I need photographs of a body in motion."

"What body?" she asked.

"Mine."

Ms. Washburn gave me an odd look for a moment, which I mentally resolved to ask Mother about later. I couldn't remember saying or doing anything that would generate such a response.

"What will you be doing?" she asked after a moment.

"Ah." I held up a finger, then walked to the desk, reached down, and picked up the baseball bat I had placed on the floor this morning. I picked it up to show it to her.

"Take it easy, Reggie," she said. She took a step backward.

"My name is Samuel," I reminded her. But I noticed—and this was due to a good deal of practice—that she was staring at the bat. It must have been a reference to the Hall of Fame baseball player Reggie Jackson. "Oh. Did you think I was going to hit you with this?"

"I was trying not to."

How odd. People don't hit people with baseball bats; they hit baseballs with baseball bats. "Of course not," I assured her. "I want you to photograph me swinging this bat."

Another odd look. "Why?"

"That is the interesting part," I told her. "Come see." I gestured toward the computer screen, and Ms. Washburn, after seeming to consider her next move, walked to the desk and looked. "You're aware that there is a new Yankee Stadium, are you not?"

"The one that replaced the House That Ruth Built? The jazzed-up version built to supplant an eighty-six-year-old cathedral of baseball? The bandbox with a Hard Rock Cafe in it? *That* new Yankee Stadium?"

It is always a mistake to assume that people will conform to stereotypes. It's taken me years to understand, but incident after incident has proven to me that one must see hard evidence before making a statement. Most women are not interested in sports like baseball, but some are. It's possible to make an assumption based on probability, but it is not a reliable way to decide a question.

"Good," I said. "So you probably also know that no home run—that is, no ball in play—was ever hit completely out of the original Yankee Stadium in the eighty-five years it stood."

"Eighty-six," she said. "Yes, I'm aware. I'm also aware that Mickey Mantle's lifetime batting average was two-ninety-eight. How does that relate to me taking pictures of you swinging a bat?"

I had to admit, her response also made me wonder if Ms. Washburn had a "special interest" in the New York Yankees, similar to mine in police procedure, baseball overall, and the Beatles.

"I have a client whose question is about the change in ballparks," I said. "He is considering making a wager that changes in the wind current resulting from a slightly different location would make it possible for someone to hit a home run all the way out of the new stadium in its first twenty years. Quite a sizable wager."

She narrowed her eyes. "So . . ."

"So I have considered all the science involved and have concluded he is mistaken. But my client is the type of man who does not believe in statistics; he is more given to visual evidence. I'd like you to take photographs of me swinging the bat, then upload them to my computer simulation of the building. I can demonstrate, then, how the air currents—which do allow for more home runs to certain areas of the park—will not compensate for the size of the building and the physics involved."

Ms. Washburn's eyes softened. She nodded her understanding. "I can do better than that," she said. "I can take short digital video and you can have a full-motion swing that you can freeze whenever you like in your simulation."

"How high will the video quality be?" I asked.

"HD," said Ms. Washburn.

"Excellent."

We spent a few minutes determining the best angle for the photography, and Ms. Washburn suggested my standing near the front window. She explained that although she could digitally isolate my image from the background, the lighting near the window would be most natural, and would not make the image we created look disturbingly different from the rest of the frame.

She took video of five different swings. I was careful to use an uppercut stroke, to simulate a batter trying to hit the ball high and far. On the fifth try, we agreed we had usable video.

We uploaded the video to my Mac Pro, but just as we were about to examine it, the front door opened, the bell rang, and a man of about fifty entered the office. I couldn't read his initial expression—his nostrils flared and his upper lip receded—but I took it to be something other than a positive one.

"This isn't Questions Answered," he said, seemingly to himself.

Again, it took me a moment to respond, since this obviously *was* Questions Answered, and the man was wrong. But in the interim, Ms. Washburn stepped in front of me and said, "It certainly is. Were you *looking* for Questions Answered?"

That seemed equally odd, since the man had walked into a building he assumed was not my business. Why do that? But after wrinkling his brow, he nodded. "Yes. I have a problem that needs to be solved."

"We don't solve problems," I said, having had this conversation with a number of people on a number of occasions. "We answer questions." Mother had suggested I say *we*, rather than *I*. She said it

13

would be more businesslike if I gave the impression of having a staff of experts on hand. I thought that was dishonest, but I acceded to her judgment, as I often do.

The man seemed to gather himself, although the top of his bald head was glistening with sweat. He was nervous, or feverish. My best guess was nervous.

"I was recommended to you by my friend Ellen Crenshaw," he said, approaching me. "I am Dr. Marshall Ackerman."

As I've practiced, I repeated my greeting, extending my hand. "Allow me to introduce myself. I am Samuel Hoenig."

"Yes." Ackerman seemed disappointed that I am myself, which made no sense at all. It was a reaction I'd seen before, but it still baffled me.

"I recall Ms. Crenshaw," I said, hoping to put him at ease. "She asked where her missing Boa constrictor might be, as I remember."

Ms. Washburn's eyes widened a bit.

I did indeed remember Ms. Crenshaw. Our business had been slightly contentious—she had wanted to receive an insurance settlement rather than retrieve the odd animal she'd been keeping as a pet, and I had spoiled things by actually finding the snake.

"Yes," Ackerman repeated. "Ellen said your service was effective and discreet."

"She had an unusual question," I said. "How do you know Ms. Crenshaw?"

"We served on the board of a foundation together a few years ago," Ackerman said. "We remained friends, and during a conversation a few weeks ago, she mentioned your service. She said your methods were impressive, if a little ... unusual."

"For service that is usual, you can go anywhere," Ms. Washburn said. Her face had an expression I read as a trifle angry, perhaps more irritated. "For service that's special, you need Mr. Hoenig." I thought that was generous of her, especially since I had not yet answered a question for Ms. Washburn. She was proving to be quite helpful.

"Pardon me," Ackerman said. "But my business with Mr. Hoenig is private." His manner suggested that he was accustomed to having people behave in the way he preferred, and not in any other.

I did notice that my own feelings were stirred. I didn't care for the way Ackerman was dismissing Ms. Washburn, especially when she had been so kind as to champion my services. "Anything you have to say to me can be said in front of Ms. Washburn," I told him. "She is my most trusted professional associate." I'm not sure exactly why I said that, but it wasn't untrue—I had been working with Ms. Washburn prior to Ackerman's entrance, after all, and since I had no other professional associates, she was by default the most trusted. She was also the least trusted, but I saw no reason to mention that.

Ms. Washburn, upon hearing my statement, coughed slightly, looked into my eyes—I made sure to be looking back—and nodded toward me. A sign of appreciation, I believed.

"And anything you say to us will be held in the strictest confidence," she added. I nodded back. "Won't you sit down?" She indicated the chair in front of my desk, where Ackerman sat. I stayed behind the desk and made a mental note to bring another chair from home to the office, since Ms. Washburn was now left standing, leaning on the baseball bat near the desk. I wondered if I should

15

offer her my chair, or if that would be considered a sexist gesture. It is difficult to know.

"Let me begin by telling you why I'm here," Ackerman said. "I am the chief administrator for the Garden State Cryonics Institute."

I had done some research on the topic on a whim one day four years earlier, when there had been a news item in the *New York Times* regarding such a facility in California. "So you are involved in freezing the bodies of people who have just died in the hope that someday there will be a means to reanimate them and cure their illnesses, is that right?"

"I don't expect everyone to agree with what we do," Ackerman answered.

"I neither agree nor disagree," I told him. "I don't think the science has been proven to either point of view yet. I just wanted to be sure that is the nature of your business."

Ackerman nodded, seeming gratified with my knowledge of his work. "That is what we do," he said. "We give people a chance at a new life, once science manages to progress to that point."

"And you charge them a flat fee, or a storage fee, in perpetuity, until that time arrives, is that so?" Sitting behind the desk might have been a mistake; I felt distracted by the image of Yankee Stadium on my computer screen, and returned to my thinking about the final presentation for my gambling client, Joseph Teradino. It occurred to me that the differences in signage at the new Yankee Stadium could make a marginal difference in the flight of the ball, but that it was probably not important to the question.

"We do charge a fee," Ackerman answered, bringing my attention back to him. "We're not a charity, and the government doesn't fund our research in any way. We couldn't be expected to keep these people preserved properly for years, or decades, even centuries, and absorb the cost ourselves. There wouldn't be enough money to keep them preserved after a month."

"Once again, I wasn't accusing you," I said. "I'm just trying to establish the basis for your question." I waved a hand to indicate he should go on.

"You'd be amazed how many people think we're charlatans," Ackerman said, apparently unable to let the point go. "I get told, to my face, that I'm stealing their money and giving their families false hope, more often than you can possibly imagine."

Perhaps he needed a prod toward business. Certainly, I was anxious to return to the task Ms. Washburn and I had been performing. "What is your question?" I asked him again.

"Well, Mr. Hoenig, one of our heads is missing."

THREE

"THAT IS A PROBLEM, not a question," I informed Ackerman.

It took him a long moment of reflection, but he composed himself and said, very deliberately, "Who stole one of our heads, Mr. Hoenig?"

"Now, *that* is an interesting question!" And it was. I had opened the office because I hoped to be challenged by unusual questions, and this was one you very rarely heard in conversation. "What makes you think someone *stole* the head, Dr. Ackerman?" I asked.

Ackerman looked stunned. "Um ... because it's no longer there," he said. "They don't just walk away on their own."

"No," I agreed, "but they could be misplaced, misfiled, misidentified. The cranium in question might have been destroyed unintentionally. It could simply have been stored in the wrong location. Why do you assume that it was stolen?"

"There's a procedure we use to log in every guest," Ackerman said. I surmised that the word *guest* was applied to anyone whose remains, either in total or just the cranium, would be brought to his facility for cryonic preservation. "It ensures that nothing can go wrong. It guarantees we know the whereabouts of every guest at every minute of every day. And yet this guest, Ms. Rita Masters-Powell, whose position was monitored at all times and had been constant for four months, suddenly vanished with no warning and no alarm whatsoever. It doesn't make sense. She wasn't being introduced to the facility, and she wasn't being moved. There's no other possibility."

It rankles me when people come to conclusions without examining every fact, but I did not express that irritation to Ackerman. It doesn't serve any useful purpose to do so, in my experience. I remembered to look him in the eye, and said, "There are any number of possibilities, Dr. Ackerman, but until I am able to see the facility, examine your security measures, and interview the personnel involved, I cannot definitively answer your question."

"Then will you come and take a look, please?"

I hesitated. There was still the Yankee Stadium question to address, and Ms. Washburn's question, whatever it might be. But Ackerman must have seen the reluctance in my expression, because he quickly said, "I'll be happy to double your normal fee."

The rent on the office was $2,479 per month. Utilities were $862 on the plan I'd chosen, which bills the user for the same amount, calculated by the utility company, each month. The drink machine cost nothing to rent, but each bottle of green tea or water cost a final amount of $0.75, and because I usually purchased at least eight drinks per day, the cost per month was approximately $132. In the interest of economy, I had resolved to buy fewer bottles of water, and refill the used ones, although the idea did make me feel slightly nauseated.

But I did not answer Ackerman immediately, as I was making those calculations mentally. Instead, Ms. Washburn said, "Triple it and it's a deal."

Startled as I was by her bold action, I tried not to swivel my head toward Ms. Washburn very quickly. I have been told sudden movements like that tend to disturb people, and I have practiced controlling my reactions for most of my life. Besides, it was best not to alert Ackerman to my surprise.

"Done," Ackerman said. He smiled strangely. "Mr. Hoenig?" He gestured toward the office door. It was interesting that he had agreed to the terms without even asking what my normal fee might be.

"We will follow you," I said, and Ackerman nodded. He walked to the door and went outside.

Ms. Washburn waited until he was out of earshot before saying, "What do you mean, 'we'll follow you'? I don't really work here."

"You said you had lost your job at the newspaper," I reminded her. "This is a chance to do some work and receive some salary. It will be just for today."

She squinted at me, as if I were very far away. "What is it I'm supposed to do?" she asked.

"At the moment, drive me to Ackerman's office. I do not drive." That was not entirely true—I have a valid license, but I almost never use it. I am a safe driver, but not a fast or comfortable one. I had not driven in months.

Ms. Washburn shook her head, just a bit, as she headed for the door, reaching for her car keys.

FOUR

THE GARDEN STATE CRYONICS Institute was located in North Brunswick, in a small gray building off US Highway 1, not far from a bowling alley and a car dealership. It took Ms. Washburn sixteen minutes to drive there, following Ackerman's car all the way.

When we found parking spaces and got out of the car, she looked at the building the way one might look at a distasteful photograph. "I don't like this," she said. "It's too ordinary to be a place where people come to be regenerated in the thirty-sixth century."

"It houses a facility that allows for the proper temperatures, backup utilities, and other necessities for maintaining the subzero conditions that make cryonics possible," I told her. "The fact is, the people who come here probably aren't very concerned with the aesthetics of the building." I thought that was an amusing remark, but Ms. Washburn stared at me a moment and then followed me as I approached the institute's main entrance, where Marshall Ackerman was standing.

"Welcome to the Garden State Cryonics Institute," he said. It seemed to me that he had given the sentence a grandeur the occasion did not merit, but sometimes inflection is a trouble area for me, so I assumed I was misinterpreting his tone until I saw the unimpressed look on Ms. Washburn's face.

"Thank you," I said, because that's what you're supposed to say when someone welcomes you, even if you don't find the surroundings particularly welcoming.

We walked inside, and Ackerman led us through the doors to the small, impersonal reception area. The building was more imposing inside than out—there was bright light and an air of more recent redecoration, and it was deceptively large. The lobby also had a reception desk, behind which sat a young woman in her mid-twenties who looked worried. Ackerman had us pass her station and walk toward the rear of the lobby.

There, a burly, bald man he introduced as Commander Johnson scowled at us and spoke only to Ackerman. He was flanked by two security guards dressed in what appeared to be the institute's uniform. They were unarmed.

"We shouldn't be letting outsiders go down there," he said. I found the statement interesting, particularly if Commander Johnson was in fact a military officer of some kind. If so, he would probably be most concerned with protocol, and I wondered, then, why he wasn't insisting the police be notified.

"They're here to help," Ackerman barked back, and it seemed to me he would prefer Commander Johnson keep his voice down, something my mother often asks me to do when I am passionate about my point, like when someone suggests U2 is a better band than the Beatles. Ackerman turned to us. "Commander Johnson is our head of security," he explained.

"Then I suppose he is at fault in the disappearance," I noted. It seemed a logical assumption to make—the head of security is responsible for any breach that occurs under his watch—but both Ackerman's and Commander Johnson's eyes widened, and Ackerman made a point of rushing us past the security personnel, through a door, and down a corridor. He ushered us into an elevator that was at the end of the corridor.

"We'll be seeing the area where Ms. Masters-Powell—Rita—was being preserved," he said once the elevator doors closed. It seemed Ackerman was being confidential, since he'd waited until we were out of the sight and hearing of any other employees before mentioning our business there again. "You can examine the security measures yourself."

I didn't say anything about that sentence containing a redundancy and concentrated my attention on the question at hand. How could I determine if Ms. Masters-Powell's head had been stolen, misplaced, or destroyed?

The answer would no doubt lie in the records kept and the security procedures. If there were, for example, a constant video surveillance system, it would have recorded the space into which the remains were deposited at the time of arrival, and then, assuming the system was being properly operated and supervised, each minute until the time the disappearance was discovered. The question would then be a relatively simple one of access, motive, and ability to tamper with the security system.

"Who has access to the security equipment?" I asked as the elevator doors opened at the B level, which I assumed stood for *basement*. The other three levels were marked with numbers, and the top level from which we'd come was designated G for *ground*.

Ackerman looked as if I'd struck him in the back. He swiveled quickly and said, "*Please* keep your voice down, Mr. Hoenig. I don't want the staff to know about the ... incident just yet."

"Would they hear us if we were just speaking normally?" Ms. Washburn asked. I was impressed, as that was the next question I would have asked, although I already knew the answer. I wanted to see how Ackerman would respond.

"Yes, there is audio surveillance in most areas, as well as constant video monitoring," he answered, pointing to video cameras mounted on the walls near the ceiling, to cover every angle. Each camera also had a directional microphone attached above the lens.

He saw Ms. Washburn reaching for her cell phone and said, "Don't bother. You won't be able to get a signal down here. Cell phones will only work internally here; you'd be able to get a call from someone else on the grounds."

"I need to call my husband," she said.

Ackerman nodded. "There are land lines downstairs; you can use those."

"I presume the hard drives storing the video records have been checked, and that no tampering has been found," I said, returning to the subject at hand.

"That's right," Ackerman noted. "I can't imagine how it ... *she* was smuggled out of here."

"Perhaps someone outside the institute needs to examine the system," I suggested. "If the thief is someone who works here, he or she could easily be covering up any tampering that was done."

"I don't believe anyone on my staff could be responsible," Ackerman said with a gruff tone.

"I don't see it as likely that it was someone else," I countered, but he simply cleared his throat and did not respond.

The elevator doors opened, and we stepped out into a hallway. Ackerman led us to the right, then down past a number of unmarked steel doors.

"Has there been any contact about a ransom demand?" I asked.

"No. I am hoping against hope that we can find Ms. Masters-Powell before there's any contact made." Ackerman took a handkerchief from his pocket and mopped at his forehead, although it was not at all warm in the institute's basement. I assumed air conditioning had to be maintained in all weather here.

I declined to comment that *hoping against hope* doesn't mean anything.

"Of course you'd want to find it soon," Ms. Washburn said, "but why the urgency about the time?"

Ackerman started to answer, but I felt it was important to impress him again, and I cut him off. "Because Dr. Ackerman has not informed Ms. Masters-Powell's family yet, and he's hoping there will never be a need to do so," I said.

Ackerman stared at me. "How did you know that?"

"Despite an almost absolute lack of competition, this facility is extremely dependent on its reputation," I said. "You've already alluded to some of the arguments against the service you provide. An incident like this one could cause considerable public outcry, and your business could very well be investigated by the authorities or disabled by a drop in confidence among your clients. You could be forced to discontinue your work altogether."

Marshall Ackerman looked positively ill at the suggestion. "The damage to our reputation could be enormous," he agreed. "This is something I . . . *we* need to be solved quickly. And there are practical, physical reasons for speed, as well."

"I would think so," I said as quietly as I could while we moved down the hallway. "If Ms. Masters-Powell's head has indeed been removed from storage and is not being cared for properly, it's very likely that you will not be able to restore it to an acceptable state even if it is returned. I'd think you need to find it within ten hours, unless you assume someone with extremely elaborate equipment is holding the item hostage."

We reached a door directly in the sight of three separate video cameras, mounted on the walls and pointed down from the ceiling. A sign on the door read PRESERVATION ROOM D. Ackerman pulled an encoded card from his wallet and swiped it through a reader on the door's right side.

A recording amplified through the corridor said, "Voice recognition pattern, please."

"Marshall Ackerman," he said in a conversational tone.

"Recognition acknowledged. Thumb print, please," the recording responded. Ackerman reached over with his right hand and placed the thumb on a scanner under the card reader.

"Accepted," the recording said. There were clicks from the door's locks as they opened, and a buzzer sounded; I cringed inwardly at the noise but tried not to show my discomfort—it is not unusual for those of us with Asperger's Syndrome to be sensitive to loud sounds. Ackerman opened the door and held it for myself and Ms. Washburn. We walked inside.

The room was similar to a physician's examination space, with stainless-steel procedure tables and a computer outfit on a workspace at one end. But one side of the room had windows instead of walls, and while they appeared to be made of glass, the thickness of the material and its color gave me the impression that it was something considerably more durable and stronger than a usual windowpane.

"That's the storage area," Ackerman explained. "As you can see, Mr. Hoenig, the security measures used to limit access to this section are extraordinary."

That was a bold statement, and I felt an inaccurate one. "I'd hardly say so," I told him. "I think the measures were quite ordinary and in use at many similar facilities striving for security. It's the number of measures that would be considered unusual, but none of them is foolproof by any means. Nothing is."

Ackerman curled his lip but did not try to debate me. "If you'll follow me, Mr. Hoenig, I'll show you the storage facility." He did not mention Ms. Washburn by name, but she followed behind me.

He indicated that we should don suits, hanging from hooks near the interior door, that were made of a yellow polymer material, with hoods that included windowed panels so we could see out. I wanted to ask if the suits had been worn by others before me, as I suspected they had been, and if so, what the cleaning procedure had been, but I held back. I'm not sure why. Ms. Washburn hesitated a moment, perhaps for the same reason, or perhaps out of claustrophobia or some general squeamish tendency, but she, too, took a deep breath and put on the suit over her clothing.

Ackerman did the same but without the hesitation; this was clearly routine procedure for him. In less than two minutes, we were all properly attired, and he reached over to a computer terminal. Even with the gloves that had been provided, he was able to punch in the proper sequence of keystrokes, and the screen read, *Access permitted.*

A red light over the interior door went on, and Ackerman walked to the door. "Don't touch anything inside," he warned. "It's all extremely cold and complex. Any inadvertent change in temperature to one of the tubes could cost these people their lives." Since they were already clinically dead, that seemed something of a hyperbolic statement, but I nodded, and he reached for the handle on the interior chamber door.

The handle turned, but the door would not move, no matter how hard he pushed.

"I don't understand," Ackerman said. "Can you help me, Mr. Hoenig?"

I didn't want to; pushing against a door that wouldn't open seemed futile, and doing so in such close proximity to Ackerman (or anyone else) was slightly sickening. But the only way to answer the question posed to me was to see the facility, and the only way to see the facility would be to open the door. I walked to his side.

"Could it be frozen?" Ms. Washburn asked.

I knew that the design of the chamber made such a thing impossible, but I did not think it was necessary for Ackerman to take a condescending tone when he said, "No, Ms. Washburn. It can't be *frozen*." I didn't think he'd been pleased to have her along during the entire trip to the facility.

"On three," he said to me. I don't understand why counting to three is supposed to increase physical strength. Why not just say, *now*? Why not count to five, or seven? Or simply start pushing and assume the other person will join the effort? But I didn't say anything, and Ackerman must have taken that for agreement. "One … two … three!"

We pushed, shoulders to the door, and it moved a few inches, not enough to get even a foot inside.

It was impossible to look through the thick steel door, but there were small glass windows on either side. "Ms. Washburn," I said, "look through there and tell me what you see." I realized later that I'd forgotten to say *please*, but Ms. Washburn did not seem offended.

She nodded and pushed her way around me to the window right of the door. She looked straight through the window, and her voice came back echoing off the glass.

"There are metal cylinders and large machines, maybe storage units," she said. "I don't see anything that looks wrong."

Ackerman and I had moved our feet to get better leverage and were still trying to push against the door. "Look down," I told Ms. Washburn. "See what is restricting the door's movement."

She did so, and gasped. "Oh my god," she said. "There's a woman on the floor."

Ackerman paled and pushed harder. The door nudged a few inches more, and I was able to get my right foot into the opening. With that, I could get sufficient leverage and open the door to the point that I could squeeze myself, even in the protective clothing, into the chamber. And I saw that Ms. Washburn had been correct: There was indeed a woman on the floor.

She was, from what I could see, quite dead.

FIVE

"DON'T TOUCH ANYTHING," I said to Ackerman and Ms. Washburn after they squeezed through the narrow opening. It was obvious now that the body of the unidentified woman had been wedged behind the door, making it difficult for us to enter. But the pushing of the door had not done significant damage to the body.

Being inside the chamber during a release of liquid nitrogen had.

"My lord," Ackerman said, instinctively putting his hand to his mouth in spite of the plastic lens covering his face. "It's Rebecca."

"What is the time?" I asked him urgently. Ackerman froze at my tone, but Ms. Washburn looked at a wall clock.

"Ten fifty-six," she reported.

"Thank you." Unlike some other people with Asperger's Syndrome, I had not required special social skills training in remembering to thank people. I had learned that at a very early age. My mother had made sure.

"Why do you ask?" Ackerman said. "Can you tell when she died?"

"No," I answered. "I have lunch with my mother every day at twelve thirty, and I wanted to be sure I would not be late."

Ackerman stared at me.

Ms. Washburn, I noticed, was standing as far from the body as she could, but I was impressed that she did not cry, she did not scream, and she did not show signs of being nauseated. I could not say the same for Ackerman. He looked like he might pass out at any moment. He seemed completely terrified.

"Who is . . . was Rebecca?" Ms. Washburn asked him.

"Rebecca Springer. Doctor Rebecca Springer. She was one of our staff specialists, part of the emergency response team that acts when one of our members is declared legally dead."

From my Internet research, I knew that Ackerman's company would send a team to the site (usually a hospital or hospice facility, but sometimes the home) where a patient was declared dead by a physician, and then would immediately take steps to prepare the body for preservation, including pumping the chest and keeping blood and oxygen flowing as long as possible to stave off an end to brain activity. Dr. Springer must have been one of the physicians, or a pathologist who would see to the body's welfare.

"You must go back out into the anteroom and call the police," I told him. "Ms. Washburn, if you would join Dr. Ackerman."

"What will you do?" Ackerman asked. Ms. Washburn looked grateful for the opportunity to leave the chamber.

"I will examine the scene for information that will help me answer your question," I told him. "And I will look for other data that might help the police answer their questions."

They squeezed through the door opening, Ms. Washburn leading the way, and I closed the door behind them, to better reproduce the conditions that were present before we had disturbed the door and the body. I did not touch anything, even with my hands in the cumbersome gloves.

The room was not as large as I had expected. There were fifteen cylinders for those who opted, like the late Ms. Masters-Powell, to have only their craniums preserved (a tactic I felt was less logical than the entire body preservation, since it assumed not only that medical science would find a cure for their terminal illness and a way to reanimate a body frozen at a very low temperature, but also that creating a body onto which a head could be transplanted would also be achieved) and ten full-body chambers.

If I were to answer the question about Ms. Masters-Powell's missing head, I would need more information before generating a theory—I didn't know which of the receptacles was hers, to begin with. But I could see the video surveillance cameras mounted on the ceiling pointed toward the storage units, and I could see the size of the room. It would have been difficult to remove anything from the chambers without being recorded.

That left a number of possibilities, but the most urgent matter at the moment was the body on the floor, so I knelt to examine it without touching it.

It didn't look different from any other corpse. I haven't seen many, but I have done some research on the subject. This one was a woman in her early forties, mouth open, eyes closed. No noticeable wounds or injuries. No marks of any kind. Just the usual waxy, stiff tone to the skin that is common to all deaths.

She was wearing relatively standard business clothing: A navy blue blouse and long black pants, black shoes with low heels, and a jacket that matched the pants. She looked as if she were heading for a meeting of executives and had fallen down, or fallen asleep.

I was careful not to touch her, so I couldn't be sure there were no signs of violence in areas I was unable to see. But there was no blood on the floor, and no evidence of a weapon in sight.

It seemed unlikely that Dr. Springer had chosen this very day, this very moment, to have a sudden cardiac arrest; from what I could tell, she was in excellent shape, and was not old. But a cause of death would probably not be difficult for the police to determine.

I stood up and looked around the room. Having discerned what I could about Dr. Springer's death, I focused again on Ackerman's question—who had stolen the frozen head of Ms. Masters-Powell? I forced myself to look at every object in the room for answers.

There was a metal tank with a nozzle on it in the rear of the room, and I walked back to gently kick it—it was empty. I was careful not to move it or interfere with its placement in any way. And while I noticed an object on the floor, one that appeared to be configured from a type of rubber or plastic, it was too dark in that corner for me to see clearly, and there was a more serious problem to consider—I was starting to get drowsy. There must still have been some nitrogen released in the room, although not enough to deplete the oxygen supply completely, and the nitrogen release must have been constant and ongoing. There was a tank with a small leak somewhere. I headed quickly for the door.

"Mr. Hoenig?" I heard Ms. Washburn's voice from beyond the door, which was now once again propped open. "The police are already at the reception area."

"Tell Commander Johnson to send them down immediately," I said. I saw Ms. Washburn's head disappear from the window, and she walked back toward the phone on the wall.

I didn't have much time—the police would not take kindly to a civilian "contaminating" the crime scene—so I focused my attention. Dr. Springer's body was sprawled in such a way that it was obvious she had been walking toward the door, perhaps even running. So I traced the path back toward the cylinders that held the frozen "guests."

Before I reached the apparatus that held them, however, I was distracted by something on the floor, where perhaps Dr. Springer had dropped it on her way; the security video would undoubtedly reveal that detail later.

It was a metal cylinder, not large enough to contain one of the totally preserved bodies, but one that was of a size to preserve a cranium. It was on its side, and appeared to have a very large crack in it.

As I moved away from the door and toward the cylinder to examine it (but certainly not to touch it), I felt my concentration wander; it was as if I hadn't slept in more than a day, which I certainly never allow to happen. It was the nitrogen leak; my time in this room would have to be short.

I examined the cylinder on the floor only briefly, but long enough to see it was inscribed with the initials R. M-P and a number, as well as a bar code.

Rita Masters-Powell.

But by then, my head was swimming, and I knew it was important to leave the room. I turned and walked, a trifle unsteadily, toward the body of Dr. Springer and the door. The closer I got to the door, the better I felt. My weariness seemed to dissipate a little more with each step.

I stepped out of the chamber just as two uniformed police officers were entering the anteroom. Ms. Washburn looked at me with worry in her eyes, and Marshall Ackerman's expression was hard for me to read—it was either disapproval or disgust. I sometimes wish I could take pictures of every facial expression I see to show Mother later, so she could confirm or dismiss my initial impressions.

"Are you okay, Mr. Hoenig?" Ms. Washburn asked.

I sat down, nodding. "Yes. I think I suffered a very mild reaction to a release of liquid nitrogen." I started to take off the protective suit, as Ms. Washburn and Ackerman had already done.

Ackerman paled. "Liquid nitrogen? Are the receptacles damaged?" He knew that the bodies and crania being preserved were kept in containers of liquid nitrogen, because it could keep them very cold without causing serious tissue damage, when done under the right conditions. A breach of the containers would be a very bad thing for him, indeed.

"Only one," I told him. "The one that contained Ms. Masters-Powell's head."

Ackerman looked even more distraught. He put his head down and started to breathe heavily.

The two police officers, who had started for the chamber door, stopped mid-stride and swiveled to look at me. One, the taller of the two, with dark eyebrows and deep-set eyes, shook his head a little.

"Someone's head was in a cylinder of liquid nitrogen?" he said. "Isn't that really cold?"

"Yes," Ackerman answered. "But that's what we do here. We preserve those who have recently experienced traditional 'death,' for the time when they can be revived." He did not raise his head to speak.

The taller officer's eyes widened, but his partner, a young African-American woman, touched his arm, and he turned his attention toward her. "It's a cryogenics lab, Jesse," she said. "It's legal."

"Cryonics," I corrected. "Cryogenics is simply the science of very low temperatures. Cryonics is the activity practiced here."

But the officer named Jesse, whose nametag read CRAWFORD, pointed at Dr. Springer's body. "What about that?"

"That is one of our doctors," Ackerman said.

"She's dead?" Crawford asked.

Ackerman nodded.

"Call it in," Crawford told his partner, and she reached for her communications link on her shoulder.

"That might not work down here," Ackerman told her, and pointed to the phone. The female officer started to call to her headquarters.

"You were coming out of there when we came in," Crawford said to me. "You shouldn't have been in there."

"We weren't sure she was dead," Ms. Washburn explained. "Mr. Hoenig was trying…"

"I answer people's questions for them," I told the officer. "I needed to be in there to answer a question for Dr. Ackerman."

"Did you touch anything?"

"No," I said. "I was extremely careful."

Crawford leaned into the preservation chamber, and Ackerman looked nervously after him. At least, I think he was nervous—it might have been an expression of disapproval.

"No blood," Crawford said. "Looks like natural causes."

"Oh, no," I told him. "Dr. Springer was murdered."

SIX

It took the Emergency Medical Services crew seven minutes to arrive, and when they did, they commanded most of the attention in the room. But they were not allowed to touch Dr. Springer's body (other than to determine that she was indeed deceased) until Det. Glendon Lapides released the corpse to their care.

When Detective Lapides, a remarkably tall man with sandy hair and a space between his front teeth, was satisfied that the police videographer had recorded the scene, he stood in front of Ms. Washburn, Ackerman, and myself. And we watched as the body of Dr. Springer was moved, on a collapsible gurney, out of the area and toward the elevator by the EMS workers.

"So, what's this about it being a murder?" he asked. I believe he was directing his question at me, but he was looking at Ms. Washburn. It was possible Detective Lapides had Asperger's Syndrome, or that he found Ms. Washburn attractive; it was hard to know.

"Is this going to take long?" I asked him in return, and the detective turned toward me with an expression I could easily identify as irritation.

"Mr. Hoenig has lunch with his mother every day at twelve thirty," Ms. Washburn explained to him. "He's concerned about being late."

"It'll take as long as it takes," he said to me, which didn't answer my question at all. "But it will go much faster if everyone just cooperates and answers the questions. Now, why do you think that woman was murdered?"

"I don't think so; I'm certain of it," I told him. "The evidence points to no other conclusion. For one thing, Dr. Springer is wearing her normal business attire. She's dressed in a sensible suit and low heels, perfect for a nondescript meeting on budget or procedure."

Lapides's eyes narrowed. "So how does that make it murder?" he asked.

"Rebecca wouldn't have gone into the chamber without a protective suit," Ackerman stepped in. "She'd know that it could be dangerous to her, and she'd know that it could potentially corrupt the guests we have preserved in the chamber." Ackerman had repeatedly asked the officers to allow him into the chamber to check for further damage but had been denied, and now he was glancing nervously in the direction of the chamber door every few seconds.

"Okay, that makes it strange, but it doesn't mean someone deliberately killed her. We're not even sure how she died—it looks like a heart attack to me," Lapides said.

"I believe you'll find that she died of suffocation," I told him. "When the liquid nitrogen was exposed to the air in the chamber, its temperature was raised far beyond its boiling point, and it transformed into a gas. That meant the percentage of oxygen in the air in the room decreased dramatically as the percentage of nitrogen increased, and Dr. Springer could no longer breathe. She was probably unconscious in seconds."

Lapides had not made eye contact with me while I spoke, studying the floor with what appeared to be great interest. It might have been his way of concentrating. It also might have been a sign that he didn't understand what I was saying, or that he was very tired.

I, meanwhile, was noting that, with the time now eleven twenty-seven, my chances of arriving in time for lunch with Mother were dwindling. "Is that all you need from me?" I asked Lapides.

Apparently my tone was less cordial than I had intended—voice modulation is sometimes a problem—because Lapides took his gaze off the floor, looked me in the eye, and said, "No, that's not *all* I need from you. Settle in. I have a lot of questions."

"Mr. Hoenig isn't trying to be rude," Ms. Washburn said. "He's just…"

"You don't need to keep defending him," the detective told her. "He's a big boy and doesn't need to hide behind a woman."

That comment didn't make any sense—I was not hiding behind Ms. Washburn. I was sitting two seats to her left. But Lapides's tone, after a moment of reflection, indicated he was being derisive.

"May I stand up, detective?" I asked, and Lapides gestured that I should. But when I did, his expression changed. I think he might have believed I was going to attack him; that's what would happen in an action motion picture starring Bruce Willis. It was not at all my intention.

41

"Let me demonstrate," I said. "Suppose that I am Dr. Springer."

"I don't think you have the legs for it," Lapides said. I stopped for a moment and looked at my legs but was unable to discern what about them might inhibit my explanation.

"It's a joke, Mr. Hoenig," Ms. Washburn told me, so I moved on.

"If I were in the chamber, dressed without any protection, my first impulse, especially given the knowledge that Dr. Springer had of the process, would be to exit as quickly as possible," I said.

"Tell me something I don't know," Lapides said.

"In a moment," I answered him. "Dr. Springer was a trained physician. Did she have a background in advanced chemistry?" I asked Ackerman.

"She did, but she wouldn't need one to know that a breach of one of the cylinders would fill the room with nitrogen gas and deplete the amount of oxygen," Ackerman answered. "Any physician— any chemistry student—would know that. She was obviously trying to get to the door before she lost consciousness. But I don't understand why you say that makes it murder. Isn't it just an accident, Mr. Hoenig?"

I shook my head. "No. The question remains: How was the nitrogen released? What happened to the cylinder that released it into the air, and who did that to Dr. Springer?"

Detective Lapides looked at me strangely, I thought. "What makes you think she didn't do it herself?"

I turned toward Ackerman. "How cold would that cylinder have been in order to keep the liquid nitrogen from boiling?" I asked.

"The boiling point of nitrogen is three hundred twenty-one degrees below zero, Fahrenheit," he answered.

Ms. Washburn's eyes widened. "Then Dr. Springer couldn't possibly have been carrying it, or handling it at all," she said.

"Not without protective clothing and equipment," I agreed. "But that's not all that indicates there was another person in the room." I stopped and looked at the three of them. A long moment passed before they realized why I wasn't continuing.

Someone had to ask the question, and it was Ms. Washburn who understood first. "What other evidence is there, Mr. Hoenig?" she asked.

I looked at her with a grateful expression, or at least that's what I intended; I'm not always sure whether I accomplish the proper outwardly appearance. "The cylinder that held the nitrogen, and Ms. Masters-Powell's head, was *behind* the body," I explained. "Even if it had been possible for Dr. Springer to carry the cylinder before it suffered a breach, and even if she had begun to fall forward, the notion that she could have tossed it over her shoulder to land behind her is virtually an impossible one."

Detective Lapides's mouth was open, but it wasn't moving. He shook his head back and forth a few times but did not speak.

"You weren't in there very long," Ackerman said to me. "How did you see that all in such a short time?"

I suppose I blinked once or twice, but I don't remember. "It doesn't take long to see something," I told him.

Lapides then seemed to regain the power of speech, but his voice was higher than before, and his face reddened. "You're taking him *seriously*?" he shouted. "That's all guesswork and tricks! I'm telling you, that woman had a heart attack—I've seen them before and I know what they look like!"

"Will there be an autopsy, detective?" Ms. Washburn stepped in between the two men and seemed to want to defuse the situation. I admired her ability to read the emotions of the people in the room and take action so quickly; it was something I would not have been able to do.

It appeared to work—Lapides's face became less angry as he pondered the question. "Any time a death occurs when no one else is present, there's an autopsy," he said, puffing out his chest just a bit. "But the results won't be public for a while. Dr. Ackerman, did she have any family we can contact?"

"I don't know," Ackerman answered. "I'll have to check..."

He didn't get the chance to finish his sentence because Commander Johnson, breathing heavily and sweating profusely, made his way past the two uniformed officers at the door and confronted Ackerman.

"What happened?" he demanded. "I *told* you we should have called the police before!"

Ackerman's face paled; Lapides's head swiveled toward Ackerman as soon as Commander Johnson's words were out of his mouth.

"Called the police before about *what*?" he demanded. "Did you know about this earlier?"

Even Ms. Washburn couldn't step in and make this situation any easier.

"No, detective. There was...an incident here at the lab, but I thought Commander Johnson and his staff could handle it internally," Ackerman said.

"What kind of *incident*?"

"Before he begins," I began, "there is something I need to address."
Lapides regarded me with a cocked eyebrow. "What's that?"
"May I go to lunch with my mother now?"

SEVEN

Ms. Washburn barely spoke as she drove, which was perfectly fine with me. A person who is comfortable with silence won't require conversation, and those of us with Asperger's Syndrome are more at ease when we don't have to worry about saying something inappropriate or overemphasizing a topic we find fascinating that others, we eventually discover, do not.

"I'll drop you off at your mother's, and then I'll head for home," she said. "I wasn't planning on being involved in a murder investigation."

That stunned me a little. I didn't think I'd missed any signals from Ms. Washburn indicating she was upset or frightened by the events at the Garden State Cryonics Institute. But I answered her as I would have even if such signals had been obvious. "This is not a murder investigation," I said. "The police are investigating the murder of Dr. Springer. I am simply attempting to answer Dr. Ackerman's question about the missing head."

Ms. Washburn did not take her eyes off the road, which was reassuring to me. Many people act emotionally behind the wheel, not realizing the enormous risk they take each time they travel in a motor vehicle of any kind. Throughout the life of an average seventy-eight-year-old, the odds of dying in an automobile crash are approximately one in eighty-three; the odds of dying in an airplane accident are approximately one in fifty-two million.

But she did open her mouth a little. I wasn't sure what that was supposed to mean, so I stayed silent.

"So you're not going to look into the murder of Dr. Springer, even though you know that the cops will treat it as natural causes?" she asked.

"I assume that the medical examiner will corroborate my findings," I answered. "And then either the North Brunswick Police or the Middlesex County prosecutor's Major Crimes unit will handle the investigation. No one has asked me who killed Dr. Springer."

"Isn't that a little callous? Don't you think Dr. Springer deserves the ultimate justice of having her murderer found, exposed, and punished?"

This was puzzling; it seemed Ms. Washburn was trying to encourage me to investigate the murder, when just a moment ago, she was threatening to end our association because she assumed I *would* be taking up that cause. "I don't understand," I told her. "Do you want me to find out who killed Dr. Springer?"

The question seemed to baffle Ms. Washburn; she thought for a moment and said, "Yes. I do. But I don't want to be involved with it."

"Because you're afraid."

Her lips tightened. I've found this is often a sign of irritation or embarrassment. "Yes. Because I'm afraid," she said briskly without separating her teeth.

"It makes sense to be afraid," I told her. "The person or people who did that to Dr. Springer are clearly violent and unpredictable. They killed someone, probably deliberately, and that means they are dangerous. I would not want to be involved with people like that."

This time, she did steal a glance—a very brief one—toward me. "So, you're afraid, too?" she asked.

"No, but I would be if I were going to investigate the murder."

Ms. Washburn nodded and did not speak again until we reached the house.

———

"Of *course* you're coming in," Mother said when Ms. Washburn tried to beg off. "When Samuel said he was bringing a guest, I made enough for three. You can't leave me with all that extra food." And she smiled her best smile, which she once told me was designed to get her out of trouble with police officers when she inadvertently exceeded the speed limit.

It seemed to work on Ms. Washburn, as well, since she acquiesced and walked into the house. Mother can be very persuasive.

The house, of course, was immaculate—Mother never allows anything other than that in her home. Mother is a short woman, somewhat stout but not dangerously heavy. I silently chided myself for not drinking enough water today, due to the distraction of Ackerman's question. Luckily, I had been on my feet for much of the morning, so my exercise was quite within my daily quota.

"It's a lovely home, Mrs. Hoenig," Ms. Washburn said to her as she surveyed the living room.

"I do what I can." Mother very rarely accepts a compliment to herself, but I have noticed that she can be downright vain about any accomplishment of my own. "Come in and eat. You must be famished. And you call me Vivian." I don't know why she believed that our activity of the morning would translate into hunger, but I have found it best not to question Mother when she says such things. She will explain, but her explanation rarely helps me to understand more fully.

While we ate (Mother had prepared turkey sandwiches, one plain, the way I prefer, and others with choices of condiments), I explained the questions I was researching today—the one about the chances of hitting a ball out of Yankee Stadium, and the one about the missing head. Mother appeared to find the one about Ms. Masters-Powell's head more interesting.

"Why aren't you looking into who killed that poor woman?" she asked me when I had completed the tale. I noticed Ms. Washburn looking away, examining my painting of John Lennon that Mother had hung on the far wall. I assumed she was doing so merely to avoid the issue Mother was raising.

"I was not asked a question," I told her. "My business is to answer questions." I was noticing that Ms. Washburn preferred mustard to mayonnaise on her sandwich, and I considered what that might have meant in relation to her overall character. I decided she was less bland than most people.

"Your business," Mother said deliberately, "is to help when you can help. This is an area where you can help."

"I don't see how," I answered. "The police are competent. They haven't asked me to assist them. I have questions I have not yet answered. It doesn't make sense for me to abandon paying clients to help an organization that has not requested my assistance."

Mother stood up and began to clear plates from the table. Normally that is a signal that I should do the same, so I stood. But Mother shook her head and gestured toward Ms. Washburn. "We have company," she said. "It's rude to leave her alone."

But Ms. Washburn had already begun to help clear. "No, it's rude for the guest to sit idly by while everyone else works on her behalf," she said.

Mother started to protest, but by that time Ms. Washburn was walking into the kitchen carrying plates. And the silent interchange between the two women was more than I could interpret, so I chose to pay no attention. I brought in a small bowl that had held chopped onions, but I avoided the one containing mayonnaise. There are limits to my tolerance, and Mother understands that.

When I walked into the kitchen, I could hear Mother saying, "… thirteen years ago, so Samuel was sixteen years old. It was the first year—" She stopped speaking when she looked at Ms. Washburn's face, which must have indicated that I was in the room. Mother looked over to see me there, smiled, and looked back at Ms. Washburn. "Not to worry, dear," she said. "Samuel knows the story."

"Yes," I agreed. "I was diagnosed with Asperger's Syndrome the first year it was listed in the DSM IV. Do you know what that is?"

Ms. Washburn nodded. "The Diagnostic and Statistical Manual of Mental Disorders," she said, then put her hand to her mouth. "I'm sorry."

I didn't see a reason for her to be sorry, and told her so. "That is what the publication is called," I said. "I believe Asperger's Syndrome is not a mental disorder, but that is the way the medical profession chooses to classify it."

Ms. Washburn nodded. Mother chuckled. "You left the mayonnaise out there, didn't you, Samuel?" she asked, then walked to the door without waiting for my answer. She left the room through the kitchen door, which swings open and closed, like those in many restaurants, including the one that was once linked to the kitchen of San Remo's, now my back room at Questions Answered.

I looked at Ms. Washburn and tried to gauge her mood, based on what I've learned about facial expressions and body language. Since I had only known her a few hours, the task was made more challenging, but purer. She stood facing away from the sink, watching Mother leave the kitchen, and then she turned toward me. Her hands were crossed in front of her, arms down, and her face turned upward slightly when she realized I was looking at her.

"You're nervous," I said after a moment. "Why are you nervous? Did I do something unusual?" Sometimes, it is very difficult to know, because I always think I'm acting very rationally.

"No," Ms. Washburn said, shaking her head slightly. "You didn't do anything. I was a little startled to see you looking at me just then."

"What do you think about what my mother said?" I asked her. Ms. Washburn's opinion was becoming more important to me. She didn't know me very well but had defended me more than once since we'd met. And she did not seem to be "weirded out" (an expression I've heard more than once) by what some would consider

51

odd behavior on my part. I was beginning to think she could be a valuable asset to Questions Answered.

"Which thing she said?" Ms. Washburn asked.

"When we were discussing the murder of Dr. Springer," I reminded her. "About my responsibility to help when I can help." It occurred to me that Mother was taking an unusually long time to fetch the mayonnaise and might have orchestrated this situation to give Ms. Washburn and myself a moment to discuss this very topic.

"I think your mother has a very high opinion of your talents," Ms. Washburn said. "And from what I've seen, that opinion is pretty well justified. But you have to decide if you're interested in making waves with the police department and doing something you haven't been asked to do simply because you might be of help to a woman who is already dead."

I nodded. "That was a concise, accurate assessment of the situation," I told her. "But I asked for your opinion. What do *you* think I should do?"

Ms. Washburn's head lowered. She was thinking.

"Don't try to determine what I want you to say," I said. "I'm asking you because your opinion will help me decide. I require your perspective." That hadn't come out sounding exactly the way I'd wanted it to, but it would have to suffice.

Her head snapped up, and she looked me directly in the eye. "All I can think," she said, "is that if it were me, I'd want you to find the person who did that to me and bring him to justice."

"Or her," I corrected.

"Or her?"

"Bring him *or her* to justice. We can't narrow our list of suspects to men."

Ms. Washburn smiled. "No. Of course not."

"All right, then," I told her. "I will take that into account as I decide how to proceed."

Mother burst in through the kitchen door, which swung wide at the force of her push. "There's nothing to decide, Samuel," she said. She advanced upon me, her face displaying determination rather than fury. She hadn't even bothered to retrieve the mayonnaise. "I have a question for you." She took a dollar from her apron pocket and pressed it into my hand.

I had worried she'd do this. "Mother..."

"Who killed Dr. Springer?" Mother asked defiantly.

Now I had no choice.

EIGHT

Marshall Ackerman's office walls held many diplomas and one certificate from the Calnor Institute of Cryonics. The diplomas indicated that he had completed various degrees, leading up to a Ph.D. in physics, but was not a medical doctor. The certificate from Calnor stated that he was a licensed practitioner of cryonics, having completed the necessary training.

Ackerman himself was seated behind a very formidable mahogany desk bearing a flat-screen computer, a scale model of a cryonics preservation tube, and a photo of Ackerman himself that appeared to have been taken by a professional photographer. In the photograph, Ackerman was leaning on the edge of his desk, with an American flag strategically positioned behind it.

When he saw me examining the photograph, Ackerman smiled and nodded. "That was for a feature article in *USA Today*," he said. "The photographer was kind enough to send me a copy."

I had spent an hour looking over three hours' worth of security video (fast forward played a major role in the process) of the preservation chamber, both from the time period during which Ms. Masters-Powell's head had disappeared, and from the moments after Dr. Springer had entered the chamber this morning. Neither tape showed so much as a person entering the chamber. Clearly, some kind of tampering had taken place, or I was examining tape from the wrong moments, which would have meant that the GSCI logs of people entering or exiting Preservation Room D were inaccurate or forged. Either was a possibility.

In short, the three hours of video surveillance had led me to only one conclusion, and it was not related to Dr. Springer's murder. At least, it was not *directly* related. Until I had more facts, there would be no way to know if it had any relevance.

"It's very nice," I said of the *USA Today* photograph, because that's what I've learned one should say when offered pictures of a person or that person's child.

Ackerman seemed pleased. "I use it for all my publicity," he said with what I discerned as pride in his voice.

"Was Dr. Springer dedicated to the practice of cryonics?" I asked. I wanted very badly to change the subject. Talking about personal matters or making small talk is very difficult for a person like me, and we try to stay "on topic," or at least the topic we find most interesting, as often as possible.

Ackerman seemed somehow confused by the change in subject, although I couldn't see why he would be—this was the subject Ms. Washburn and I were there to discuss. But he recovered after a moment. "Of course she was," he said. "Why do you ask?"

"I noted that you made no effort to freeze her body after she was killed," I said. "It seems to me that someone who would work in the field might well have desired to experience it herself when necessary."

Ms. Washburn's eyes narrowed. I took that to mean she hadn't considered the question until I'd posed it.

"In fact, Rebecca *was* on the list for preservation," Ackerman answered. "But the way she … What happened to her made it impossible. With oxygen deprived to the brain for so long, there would never have been a way to revive her and keep her mind intact."

It occurred to me to mention that such technology or science did not exist at this time for anyone, no matter how death occurred, but that would have added little to the conversation, and if past experience was any indicator, would probably have annoyed Ackerman.

"How many people were in the building during the period between the time Dr. Springer went into the chamber and the time we discovered her body there?" I asked.

Ms. Washburn offered a clipboard. "I went to the security desk and asked for the log-in sheet," she said. "This is the one that begins at seven this morning."

I nodded my thanks to her and scanned the sheet. "There were seventeen people signed in, excluding Ms. Washburn and myself," I told Ackerman. "Please look at this list. Are they all employees of Garden State Cryonics?"

Ackerman took the clipboard from my hand, put on a pair of reading glasses, and studied it. "No," he answered. "Fourteen are employees, plus myself. The other four are visitors—a blogger on medicine, you two, and Commander Johnson's wife."

"Why was she here?" Ms. Washburn asked. I would have asked about the blogger first, but only because Ackerman had mentioned that person first. I tend to react to lists in order.

"She drops by from time to time." Ackerman said. "Amelia is very smart and very dedicated to her husband. She likes to see what he's doing here. I approved the visit two weeks ago. We get a lot of that from employees, especially new ones. Everyone's curious."

"Is Commander Johnson new here?" I asked.

Ackerman nodded. "Relatively. I think he's been working here about five months."

"What happened to the last head of security?" Ms. Washburn asked.

"Mr. Monroe left to pursue other interests," Ackerman said. "I can get you his phone number if you like."

I indicated that he should, and Ackerman made a note of it on his pad. "May I have a list of every employee of the company, and contact information for the other two guests?" I asked.

"Of course," Ackerman nodded. "I'm so glad you decided to help in the investigation. Frankly, I didn't see much hope with Detective Lapides as the lead investigator." He made another note.

"It would be best not to underestimate the detective," I said, although I did not think Lapides was an excellent investigator. "He might very well be an astute observer, or he may have not developed his skills yet. Time will tell."

"I don't understand," Ms. Washburn said. "We looked at the video. There's one point where Dr. Springer walks in wearing the protective suit, then she goes back to the tank—"

"The receptacle," Ackerman corrected her. I had been careful to note that terminology when he had used it previously.

"The *receptacle*," Ms. Washburn said. "Why would she walk to that receptacle when you already knew the head was missing?"

Ackerman cupped his hands together, as if he were about to begin applauding, but he did not move them. After a moment, I realized that meant he was thinking. "It's possible Rebecca didn't know about the theft," he said. "I tried to keep it very quiet around here, and I know I didn't tell her. She might have been doing a routine check. We look in on all our guests at least once a day to monitor their condition. But I don't understand." He swiveled his chair to face me more directly, and I wasn't sure if he was trying to dismiss Ms. Washburn. I was starting to think Ackerman was something of a pompous man who held a dim view of those without professional credentials. "It doesn't make sense that the cylinder in which Ms. Masters-Powell's remains were being preserved would simply rupture like that. We are very careful about our equipment."

"Is it possible someone could have deliberately caused it to develop a crack?" I asked. Before Ackerman could answer, I turned to Ms. Washburn. "Make sure you research that possibility when we return to the office," I said. Ms. Washburn nodded. We hadn't discussed such a scenario before, but I suddenly wanted Ackerman to see Ms. Washburn as a valuable associate, not a servant.

"It's very unlikely," he said. "Those steel receptacles are very thick, and very strong. Otherwise, they wouldn't be able to sustain the extremely low temperatures we require of them for such a long period of time."

"Still," I said. "It is curious that Dr. Springer appeared to have been looking at Ms. Masters-Powell's receptacle, but not to have noticed it was empty. That is very odd."

Ackerman nodded. "I agree. I wish I could explain it. What's next in the investigation, Mr. Hoenig?"

"I'd like to start interviewing employees and the two guests who were present today," I said. "Can we set up an interview room with video security intact?"

Ackerman seemed quite pleased with the notion. "Certainly!" he said. "We have many rooms that can be made available. Who should you interview first?"

"You," I said. "May we begin now?" I rose to walk to the door.

Ackerman looked stunned that he was being considered a suspect, but I couldn't imagine why he wouldn't anticipate that—he worked at the Garden State Cryonics Institute, he had a financial interest in the facility, and there was no concrete evidence that he hadn't committed a crime. It was only sensible that I would want to talk to him as well as the other GSCI employees.

He stood. "Of course," he said. "We can use the level-three conference room."

Before we could leave the room, however, Ackerman's desk phone rang, and he picked it up on the second ring. After the usual greeting, he said, "Hello, detective," and then listened for quite some time. He thanked the other party and ended the phone call looking a bit shaken.

"Was that Detective Lapides?" Ms. Washburn asked.

Ackerman nodded. "They found something in the empty receptacle for Ms. Masters-Powell," he said and sat down hard, exhaling.

"Was the head put back?" Ms. Washburn asked.

Ackerman squinted at her, incredulous, then shook his head. "No."

"What did they find in the receptacle?" I asked him. A direct question is always the best option.

"A bullet," he said.

NINE

"IT WAS A THIRTY-EIGHT caliber bullet, and that's really all I know," Ackerman said. "Detective Lapides called to tell me not to let anyone into the chamber, as he now agrees with you, Mr. Hoenig, that it is the scene of a murder. He'll be back here shortly."

We sat in the conference room at Garden State Cryonics, a much more expensively decorated room than any other I'd seen in the facility. I assumed this was the area in which potential clients and their families were given information intended to persuade them to buy GSCI's services. Ackerman sat at the head of the table, where a telephone console was at his fingertips, along with controls that I assumed ran an audio/video system. There were high-definition television monitors placed throughout the room, which had a polished wood conference table and upholstered chairs, as well as a thick carpet and, it appeared, soundproofed doors. As most people are upset by the thought of death, I concluded that some of the conferences held here were quite emotional.

"That explains how the receptacle was ruptured," I said. "Someone either fired a bullet directly into it, or fired at something else and hit the cylinder by mistake."

"But there were no bullets in Dr. Springer's body," Ms. Washburn said. "She wasn't shot, was she?"

I shook my head. "Dr. Springer's body had no bullet wounds." I turned toward Ackerman to begin the interview. "First. What is your favorite Beatles song?"

Even Ms. Washburn looked a little stunned, but Ackerman was more so—he stared at me and knit his brow. "My what?"

"Your favorite Beatles song. Please," I reiterated.

"I listen to classical music," he answered. "Why?"

"If you had to choose one Beatles song," I persevered, "what would it be?"

Ackerman looked at Ms. Washburn, perhaps for some assurance that I was not insane. "I just told you, I listen to classical music," he repeated. "I really can't answer ... "

"But you have heard of the Beatles?" It was no idle question; I am able to discern quite a bit about a person's character from their answer to this question.

"Yes, of course."

"Then, if you had to choose just one song as a favorite?"

He shook his head and let out his breath. "I don't know," he said. "I guess 'Eleanor Rigby.' Why?"

Pretentious. Terrified of death. Perhaps sees himself as lonely.

"It's a device I use," I told him. "It's the way you answer, rather than the answer itself." That wasn't entirely true, but I did not want to tell him what I'd discovered until I could answer the question

62

about Dr. Springer. So I quickly changed the subject. "Who was Rita Masters-Powell?" I asked.

The question must have seemed abrupt to Ackerman, because he started a bit and then regained his composure. "She was the daughter of Leonard Masters and the granddaughter of Julius Masters," he said. "Do you know who they were?"

"I believe Julius Masters founded International Data Associates, a company started as a bookkeeping concern during the Second World War. It grew into a computer keypunch operation in the 1960s, and eventually into a very large manufacturer of microprocessors during the 1980s. His son Leonard succeeded Julius as the chief executive officer of the firm and navigated it through the transition to computer hardware, and both of them became extremely wealthy men. Am I correct so far?" I asked Ackerman.

"Impressively so," he replied.

"There had been rumors that the company was about to be sold to a Chinese concern, and I believe that sale is pending at the moment," I added. I read the business pages of the *New York Times* every day, and I monitor computer- and hardware-related businesses. Some of my investments are in such businesses. "What caused Ms. Masters-Powell's death?" I asked Ackerman.

He hesitated only a moment this time. "Cancer," he said. "Apparently, Ms. Masters-Powell was a heavy smoker." He shook his head mournfully, in a move that I'm sure he had used in this room many times before, and just as persuasively.

"She changed her name. Was she married?" Ms. Washburn asked. An excellent question, as a husband would probably stand to gain a great deal financially from the death of such a wealthy wife.

"Ms. Masters-Powell was divorced," Ackerman answered. "She was only forty-one years old when she passed away, but I believe they had been divorced almost three years."

Ms. Washburn looked thoughtful. "But she kept her husband's name even after the divorce. Do you know why?" Ms. Washburn was becoming more of an asset with each passing minute. Her training in journalism, even if her work was photographic in nature, was surely shining through.

"I have no idea," Ackerman said. "I never met Ms. Masters-Powell. She was already very ill when her brother Arthur contacted us on her behalf. He was absolutely distraught over his sister's impending death and said she saw our service as a way to maintain hope." Ackerman looked quite pleased with himself.

A buzzer on the table's console sounded, and Ackerman reached over to pick up the phone. After a brief conversation I could not hear, he hung up. "The police are here," he said. "I'm afraid we'll have to continue this talk later." He stood up.

Ms. Washburn and I followed suit. "Very well," I said to Ackerman. "Would you send Commander Johnson in to talk with us?"

Ackerman nodded and walked toward the door. Just before reaching it, he stopped and turned to me with an expression on his face that Ms. Washburn later told me was one of concern. "All these questions about the theft, and not the murder," he said. "Shouldn't we be most concerned with Rebecca, and not the question of Ms. Masters-Powell's remains?"

"I believe the two incidents are connected," I told him.

His eyes widened. "Really!" he said. "I guess I shouldn't be surprised. But you've seen the security tapes. How do you think Ms. Masters-Powell's remains were smuggled out of the facility?"

It was a question that deserved an answer. "I don't believe they were," I told Ackerman.

TEN

ACKERMAN LEFT TO TALK to Detective Lapides, and for a moment before Commander Johnson arrived, Ms. Washburn and I had a moment to talk privately.

"What did you mean, you don't think the head was taken out of the facility?" she asked me. "Do you think it's still here?"

"I was trying to gauge Ackerman's response," I answered. "I wanted to see if he looked surprised, or worried. If he looked surprised, he is probably an incompetent manager and doesn't know what is happening under his own roof. If he looked worried, he most likely has some knowledge he'd prefer we not find out."

"How did he look?" Ms. Washburn asked.

"Confused."

Before she could question me further, the conference room door opened and Commander Johnson, lit from behind, stood in the doorway, seeming to survey the situation before he entered. It occurred to me that if this were a satiric motion picture like *Dr. Strangelove: or*

How I Learned to Stop Worrying and Love the Bomb, he would have a great number of medals pinned to his shirt and might even be carrying a riding crop. He had neither.

Instead, the commander was wearing the company uniform—a light blue denim shirt with short sleeves and the initials GSCI embroidered on the left breast pocket and a pair of cargo pants. He was wearing a pair of Nike cross-trainers with a blue "swoosh" across the sides.

Commander Johnson stood straight and tall to the left side of the conference table where Ms. Washburn and I sat. He clasped his hands behind his back and stared straight ahead, over our heads.

"There is no need to stand at attention, commander," I suggested.

"I am at ease," he responded, and I made a mental note to ask Ms. Washburn later if his voice had a tinge of condescension in it.

"Please sit down," I said. "I am not a police official. This is an informal inquiry commissioned by the institute."

The commander grimaced, as if I had suggested he remove his pants. But he sat down in a chair immediately to our left and folded his hands carefully on the table before him. I thought he looked very formal.

"Commander," I began. "Is that a rank you acquired in the service?"

His mouth tightened just a bit, which I noticed because I was being careful to observe his facial expression. It was difficult for me, because I usually prefer not to see a person's emotions on his face; I find it terribly personal and embarrassing. In this case, however, it was necessary in order to answer the questions at hand.

"No," Commander Johnson replied. "'Commander' is a title given to me by members of my neighborhood watch committee. When I served in the Army, I was a corporal. I served during the first Gulf War."

"Where were you stationed?" Ms. Washburn asked. The information was not relevant to the questions I had to answer, but it was possible she could discern something about the commander's character from his answer.

He looked away, much as I usually do when someone is speaking to me. "Fort Dix," he said softly.

"Here in New Jersey?" Ms. Washburn said. I thought she sounded surprised.

"Yes," Commander Johnson acknowledged.

"You became chief of security here five months ago, is that correct?" I asked him. I took no notes, but Ms. Washburn had a pen and notebook provided by Ackerman.

"Yes. It was my understanding that Miles Monroe, the previous chief, was dismissed, but I never met him."

"Was he incompetent?" I asked.

The commander's face did not change. "I would have no way of knowing," he said.

"When did you first find out about the disappearance of Ms. Masters-Powell's remains?" I asked.

Commander Johnson seemed to be anticipating that question, because the answer came quickly and without hesitation. "This morning, at approximately oh-seven-thirty," he said. "I was not scheduled to come on duty until oh-eight-thirty, so the night shift commander, Mr. Feliz, called me at home."

That was when something occurred to me. "Quickly," I said to the commander, "what are the dimensions of this room?" I stood up straight.

Ms. Washburn started at my action, which made me wonder if I'd done so too fast. Commander Johnson barely reacted at all. He merely said, "Twenty feet by fourteen." He did not have to consult any data source; he knew the dimensions "off the top of his head," a common expression that suggests very strange images.

I'd realized that I hadn't gotten my body into motion even once since lunch. I was behind on my day's exercise. So I began to walk purposefully around the perimeter of the room, making sure to bend my knees properly and raise my arms over my head with every other step. Calculating mentally, I concluded that twenty-six laps around the room would equal the third of a mile I should be doing at this time of day.

While I walked, however, it was still necessary to continue the questioning of Commander Johnson. "So when Mr. Feliz called you about the missing remains, how did he say the loss was discovered?"

There was no answer, which forced me to look down, although it is always better to keep one's neck straight while exercising. Ms. Washburn and the commander were watching me walk around the room with similar facial expressions, which I believe indicated they were surprised by my actions.

"It is my time for exercise," I explained. Ms. Washburn immediately smiled and nodded, but Commander Johnson's demeanor was unchanged. "So please, commander, if you would?"

"Oh! Yes. Well, when I arrived, Feliz told me he had run the routine sweep of the facility at zero hour and at oh-three-hundred, and had found nothing amiss. But when he returned to the storage chamber at oh-six-hundred, he found the door ajar and the power disconnected from one receptacle."

Johnson watched me until I was behind him, shook his head a bit, and went on. "Thinking that someone had badly handled the one receptacle, and fearful that the guest inside might be damaged, Feliz reconnected the power cable immediately, and then called Dr. Lanier to check on the guest. He said she arrived very quickly, and upon examining the container, discovered it empty."

"So it was Dr. Lanier who confirmed that nothing was in the disconnected receptacle?"

"Yes," Commander Johnson nodded. "As the ranking medical expert on that shift, she would be the one to look into any unusual activity among the guests."

I was on my eighth lap around the room. This was not going as quickly as exercising at my office, because the room was smaller and more fully furnished, and I had to dodge chairs whenever I passed Ms. Washburn or Commander Johnson. But another eighteen laps were necessary, and there was no avoiding them.

"Did you examine the chamber and determine how someone got in to do the damage?" I asked, breathing just a little heavily.

I couldn't see Commander Johnson's face at that moment, but his tone suggested he was insulted. "Of course!" he bellowed. "It was a serious security breach, and I am the chief of security."

A moment passed before I realized that he was not going to elaborate further. I'd made up almost a third of a lap before I asked, "How did you determine the break-in was accomplished?"

"There was no evidence of a break-in," the commander said, his voice once again taking on a conversational tone. "No scratches on the doors or the locks, the keypads, or the windows. Nothing."

"And when you reviewed the video taken at the entrance to the chamber?"

"No one entered through that door between the time Feliz did his oh-three-hundred sweep and the time he returned at oh-six-hundred," Commander Johnson replied.

"On the contrary," I said. "Someone must have entered, or the damage would not have occurred. What you're saying is that the video recorders did not register someone entering during that time period."

"I suppose so," he allowed.

I was on lap number thirteen, the halfway point, when I asked, "What about an analysis of the video surveillance from after the break-in?"

"Why would I look at the video from after the break-in?" Commander Johnson wanted to know.

Ms. Washburn answered for me. "Because that is when Dr. Springer came back to the storage chamber and someone killed her," she said.

"That's a matter for the police," the commander sniffed. "They are no doubt looking at those time periods now."

"Why didn't you call the police when the head was discovered missing?" I asked. "Wouldn't that be standard procedure?"

Commander Johnson nodded enthusiastically and pointed a finger at me, which was confusing. I hadn't had anything to do with the decision not to inform the authorities. "That's exactly what I told Dr. Ackerman we should do. But he was so worried about anybody finding out—and if it were in the police reports, the newspapers would know—that we never called the police. But I made sure my objection was on the record."

Six laps to go. My arms were getting tired, and I felt a comfortable bead of sweat just under my hairline, which indicated the exercise was having its desired effect. I asked the commander what steps he had taken to secure the area after Ms. Masters-Powell's remains had been discovered missing.

"I sealed the storage compartment myself," he answered, and I believed his tone indicated a perceived insult. "There was video surveillance throughout, as you know. No one could have gotten in."

"And yet," I said, my breath coming just a little heavier now, "Dr. Springer entered not only the outer room, but the chamber itself, and so did someone else, who killed her. How is that possible?"

"I have no idea," Commander Johnson said. He spoke through clenched teeth. I thought for a moment, with three laps left before I could sit again, and asked him the only question I thought he might be able to answer.

"Is there a vending machine with water bottles on the premises?"

His eyes widened for a moment, for reasons I could not discern, and then he shook his head. "But you can find water in the breakroom, one level up," he said. He pointed to the ceiling, as if I had no idea where "up" might be.

Ms. Washburn cleared her throat, which I've learned is a signal that someone might want my attention, so I turned toward her. "I think Detective Lapides wants to talk to us," she said and pointed at the door. Sure enough, the detective's face was visible in the window.

Commander Johnson stood. "He's already questioned me, so I assume he's looking for one or both of you," he said. He stood stock still, as if waiting to be dismissed.

I finished my last lap and sat. I wasn't exhausted, but I had exerted myself. "Very well, commander," I said. "Thank you for your time."

Commander Johnson turned toward the door, but Ms. Washburn cleared her throat again. "Just one last thing, commander," she said.

He turned back, looking confused. "Yes?"

Ms. Washburn pointed to her notebook. "For my records, sir. What is your first name?"

The commander, as he had so many times in the past few minutes, looked pained. "Alvin," he said, and left.

ELEVEN

DETECTIVE LAPIDES SAUNTERED—I BELIEVE that is the correct term—into the room with his hands in his jacket pockets. "So, Mr. Hoenig," he began.

"Come with me," I said and walked directly past the detective and into the hallway. Lapides looked somewhat surprised, something I'm accustomed to seeing, and followed me. I wasn't sure, but I thought Ms. Washburn also joined us as we walked.

"Where are we going?" Lapides asked. "Have you found something?"

"Not yet," I told him. "I'm still looking for it, but I have every confidence I'll be there soon."

"Where?" the detective wanted to know.

"The breakroom, one level up," I answered. "I'm told there is cold water to drink there. Now, what were you about to say, detective?"

We reached the elevator, and I pushed the elevator call button with my knuckle. There was a silent moment, as I think the detective was catching his breath. He stared at me briefly.

"Well, first of all, Dr. Springer's death is being investigated as a murder," he said.

"Of course," I nodded. What else could it be? "The bullet in the empty containment case would mean it could be almost nothing else."

"Yeah." Lapides seemed disappointed. "And I want you to know we have eliminated you and Ms. Washburn as suspects."

Ms. Washburn bit her lower lip. I thought she might be trying to suppress a laugh.

"I wouldn't think we were ever considered suspects," I told the detective. "Clearly, we were not on the premises when the crime was committed."

"Yeah," he repeated, again with a slightly melancholy tone in his voice. I wondered what was making him sad. "But I'd like to ask a few questions about your discovery of the body."

The elevator doors opened, and we moved inside. Ms. Washburn pushed the button for the next level up, for which I was grateful. So many fingers push elevator buttons that having to press one myself is an unpleasant task.

"Please feel free," I told Lapides, since he had not yet asked a question.

"Here? In the elevator?"

"Why not? We know the same information in the elevator that we do outside, but if you'd prefer to wait..."

In that period of time, we had made it to the next level, and the doors opened. So we left the elevator anyway. But secretly, I had to admit the detective was starting to amuse me.

"What is your favorite Beatles song, detective?" I asked.

"'Help!'" he said. "Why?"

Energetic. Articulate. Possibly sees himself as a victim. Aware of his own limitations.

"It's a game I play." Lapides probably identified with the need for assistance and took the song on its most literal level. "Please go on," I urged him.

"Why were you going into the storage chamber before you knew Dr. Springer was inside on the floor?" Lapides asked as we walked down the hallway in search of the breakroom. It appeared to be an open area at the center of the level.

"We had been called in to answer a question about the disappearance of Ms. Masters-Powell's remains," I said. "I was about to examine the area in which her head had been preserved. But you knew that. You asked us that when you questioned us earlier."

"Yeah." This was getting to be a habit with him. "Did you smell anything in the chamber when you were in there?"

We reached the breakroom, which was simply an area that held a small table, three molded plastic chairs, a microwave oven, and small refrigerator. "Smell something? We were in protective suits with hoods, detective. It was not possible for us to smell anything."

I opened the refrigerator. It contained a single apple, three cans of soda (all diet), and a brown paper bag marked *JS*. I looked at Ms. Washburn. "There are no water bottles," I told her.

"No, but there is a water cooler in that corner." She pointed. A half-full five-gallon bottle sat on top of the cooler, which was humming. "You can have a drink from that."

"I won't know for certain the amount I'm drinking," I said. "I always have sixteen ounces of water at a time."

"I guess you'll have to estimate," Ms. Washburn answered.

"I don't like to estimate. It's not exact." I started to feel anxious, a clenching sensation in my stomach. I learned during childhood what that feeling meant, but even now, it wasn't always possible to control it completely. I began by trying to play "Here Comes the Sun" in my head. But Lapides interrupted George Harrison's lovely introduction, the acoustic guitar holding a capo on the seventh fret.

"Don't worry about the water," he said, reminding me of the matter that was causing my anxiety. "Think about the storage chamber. Was there any blood on the floor when you were in there?"

"Of *course* not," I said a little too loudly (I could tell because Ms. Washburn's eyes narrowed in concern). I walked with great purpose toward the water cooler and picked up one of the paper cups stacked next to it. "There is no indication of the capacity of this cup," I told Ms. Washburn.

"It's a four-ounce cup," she said. "Drink four of them, and that will be sixteen ounces."

The unease in my stomach was causing a slight sweat on the back of my neck. "How do you know it's a four-ounce cup?" I asked.

"Will you stop worrying about the cup?" Lapides said. "Just drink some water until you're not thirsty, and that'll be enough."

"No, it *won't*!" I shouted, unable to contain myself any longer. I turned back toward Ms. Washburn. "How do you know this is a four-ounce cup?"

She walked around Lapides to look me in the face, because I was trying to avoid eye contact. "I know because that's the same size and brand I use at home, and I use four-ounce cups."

I heard myself breathe out, heavily. "You're sure?" I asked her, and I watched her eyes. Her gaze was steady.

"Sure," Ms. Washburn said.

My stomach stopped churning. I walked to the water cooler, took a cup and filled it. When I drank, I noticed the water was cold but had a slightly different flavor than the bottled water I get from the machine in my office. Still, it was a relief to drink that cup and the one I filled after it.

"Blood," Lapides said, trying to remind me of something I had not forgotten. "On the floor. Of the chamber."

"Just a moment," I told him. "Two more cups." I filled the third and emptied it as Lapides, seeming impatient, watched. After I'd completed the sixteen ounces of water I'd set out to drink, I turned to him.

"Dr. Springer had not been shot," I said. "The empty containment vessel had been shot. There was no head inside, and even if there had been, there would have been no blood in it. Fluids are drained before the freezing process is initiated."

"But liquid nitrogen had been released into the room," the detective countered. "Wouldn't the air have been freezing? Why wasn't there more of a wound to her head when she hit the floor?"

Clearly, Detective Lapides was a person whose idea of science was formed by watching a good deal of television. "First of all, the liquid nitrogen released into the room would immediately have boiled, because it was no longer being kept at a temperature that could sustain it in a frozen state," I said. "But even if the room had been that cold, a person's head doesn't simply shatter because it sustains an impact in cold weather. There was no blood on the floor because Dr. Springer's head did not receive a severe blow; it was the lack of oxygen in the room that killed her."

Lapides, who had been taking notes while I spoke, kept scribbling, but he managed to ask, "Did you notice anything unusual in the chamber?"

"Besides the woman's body on the floor?" Ms. Washburn asked.

Lapides looked up sharply at her, and I decided I didn't care much for the way the detective was interrogating us. He was doing his job, but not well. I wondered if his superiors would have sent him to the scene if it had been known from the outset that this was a case of homicide.

"I had never been in the chamber, or any other such area, before in my life," I told him, deflecting his attention from Ms. Washburn. "So I have no basis of comparison to judge what is unusual and what is not."

I believe Detective Lapides sighed. "You know what I mean," he said.

"I assumed you meant what you said. Was I in error?" I looked at Ms. Washburn for concurrence, but her hand was at her mouth—perhaps suppressing a smile—so it was difficult for me to determine whether I'd said something inappropriate. Sometimes I do take conversation more literally than it is intended, because many expressions do not really mean what they appear to mean. When was the last time, for example, that someone actually pulled your leg?

Now that I'd taken in sixteen ounces of water, it would not be terribly long before I would need to find a restroom, and I had not noticed where the facilities were in this building. It would be awkward to ask Ms. Washburn if she'd noticed, because she was a woman, and pointless to ask Lapides, since I did not believe he would have observed the area closely enough to know. I would have to ask a GSCI employee, and the prospect was not pleasant; I am not always comfortable asking strangers for information.

"Let me ... rephrase my question," Lapides said. "Did anything you saw in the storage chamber—with the exception of Dr. Springer's body—seem worth noting? Is there anything you think that I should know?"

There were a great many things I believed Detective Lapides should know, but I knew enough about conversation after many hours of social skills training to realize that he meant something else by his question. "It seemed odd that Dr. Springer was in the room with Ms. Masters-Powell's receptacle the only one out of place," I said. "The administration of the facility and its security team already knew the remains were missing. Why would she be going in to examine an empty vessel?"

Lapides mumbled "empty vessel" as he scribbled, then asked, "What else did you see?"

I closed my eyes to better picture the room. "There were full-body receptacles at the far end of the chamber, and the partial remains—the crania—were kept nearer the door that could open, I presume to better accommodate any slight changes in temperature created by the inner door opening and closing as staff entered or left the room. The chamber had a relatively low ceiling, not terribly so, but certainly not high; I would estimate it at eight feet. The walls were painted a pale blue. The floor was a nondescript linoleum pattern, but not tiles; it was rolled out. The receptacle lay on the floor behind Dr. Springer, was clearly damaged, and had the patient's initials engraved on it. The lighting was from the ceiling, and recessed. And there was still some nitrogen in the air when we entered."

When I opened my eyes, I added, "And now you must excuse me." I walked briskly into the hall to make an attempt at locating a bathroom without having to ask anyone for its location.

"Mr. Hoenig," I heard Ms. Washburn say behind me, "there is a restroom just around this corner; I noticed it as we walked from the elevator." Ms. Washburn was proving to be invaluable.

"*Wait* a second!" Lapides shouted at me as I reached the door. I turned. "I'm still questioning you."

"And you may continue to do so when I come out, but I sincerely believe this takes precedence, detective." I did not wait to hear his response.

Suffice it to say, it is not normally my first choice to use a public restroom. Such a situation, in which I am unable to rely on my mother's impeccable cleanliness, is at best distasteful, and more often borders on horrifying. But there simply wasn't time now to leave the building, drive to my mother's house, use the bathroom, and then drive back to GSCI. Luckily, the facilities here seemed well cared for, no doubt because the institute required certain baseline standards of germ containment. Still, I spent no more time there than was necessary and was careful to wash my hands carefully before exiting.

I presume Lapides had taken it upon himself to ask Ms. Washburn about the chamber, because when I emerged from the bathroom four minutes after entering, she was saying, "The suit made it hard to see in great detail anything but what was right in front of me. I had very little peripheral vision."

It was one thing when he was questioning me, but his hectoring Ms. Washburn again seemed unfair. "Come now, detective," I said to Lapides. "You've asked us all this before, and you've gotten our answers. Tell me: What is it you *really* want to know?"

The detective looked either confused or insulted. "I'm conducting a murder investigation," he said with a great sense of pomposity in his voice, enough that I could recognize the inflection. "I don't have to explain my methods to *you*."

It was true; he had no obligation to me at all—I am not a resident of his jurisdiction. Still, I felt it was important to press on. "I am not asking you to explain your methods, since they are quite obvious," I said. "I am asking you to get to the point, as I also have questions to answer, and a much stricter deadline than yours. What is it you want to ask me?"

"I'm trying to gather any information you and Ms. Washburn might have from your time inside the storage chamber," he reiterated. But his hairline was already dark with sweat.

"Detective," I admonished. Ms. Washburn gave me a look that indicated she was appreciative but did not really see which direction I was taking.

"Oh, all right," Lapides said, curling his lip.

I looked at him, all attention.

"Mr. Hoenig," he began, "I've been a detective on the force here for six years, and a cop for fourteen."

I didn't see how this professional biography was relevant, but I let him talk without interruption.

"In all that time," Lapides continued, "I've never worked on a homicide investigation before."

"Never?" I asked.

"We have two murders here every *decade*," the detective lamented. "And most of those are obvious—family members taking a knife to each other, that kind of thing. It's never fallen on me before."

"I don't see how this has anything to do with us," Ms. Washburn said. "Mr. Hoenig and I didn't kill anyone."

"I don't think you did," Lapides answered. "But I do have a question for you." He turned to face me directly, and I fought the urge to look away.

"Yes?" I asked, my voice sounding steadier than my eyes felt.

"What do you think I should do next?" Lapides asked.

TWELVE

Ms. WASHBURN INSISTED ON our leaving the building before I could answer Lapides's question. She argued that it was possible the entire facility was wired for surveillance—which Ackerman had indicated was the case—and that our conversation could not be confidential if we remained inside.

She also mentioned that she wanted to make a cellular phone call to her husband, and that she was unable to receive a proper signal inside GSCI. In what I thought was a friendly gesture, I did not mention that any electronic surveillance inside the facility was probably being done on the outside grounds as well.

I believed that any conversation I could have with Lapides would be uninteresting to anyone listening in, anyway.

Ms. Washburn stood to one side, talking to her husband. I did not attempt to hear her side of the conversation, as it was not relevant to my business, but I was surprised at how quickly I had started to think of her as an associate in Questions Answered. I realized we had agreed that she would work with me only for this day, but perhaps it would make sense to make the arrangement indefinite. I would talk to her about that later, assuming I could consult with my mother at some point. Mother is very good at noticing when I am acting impulsively or misjudging the intentions of another person I have met.

Lapides, his shoes sinking slightly into the mud in this desolate field behind the facility, looked at me for some time before I met his eye and saw his expression was an expectant one. He was waiting for an answer to his question.

"You realize that my business is answering questions for other people," I began.

Lapides started to reach into his inside jacket pocket. "How much do you charge?"

I held my hands up, palms out. "I was saying that only because I want to emphasize that I am not a criminal investigator," I said. "I am not trying to charge you for the question you asked."

"You notice things," Lapides answered. "You seem to understand things. If there's something you've seen that can help me figure out what to do, I need to know about it."

I did not take the opportunity to explain about Asperger's Syndrome, nor to suggest that my knowledge of human behavior was academic, not instinctive. I made sure to look the detective in the eye and told him, "Very well, then; I will tell you what I think you should do, but I do not guarantee success."

A few moments went by as I awaited a response, but I got none, other than Lapides taking a reporter's notebook out of his back pocket and digging a pen out of his jacket to take notes.

"First, find out how many storage chambers like the one we saw are on the premises. I counted three, but I have not seen the entire facility. Then, call in a security expert other than Commander Johnson or anyone on the GSCI payroll, and have that person check the wiring on all the video and audio surveillance used on the level where the murder took place. Find out from employee records if Dr. Springer was married or had family nearby, if you haven't done so already."

"She was divorced, no children," Lapides said. "The ex-husband lives in Missouri, and is there now. He's not a suspect at the moment."

"Good," I continued. Lapides looked pleased with himself, like a pupil who has unexpectedly given the teacher a correct answer on a difficult arithmetic equation. "Concentrate on interpersonal relationships among the employees here. Were there any romances going on? Is there some jealousy that might have been a motive? Or is this strictly tied to the disappearance of Ms. Masters-Powell's remains? Talk to Commander Johnson's wife. It's a coincidence that she was present today, and any coincidence, especially when her husband was called in early to deal with an extraordinary situation, is suspect."

Lapides was rapidly scribbling down as much as he could remember. "Am I talking too fast?" I asked him. He shook his head violently as he scribbled more.

"Then I would look into the possibility that Ms. Masters-Powell's family might be upset with the kind of service her remains have been given here, and therefore might have taken out their aggression on Dr. Springer," I continued. "Summon her family here and question them separately, so they can't coordinate their responses."

"Wouldn't they be able to do that on the way over here?" Lapides asked without looking up from his pad.

"You're assuming they all live together and will come here in one vehicle," I answered. It was becoming difficult to imagine how Lapides had been promoted to detective to begin with. "I doubt that is the case."

Lapides stopped scribbling long enough to reach into his jacket pocket and pull out a pack of cigarettes. I felt my eyes widen.

"Please don't smoke," I said. "I won't be able to think of anything except your lungs filling up with tar."

The cigarette packet disappeared into Lapides's coat. He stared at me. "What's *wrong* with you?" he said.

"Nothing is wrong with me," I responded. "I have what you would call a disorder, but I consider it merely a facet of my personality."

I wasn't sure Lapides would ever close his half-open mouth. "Uh-huh," he said.

But there wasn't time to respond before I heard Ms. Washburn raise her voice into her cell phone. "There's no reason to yell at me!" she said, and both Lapides and I turned our heads in her direction. "I'll call you when I can!" She closed the phone and was putting it back into her purse when she realized we were looking in her direction.

Ms. Washburn walked to where the detective and I were standing. I could not read her expression, but given the context (as I have been taught to do), I believe she looked a bit embarrassed. "My husband is a little excitable," she said.

"I guess," Lapides said. He turned to face me again. "What else do you recommend, Mr. Hoenig?"

"That's all for now," I answered. "If you feel you've run into trouble again, let me know and I will do what I can."

"What are you going to be doing?" the detective asked.

"I have to answer the question about the missing remains," I told him. "I will be here questioning witnesses, as you will, but about the other issue."

Lapides nodded with an air of resolution and began walking back toward the building. When I did not make a move to follow him, Ms. Washburn put a hand on her hip and studied my face.

"Why aren't we heading back?" she asked.

"Why is your husband concerned about your working with me?" I countered.

"How . . ."

I think I grinned at her. Sometimes I can be immodest. It comes from people having lowered their expectations of me because of my Asperger's Syndrome. "During your conversation with your husband, you glanced in my direction nine times. Each time, your expression was either anxious or angry, in my judgment. I hadn't given you any reason to be angry with me, so I determined you were angry with your husband, and it had something to do with me. And since I have never met your husband, it's logical to conclude that he was concerned about your working with me. Just because I don't always make eye contact, Ms. Washburn, does not mean I'm not observing."

She studied me for a moment, and said, "I was going to ask, rhetorically, how my husband could have the nerve to suggest I shouldn't take any kind of work I see fit. I was making those faces at you during the conversation because I thought you'd understand that I was annoyed with him."

As I said, there is a danger in making assumptions about human behavior. "How did you resolve the matter with your husband?" I asked.

Ms. Washburn started back in the direction of the GSCI facility. "Let's go question some witnesses," she said.

THIRTEEN

"I AM NOT A blogger," Charlotte Selby said. "I am a *citizen journalist.*"

Charlotte, a woman in her early forties, I'd judge, and just barely taller than five feet, sat across the table from Ms. Washburn and me in the conference room at GSCI. She had dark brown hair and a face that was almost diamond-shaped, with a pointed chin and a narrow forehead. Given the usual stereotype, one might have expected to find a younger person in the role of blogger on "technological and spiritual issues," as Charlotte called her topics, but again, it is always a mistake to assume something without having facts to back up the theory. Charlotte was, certainly, not the usual blogger. Or citizen journalist.

Some people with Asperger's Syndrome call themselves Aspies. I don't. The words one uses to identify oneself is a personal choice.

"As a citizen journalist," I responded, giving her the courtesy she had requested, "what was your purpose in being here this morning?"

"I work for Eyeintheskyonline," she said, jamming all the words together the way they would appear on a Uniform Resource Locator (URL), or web address. "We cover all news, with a particular interest in life preservation and the afterlife."

It would have been counterproductive to voice any skepticism, so I pressed on. "And you considered Garden State Cryonics Institute a story?" I asked. "The facility has been here for seven years."

"I heard about the missing head," Charlotte said plainly. "I was here waiting for an interview with Ackerman, but he was out."

"Yes," Ms. Washburn said. "He was out getting Mr. Hoenig to look for the remains."

"You're not with the police?" Charlotte asked me. I indicated that I was not, and she immediately reached into her purse and pulled out the same kind of reporter's notebook that Lapides had used during our interview. "So tell me: What have you found out about this missing head and the dead scientist?"

I stopped for a moment, gave the matter some thought, and replied, "I think I prefer not to be a resource for your journalism."

"You want to be off the record?" Charlotte asked.

That was very clever; most people would have accepted the term as meaning what I had said. But I was familiar with the ethics of journalism, citizen or otherwise, having studied the topic as a student and recently for a question a client had asked about what he considered the "outmoded" concept of print reporting.

I shook my head. "No, I prefer not to supply you with any information, either for publication or for background," I said. "Please tell me—"

"I don't think so," Charlotte said. She put down her pen and folded her arms.

That was odd. "I'm sorry?" I asked.

Ms. Washburn, who had been watching quietly and tending to the small recorder I was using to tape the interviews, looked at me and said, "I think Ms. Selby is saying she won't cooperate if you won't allow her to write about it, Samuel."

"Damn right," Charlotte agreed.

That position did not make any sense. I needed the information Charlotte had to complete my answer of Ackerman's question. Why would I share all my research with her?

"I don't understand," I said.

"What's to understand?" Charlotte asked. "You want something, I want something. If we both cooperate, we both get what we want."

The way she had explained it, the theory seemed to make sense. But I was sure it did not. I am not terribly skilled in quick conversation, however, as I tend to think through each word the other person has said. So I was pleased that Ms. Washburn jumped into the fray.

"Let's look at it this way," she began. "If you give us any information that helps Samuel answer the question at hand, he will give you an interview that you can use on the record."

"But—" Charlotte tried to interrupt her, but Ms. Washburn was already continuing.

"The interview will take place only after the question is answered, and will last no longer than twenty minutes. Samuel's representative will have the right to examine any quotes you intend to publish before you do, and to veto any section Samuel believes is inaccurate or does not represent his intention when he was speaking. Is it a deal?"

Charlotte appeared to be either stumped or irritated. "That is not acceptable," she attempted. "I will not allow for an interview subject to see the material before publication. I have journalistic ethics to consider."

"And if Samuel does not talk to you, you'll have only your own ethics to consider," Ms. Washburn countered. "Samuel is very careful about his image. Because of certain aspects of his personality, he is inclined to respond in unusual ways. If he does not understand your tone of voice or an idiom you happen to use, he might answer you with a response that would not represent the answer he would give if he understood the context. So those are the conditions. Take it or leave it, Charlotte; that's all you're going to get."

Charlotte's eyes narrowed. I didn't have to read her expression to understand her thought process: She could refuse to cooperate, but she would come away with nothing for her trouble. She could try to negotiate, but Ms. Washburn was clearly not giving up much of my time or expertise. So she pursed her lips, emitted a sigh, and nodded.

"All right, but I get to watch him conduct the other interviews for my reportage."

Ms. Washburn smiled. "Not a chance."

"Oh, fine. You can't blame a girl for trying. God, I need a cigarette." The institute was a complete nonsmoking facility; she would have to wait.

Now that the ground rules had been established, I could continue with the questioning and assume Charlotte would be more forthcoming with her answers. I made a mental note—hardly my first of the day—to thank Ms. Washburn for her efforts on my behalf.

"Very well," I began. "How did you find out about the missing remains of Ms. Masters-Powell?"

"I have sources in the facility and no, I'm not going to tell you who they are," Charlotte said. Perhaps her answers would not be more forthcoming after all. "I got a call this morning that there was a head missing, so I hopped in the car."

"Was this the first time you've been to the facility?" I asked.

Charlotte waved a hand. "Hardly. Check the visitor records. I've been here five, six times in the last year. I find the process fascinating, and my readers like to know about any possibility that death might be reversible."

Reversible death. The phrase itself seemed oxymoronic, and yet, this entire facility and a number like it were counting on exactly that becoming possible. "Have you posted about the institute before?"

She nodded. "Twice. Once just a general feature that it existed, and then about two months ago, I ran a lengthy interview with Marshall—Dr. Ackerman—and a couple of the family members of people who were being stored here. I think Rita Masters-Powell's brother, Arthur, might have been one of those."

"Do you have a laptop with you?" I asked. "I'd like to see those postings."

"I have one, of course," she said, pulling a Dell laptop from the bag she had stored under the table. "But I can't access the Internet. This building's Wi-Fi network requires a password, and I don't have one."

"Perhaps we can get a look at your posts on one of the institute's computers later," I said. "Now tell me, once you arrived here this morning to cover the story, what did you discover, and to whom did you talk?"

Charlotte made a face that indicated she was thinking, and out of the corner of my eye I noticed Ms. Washburn raise an eyebrow.

"Well, like I said," Charlotte began, "Marshall—Dr. Ackerman—was out when I got here. So I talked to Commander Johnson and his wife for a few minutes, after I got past Lorraine, the receptionist."

"And what did the commander and his wife tell you?"

"Amelia didn't know anything," Charlotte answered, with a tone that I believe indicated she had no high regard for Commander Johnson's wife. "But the commander was very upset because he said he was being bypassed on the most important security problem that had arisen since he has worked here." She consulted a page on the reporter's notebook. "Yes. Here. 'He didn't even ask for my advice. He won't even let me down there.' You see he was quite upset."

"Marshall Ackerman wouldn't allow his head of security into the area where valuable human remains had vanished?" I asked. Commander Johnson had not mentioned that when I'd questioned him. Why wouldn't the head of the facility let his handpicked security officer investigate? Why come to me first?

"That's what Johnson said," Charlotte answered. "I asked him why that was, and he sort of grunted at me and left the room."

"Do you know how Ackerman met the commander?" I asked. "I understand he's been working here only five months."

Charlotte nodded. "After he fired Miles Monroe, Marshall wanted a military man to head the facility's security team. But most of the good ones are either still in the military or priced too high for the institute, so he ran an ad in one of the enthusiast magazines, and he found the commander."

Marshall Ackerman had said his previous security chief had "left to pursue other interests." "Ackerman dismissed Mr. Monroe?" I asked.

Charlotte looked at me with an expression I recognized—she clearly thought I was not as competent as I should be. "Yeah. There were allegations employees were mistreating some of the 'guests,' and Marshall wanted that stopped. So he got rid of Monroe and brought in Johnson."

"What do you mean, 'mistreating the guests'?" Ms. Washburn asked. It was an excellent question, one I had been planning to ask.

"Some employees—two of them, both fired now—were accused of . . . using one of the heads in a game of office basketball," Charlotte said. She did not look me in the eye when she said it; she seemed instead to be profoundly interested in the American flag on a pole in the corner of the room.

Ms. Washburn, however, looked directly at Charlotte, and she whitened. She began to say something, stopped, and shook her head. It was obvious to me that Ms. Washburn was appalled by what she'd heard, but it was not an isolated tale. There had been allegations of similar atrocities at the facility where the Red Sox slugger Ted Williams's cranium was being stored, although they were never substantiated. Someone at GSCI might have gotten the idea for a grotesque prank from those stories.

"Do you know the names of the dismissed employees?" I asked. "Could one or both of them be responsible for the theft of Ms. Masters-Powell's remains?"

Charlotte began rummaging around in her purse. "I don't think so," she answered, "because one of them moved to Nevada and the other was dumber than a post. Ernie Deshales wouldn't have been able to mastermind shoplifting a Snickers bar from a 7-Eleven." She pulled a snip of paper from the purse. "Here ya go. These are the two guys who got canned for the vandalism. Deshales and Randy Morton." She gave the paper to Ms. Washburn, who, having recovered from her shock, copied down the information on it and handed it back to Charlotte.

"Do we have contact information for both?" I asked Ms. Washburn, and she nodded. "Good. Now Charlotte, it sounds like this facility has been under clouds of suspicion for some time. Why did you not report on these allegations on your blog?"

"I didn't see the point," Charlotte answered, with a tone I recognized as impatience, probably with my perceived stupidity or naïveté. "I knew the rumors were false. Nobody did any damage to the people being stored here."

"How did you know that?" Ms. Washburn asked.

"Marshall told me," Charlotte said, her tone indicating that Ms. Washburn was no more intelligent than she thought I was, and that it was a sad state of affairs.

"Of course," I said. "Are you having an affair with Marshall Ackerman?"

Charlotte's head receded; she reacted as if struck. "I beg your pardon?"

"Are you and Marshall Ackerman lovers?" I asked. Perhaps my wording had been imprecise the first time I'd asked. I had no idea if either Ackerman or Charlotte was married, so the word *affair* could have been used out of its proper context.

"I will not dignify that disgusting question with an answer," Charlotte said, indicating that the truthful response would have been yes.

"As a citizen journalist, is it not your responsibility to your readers to double-check every fact and get more than one source on everything you report?" I was attempting to appeal to Charlotte's sense of professional ethics.

Unfortunately, she did not appear to have such a sense. "It is only my responsibility to get the information right," she answered. "In this case, the word of a respected industry leader like Marshall Ackerman was enough to put the entire silly rumor to rest." Her voice was so matter-of-fact, it almost obscured the truth, which was that what she was saying made no sense.

"I see. Well, thank you for your help on this matter, Charlotte."

But the blogger simply sat there staring at me for a long moment. So, in a signal that the interview was concluded, I used a tactic that I'd been taught in Dr. Mancuso's social skills training sessions. I stood up and extended my hand. "Thank you," I said again.

"That's it?" Charlotte asked, seeming incredulous.

"Have I missed something I should have asked?"

"Don't you want to know who I think stole the head?" she said.

If it was just Charlotte's opinion she was offering, I must confess to being less than breathless in my eagerness for its revelation. But if it would help get Charlotte to leave the room more quickly, I would have to accept the offer and move on.

"Of course," I said. "How silly of me. Who do you think is behind the theft?"

"Rita's brother, Arthur. The little weasel hated his sister and would never want to see her come back from the dead."

There was silence in the room for some time after that. Eventually, I looked to Ms. Washburn and said, "We should make sure that Arthur Masters comes here for questioning immediately. Thank you for your help, Charlotte."

She looked quite pleased with herself as she stood up and gathered her belongings. "Don't forget, we have a deal on an exclusive interview."

"Charlotte," I said, "what is your favorite Beatles song?" I didn't really care about the answer, but the question was worth asking.

"Is this part of your investigative process?" Charlotte asked.

"It is."

She barely took time to think. "'You Know My Name, Look Up the Number,'" she answered. "That thing cracks me up every time."

Complete and utter lunatic.

"Once again, thank you." I watched as she walked out through the conference room door.

"What does that song mean?" Ms. Washburn asked.

"That she is a very strange woman," I told her.

"News flash."

FOURTEEN

"The clock is ticking," Marshall Ackerman said. "We're not sure how many more hours we have before it will be impossible to properly preserve Ms. Masters-Powell."

"Based on the information you gave me, we have exactly five hours and thirty-seven minutes," I corrected him. Ackerman had summoned Ms. Washburn and me back to his office only seconds after the interview with Charlotte had ended. "If you do not receive a ransom demand or some such communication from the people involved indicating the remains are being properly cared for, we will have a very poor chance of finding them intact after that. So I believe we are wasting precious time rehashing these facts. Is there new information relevant to the question that you can tell me?"

Ackerman looked oddly surprised. Later, I realized he probably wasn't accustomed to being spoken to quite like that, but at the time I felt I was merely stating facts. People's emotions are tricky things, and sometimes I forget that.

Ms. Washburn, standing to my side, told Ackerman, "Mr. Hoenig is concerned about the urgency of the situation and is doing everything he can to answer your question while there is still time to bring the matter to a satisfactory conclusion."

"He doesn't need an interpreter," Ackerman said with a growl in his voice. "He's told me off quite effectively." He turned his attention to me. "Yes, Mr. Hoenig, as a matter of fact I *do* have some information for you. Arthur Masters is on his way here, along with Ms. Masters-Powell's mother, Laverne. And I thought I had asked you not to contact them if at all possible."

"I didn't contact them," I told him. "I assume Detective Lapides did so."

Ackerman nodded. "Yes he did, and when I asked him about it, he told me you had suggested it might be a good idea. Why would you do that when I asked you not to?"

"You asked me not to contact them about the disappearance of Ms. Masters-Powell's remains," I reminded him. "I have not. Detective Lapides is investigating the murder of Dr. Springer. That is a completely separate affair."

Ackerman gasped, not in surprise, but almost as if he were fighting for breath. He made some noises that did not resemble speech, and the veins in his neck became visible. I looked to Ms. Washburn for some explanation, but she had turned away and had her hand to her mouth. She appeared to be suppressing a laugh.

"Just … just … just try to be discreet about this matter," Ackerman finally pushed out of his mouth. "My business, this institute, relies on patrons like Rita Masters-Powell for its very survival. A challenge to her endowment for us could be crippling."

That should have immediately reminded me never to take any piece of a question for granted. I felt my hand go to my chin and stroke it, which I've been told means I am thinking more deeply than usual.

If it was Ms. Masters-Powell's endowment that was paying for the preservation of her remains, that meant her family either was not paying the monthly (or annual) bill issued by GSCI, or had provided the endowment for her before her death. So Ackerman's concern about Lapides contacting her family probably would not be motivated by a fear that his stipend would end if they were dissatisfied with the service for which they were paying; it would be because he was afraid they'd challenge her posthumous desire to have it paid. He was worried, in other words, that he would be sued.

In moments like this, I especially missed having my mother nearby, since she understood human behavior and things like anger much more completely than I do. I get "agitated," Mother says, when something is not logical, or when people act in an irrational way that keeps me from completing a goal. I know I should react differently, and had been working with Dr. Mancuso to find better outlets for the feelings of frustration and irritation. Some very interesting techniques had been suggested and attempted, but so far, my success had been somewhat limited.

The best analogy would be the kind of emotion that Paul O'Neill had exhibited during his days playing for the New York Yankees. Even watching on television with the sound turned off, I understood his frustration with making an out in a crucial situation, but knocking over a water cooler or throwing a batting helmet would not help to alleviate—

"Samuel," I heard Ms. Washburn say just to my right, "Dr. Ackerman asked you a question."

I turned my attention toward Ackerman, who had reddened considerably in the face since he last spoke. I wondered if he had expressed some anger toward me. "Excuse me, Dr. Ackerman," I said, as I have learned to do in such situations. "What was the question?"

His eyes widened and seemed to bulge from their sockets, although I'm certain that did not literally happen. "What do you plan to ... *do* about this?" he asked.

"Do about what?" I honestly had no idea what reference he was attempting to make.

Ackerman began to gasp for breath again, so Ms. Washburn spoke before he could. "About the impending arrival of the Masters family," she said.

"They'll be here in less than ten minutes," Ackerman added, his head trembling slightly.

"Excellent," I told him.

"*Excellent?*"

"Certainly. That will allow me to question Commander Johnson's wife while Detective Lapides is talking to Mrs. Masters and her son. And when he has concluded his questioning, I will be able to talk to them about the missing cranium."

Ackerman opened a drawer in his desk—the middle one on the left side—and pulled out a plain brown paper bag. He was still breathing into it when Ms. Washburn and I left his office.

FIFTEEN

AMELIA JOHNSON HAD AN expression that my mother would say "looks like she's sucking lemons." Her lips were pinched tightly into an oval shape and her hair, severely pulled back off her face, was beginning to go gray. If I were reading her face correctly, Amelia had not been pleased by anything for years, if ever.

"My husband has been treated abominably," she said, although I had not yet asked a question. "He is the chief of security for this organization. Yet when a situation arises, he is supplanted by an inexperienced *civilian*"—at this point she gave me an especially displeased look—"and will probably be blamed for everything that has gone on here, when it was all beyond his control."

"I have not heard anyone blame your husband for either of the incidents that have occurred here today," I told her honestly, although I had implied that he was responsible because as head of security, he should have prevented them from occurring. The fact that his wife was aware of the issues was probably a breach of contract, and could have been grounds for dismissal, but I have observed that marriage seems to have different boundaries than other types of relationships. It was, therefore, logical to assume she would have other types of information to convey. "Have there been problems with such things in the past?"

Amelia closed her eyes briefly, as if absorbing a hard blow. "How dare you suggest such a thing?" she asked. Her voice was harsh, it seemed to me, and there was an air of suspicion in her manner.

We had verified that one of the disgraced security officers from GSCI, Randy Morton, had relocated in Reno, Nevada, and was not on the East Coast when the incidents occurred. Ernest Deshales, the other, was in the Ocean County jail and had been for six months, having been convicted of armed robbery; so, strangely, he was cleared of any wrongdoing at the institute as well.

Amelia had insisted on being interviewed in her husband's office. It was a dark, wood-paneled room, considerably smaller than Ackerman's, with no photos on the wall to remind the commander of past triumphs, nor citations for past valor. It had no window, being below the street level. It was, in essence, a large closet.

Some interrogators who work for government agencies would have frowned on my allowing the interview to take place here, feeling the subject might be too comfortable in familiar surroundings. But I was not interested in intimidating Amelia Johnson, and she did not seem the least bit comfortable.

"I have suggested nothing," I answered her. "I was asking if there is a reason you would suspect others in the institute of placing unwarranted blame on your husband, and you have given me no examples of past incidents that would suggest this is an established pattern."

"Alvin has been the head of security here for only twenty-one weeks," Amelia said without changing her facial expression from the previous level of disapproval and acrimony. "During that time, there have been suggestions that he has run a lax operation and that access to the secure areas of the building has been far too open. Neither of those things is the case."

"Who made those suggestions?" Ms. Washburn asked. "Was it Dr. Ackerman?"

"Marshall Ackerman is a pompous windbag and a liar," Amelia said in response. "But he is too easily swayed by those who work under him. He agrees with the last person who spoke with him, every time."

"Who was the last person to speak to him about your husband?" I asked.

"Rebecca Springer," Amelia answered. She looked me directly in the eye, with an edge of defiance.

I chose not to react. I would have chosen to react if I had thought it would further the investigation, but it probably would not, and simply would have inflamed Amelia's passion, whatever it might be. "So you believe that Dr. Springer had some reason to deride your husband's performance to Dr. Ackerman?" I asked.

"I think she was in love with my husband and angry that he spurned her," Amelia said.

Ms. Washburn's eyes blinked three times.

"Are you suggesting that Dr. Springer approached your husband about having an affair and he rebuffed her?" I said, simply to be sure I understood correctly.

"I'm not suggesting it; I'm saying it," came the reply.

"You realize that if what you're saying *is* the case, it gives both you and your husband a very strong motive to want Dr. Springer dead," I said.

"Maybe, but I didn't kill her, and neither did Alvin."

"I'll accept for now that you're telling me the truth," I answered. "But assuming you did not kill Dr. Springer, how do you know your husband didn't?"

Amelia raised an eyebrow. "He told me," she said, as if that settled it. The women I had interviewed about this question were either unrealistically trusting, or lying.

"You asked your husband if he killed Dr. Springer, and he denied it?"

"Of course," she said, waving a hand. "He wouldn't have done something like that. This is just a plot to make him look bad."

Some people are conspiracy theorists. They believe that no crime is as simple as it might appear. Others are paranoid personalities who think there is a threat to them personally in almost everyone they meet. What appeared to be the case in Amelia Johnson was a combination of the two: a woman who believed that everyone was interested in hurting herself or her husband, and that no matter how simple an explanation was available—like the idea that her husband was merely an incompetent security officer—there had to be a more complex solution.

"Well, I'm not trying to answer the question of who killed Dr. Springer," I told Amelia. "I'm trying to answer Dr. Ackerman's question. So do you know what happened to the missing head?" I was no longer asking Amelia questions and expecting helpful answers. I was now asking questions simply to observe her reactions and see how her thought process operated.

"If you like," she said, "I'll show you."

———

The storage chamber was empty when we arrived, having taken some time to get security clearance, first from Commander Johnson and then from Ackerman when the commander decided that he would recuse himself from security decisions involving his wife. Both men had offered to join us in this "demonstration," as Amelia Johnson insisted on calling it, but I had declined their offers, believing that the fewer people in the room, the easier it would be to concentrate on the matter at hand. I am not fond of being in crowded spaces, and too many voices speaking at the same time can have an adverse effect both on my ability to focus and my nerves.

"This is not the same chamber in which Ms. Masters-Powell's remains were being stored," I mentioned. We had gone through a door marked C, not D, and the police tape marking the quarantine was not present here.

"No, but it is identical," Amelia answered. "Alvin told me that all the storage chambers are exactly the same, and the security equipment used in each matches as well."

Ms. Washburn, remaining somewhat apart from Amelia and myself, seemed nervous in this room. This was understandable, given the events that occurred the last time she and I were in such a facility. She was taking notes, however, clearly making an effort not to let her emotional state interfere with her work.

Amelia walked to the door to the inner chamber, picked one of the protective suits off the hook, and threw it toward me. Startled, I let it fall to the floor. "Come on," Amelia said. "We're going in."

As squeamish as I had been the last time I'd had to wear a suit that many had worn before, this time my distaste was compounded by having to pick the clothing up off the floor. I knew the floor must be extremely well scrubbed on a regular basis, but that did not help very much. I hesitated as I bent to retrieve it.

"Would you like a different one?" Ms. Washburn asked quietly so Amelia wouldn't hear.

I shook my head. "But thank you," I told her.

It took one minute and twenty seconds for Amelia and me to don the suits. It was agreed that Ms. Washburn would wait outside in the antechamber, since three people would make movement inside difficult. We knew the commander and possibly Ackerman were probably watching on security monitors somewhere else in the building.

Of course, it was considerably easier to open the inner door this time, with no corpse blocking the way on the floor. Amelia entered first, ostensibly leading the way to what she considered enlightenment, and I closed the inner door behind me once I was inside.

"How do you know what happened?" I said through the protective mask. I was aware of some communications link that existed in the suits; I was able to hear Amelia's voice, but it sounded amplified and nondirectional. This had been the case with sound the last time we'd entered the storage chamber as well.

"My husband is the head of security," Amelia said. "I know all there is to know about the facility and the way it's watched. There is only one way to remove a specimen without setting off loud, very effective alarms."

"So you are speculating," I answered. "You don't really have any first-hand knowledge of the crime."

"Believe me, this is more than a guess," Amelia said. "Any other theory can be proven impossible. I'm sure this one can't."

That statement did not increase my confidence in Amelia's reliability or her husband's ability to maintain security, but there was no harm in seeing what she thought was the *only* solution possible. Just because it came from an unreliable source did not make the idea itself incorrect.

She walked to the second-farthest chamber from the door. "This is the same location as Rita Masters-Powell's, yes? You'll notice the surveillance cameras there and there." She pointed to two locations on the ceiling, where indeed high-definition video cameras were mounted.

Amelia turned her back slightly to me, making it impossible to see her face or her hands. "Look at the cameras now," she continued. "Can they see what I'm doing?"

"Their view would be somewhat obscured, but you are hardly invisible," I told her. "If you are suggesting that the surveillance material showed no break-in simply because the intruder's back was turned—"

"I am not suggesting that at all," Amelia cut me off. "But I am suggesting that anyone entering the chamber with the intruder would not necessarily be able to see what was happening very well."

I acknowledged that with a nod. "Proceed," I said.

"Let's say there wasn't one intruder, but two," she went on. "Perhaps there was a routine check to be made on the specimen, or they had reason to think something was wrong. They would have entered in this order, the way we did, with the person who was planning to steal the specimen coming in first."

"So we are assuming that both people in the chamber were not involved in the theft?" I asked.

"I think that's unlikely," Amelia answered. "If more than one person working at the institute had been involved, there would have been gossip by now. There would have been rumors. There's been nothing."

"Why couldn't it have been one person, then?" Ms. Washburn's voice came through the speakers in the suit's headpiece. I glanced through the glass and saw her speaking into a microphone, her finger on a button on the control panel.

"I'll show you," Amelia answered. I thought her voice sounded annoyed, and that seemed odd. Ms. Washburn had not asked an inappropriate question; in fact, it was exactly what I was going to ask.

Amelia reached toward the container in front of her. "One person reaching in and breaking the infrared seal around the container would set off the alarm, assuming the container had not been cleared ahead of time by security. But if two people were here, one could break the seal while the other neutralized it."

"How is that possible?" I asked before Ms. Washburn could break in. Perhaps it was the fact that another woman was questioning her that made Amelia angry.

"Look." Amelia carefully pointed with a gloved hand at very small openings in the walls surrounding the container. "These are infrared signal sources."

I nodded. "Yes, I saw them before. They will register any movement around the container. I assume they have to be turned off before any routine maintenance is done."

"That's right," she agreed. "But the security log will show that the infrareds are usually disarmed from the outside chamber. If someone wanted to do something *without* it showing up on that log, they'd have to disable the sensors from in here."

It occurred to me that this was only one of numerous obstacles in removing the head from the chamber without being detected, but it was worth knowing how it could be done. I nodded toward Amelia. "How?"

"It's possible to blind the sensors without tripping them," she answered. "You can use spray bottles to identify them, and then mist enough to convince the sensors there is no movement when you're moving the container."

"Why would I want to disable the sensors?" I asked. "I am not under suspicion for the theft."

Amelia stood looking at me for a long moment. I couldn't see her face, so it was impossible to read an expression. "I meant *a person* could do it. Not you."

"I see. But wouldn't even bringing a metal can of aerosol spray into the chamber violate numerous security regulations and set off alarms?"

She nodded. "But a small plastic spray container probably wouldn't be detected," she said. She held up just such a bottle, which appeared half filled. "Like this one."

Before I could even contemplate what she might do, Amelia sprayed mist, which I assumed was water, into the path of the infrared sensors. I gasped, hopefully not audibly, fearing that her theory was incorrect and the alarm would sound. But thankfully that did not happen.

"One person would have to keep the mist flowing at just the right level, not so heavy that the sensors would notice movement from the water bottle. They couldn't stop until the cylinder was removed from the chamber and there was no more movement."

"Wouldn't the security system notice the absence of the cylinder once the mist was discontinued?" I asked.

"Certainly," Amelia said. "I figure they brought another one, weighted properly, to replace the original one." She demonstrated by miming such a move without actually putting her hands in the range of the storage assembly.

Amelia was making enormous assumptions about a crime of which she claimed to have no knowledge aside from a secondhand analysis of the facility's security measures. "That doesn't explain a great many things," I told her. "You don't have a way for these people to have gotten into the chamber with a second cylinder. You don't have a motivation for the second person, the backup, to help with the crime, since you believe that person was innocent. There are numerous security procedures being breached that you have not acknowledged. This sounds a little suspicious to me, Mrs. Johnson."

She turned her head, but kept her hands out of my sight. "What do you mean by that, Mr. Hoenig?" she asked.

"Frankly, it sounds to me like you're trying to cover up for your husband, yourself, or both."

Amelia Johnson laughed. "I don't know what you're talking about," she said. "I'm trying to help you."

"You're trying to lead me," I countered. "That's different. You want me to believe your theory, and you're kind enough to provide just enough plausible detail to pique my interest. But the fact is, this little performance is all about trying to get me to think the way you want me to think, and not the way the facts in this situation would otherwise point me. I think you know a great deal more about this incident than you are allowing, Mrs. Johnson."

"Oh, seriously." Amelia tried to turn toward me quickly, and in the course of doing so, swept her hand through the field of infrared sensors.

I had only a split second to think, and that wasn't going to be enough. I had barely turned toward the chamber door when the alarm sounded. It was loud and piercing and extremely disturbing. I felt my legs stiffen and my hands go to my ears.

Worse, I could hear the door lock automatically. There would be no way to get out until the alarm was disabled.

The alarm continued as I sensed myself drop to my knees. Amelia's voice was ringing in the internal speakers, but I couldn't make out the words. I believe Ms. Washburn's voice blended in at the same time. Lights were flashing. The intolerable sound of the alarm seemed to get louder as it continued.

Amelia's legs passed by me on her way to the chamber door, and she practically had to step over me, immobile as I was, now on all fours.

I was probably screaming. I forced myself up to a kneeling position again, but my hands were flapping at both sides and I felt like I could not stand. The alarm went on and on, and I was aware of people running toward me. I thought I saw gray GSCI uniforms gathering in the antechamber on the other side of the glass. I put my hands back up to my ears. It didn't help much, but it was something.

Amelia appeared to have a key card, because she managed to unlock the inner chamber door even as the alarm continued to sound. She stepped out and I lowered my gaze to the floor, trying desperately to ignore the horrible noise and stand up.

Ms. Washburn's face appeared in my visor. She was not dressed in a protective suit, and she was holding her hand out to me. I shook my head. Instead, I turned to watch the commotion in the antechamber. At some point, this nightmare was going to end, and I had to concentrate on that. It was the only way to stay sane.

Men were rushing around the room, but the screaming, blaring, horrifying alarm continued until Commander Johnson strode in, unwavering, and walked to a panel near the rear of the room, where no one else was standing. He worked a series of levers, in succession, from left to right, and then took a key card from his pocket and swiped it in a built-in socket next to the levers.

The alarm stopped.

My breathing was still heavy, but after a minute, I could stand. Ms. Washburn held out her hand again, but I did not need assistance in getting to my feet. I let out my breath and removed the head covering of the protective suit.

"Are you all right?" Ms. Washburn asked.

I nodded. "The alarm has stopped," I said.

"I was worried about you."

"I understand. Thank you for your concern."

She looked toward the antechamber door. "We should go out," she said. "If you're feeling all right."

"I am better than that, Ms. Washburn, I assure you," I told her. "I just discovered how the alarm system in these chambers is activated, and how it is disengaged. That might be useful information going forward."

She narrowed her eyes and stared at me. "You mean that whole scene was a fake?" she asked. "You really weren't paralyzed in terror?"

"Oh, no," I assured her. "That was quite real. But just because my Asperger's places me in a difficult situation, it doesn't mean I can't *use* it."

SIXTEEN

IT WAS GETTING LATE in the day, and I began to be concerned that I would not be at my home for dinner at seven, as was the custom with Mother and me. But Marshall Ackerman had a more pressing deadline, and he was not being shy about it.

"It's only a question of hours before that cranium is no longer viable, and you are falling to your knees in a storage unit because the alarm went off!" Ackerman's hands were up at the sides of his head and his eyes were wide. There was a drip of sweat coming from his temple. He was biting both lips.

I began to wonder if he might be undiagnosed with Asperger's Syndrome.

"That will become fact within three hours," I told him. "And I see very little hope of recovery before that time if there is no contact from the people who took the remains."

Ackerman blanched and sat down behind his desk.

He had summoned Ms. Washburn and myself here after the incident in the storage chamber. For some reason, he seemed less confident of my abilities now, despite my having gained useful information through my observations during the alarm period. It did not make much sense, but it certainly seemed to be the case. I had to make sure not to fixate on that puzzle, because it would distract me from the larger question.

When Paul McCartney needed help with a lyric, he could consult John Lennon. In fact, he could ask George Harrison, Ringo Starr, George Martin, or any of at least a hundred other people involved in and dependent on the success of the Beatles. If a member of the New York Yankees was having a hitting slump, he could count on one of the others to "carry" him until the problem was resolved.

I had been working completely alone until this morning, and while Ms. Washburn had proved extremely helpful during our quickly developing professional relationship, I could not yet rely on her for answers to questions I could not answer on my own. But I was beginning to see the merit of working with others, no matter how difficult that might make certain circumstances.

"Samuel," Ms. Washburn said. I regained my focus on the room.

Ackerman had raised his head and did his best to hold me in his gaze, but I was reading the small print on the diploma hanging on a wall opposite the chair in which I was seated and was uninterested in looking at his face.

"If your symptoms make it impossible for you to do your work, Mr. Hoenig, I don't see how we can continue now, and it's much too late for me to hire someone new," Ackerman said.

"I do not have symptoms," I informed him calmly. "I have personality traits that serve me quite well. And it is not my effort that is impairing our progress, Dr. Ackerman, but a serious dearth of facts as opposed to opinions."

"Have you even formed a theory?" Ackerman asked.

"Not yet," I told him. "There is no point in forming a theory when you don't have enough facts. All we know at this point is that the cranium was removed from the storage chamber at some point between the final security check on camera last night at eleven fifty-two p.m. and the time Dr. Lanier discovered the specimen missing at approximately five thirty-seven this morning. We know that Dr. Springer was murdered in the storage chamber while the specimen container for Ms. Masters-Powell was out of its designated area. A gun was fired and there was a leak of liquid nitrogen, which caused the oxygen level in the small chamber to decrease sufficiently to suffocate Dr. Springer."

"We knew all that this morning," Ackerman protested. "All these interviews and you've made no progress?"

"All these interviews, and we have established no further facts," I clarified. "I have heard the accounts of those involved, and will hear more accounts as soon as you decide this meeting is concluded, but all I know right now is that these people have chosen to tell me these things. I do not know which ones are true, which ones are impressions the witnesses had that are incorrect, and which ones are simply lies. That will require more time."

Ackerman looked more tired than desperate, although I am certain that was just a function of his stressful day, and not his level of concern. He stared at me for a moment. "Go do more interviews," he said. "I wouldn't want to hold you up."

"I wouldn't think so," I answered. "Robbing me would serve you no purpose."

Ms. Washburn appeared at my right elbow. "It's an expression, Samuel. Let's go."

While we were leaving the room, I believe I heard Ackerman mumble, "*Hold you up*, jeez."

An interview with Dr. Harold Lanier proved completely unenlightening. The doctor, a second-rate medical man from my observation, had been filling in for Dr. Springer and others on sporadic basis for two years and barely seemed to know anyone who worked at GSCI. When I mentioned Dr. Springer's name, he asked me who that was, and when I mentioned the missing specimen, his reaction was simply that he'd discovered it missing while performing a routine check and had "no idea at all" what might have happened to it. Once dismissed, he went quietly back to his post, which, according to every other GSCI employee I spoke to, was what he always did. "Hal Lanier is roughly as interesting as oatmeal," one of them had said.

I was less anxious to continue the interviews with GSCI employees, most of whom would not have had access to the secure areas, than I was to check on the progress of Detective Lapides, so Ms. Washburn and I took the elevator to the second level, where he was conducting his interrogations in the common area usually reserved for employee breaks and informal meetings with business associates, Ackerman had explained on our tour.

It was a mistake. Interviewing possibly hostile subjects (in this case, the Masters family members) in an open, inviting space decreases the interviewer's ability to intimidate. It makes the subject relax, and—even more seriously—allows the subject to become distracted by outside motions or sounds. Lapides was not a very good detective, but at least he knew it.

"I've done as you suggested," he told me quietly while one of his uniformed officers sat with a man of about forty and a woman who, judging from her age, was probably his mother. "I have Arthur Masters here, Rita Masters-Powell's brother."

"And the older woman is his mother?" I asked.

"Yes. Laverne Masters. When I called Arthur, she was over at his house and insisted on coming along." Lapides looked almost apologetic, as if he had somehow let me down. "I couldn't talk them out of it. I know you said they shouldn't come together, but there was no other way."

There was no point in explaining the difference between what I'd said and what he had heard in our previous conversation. "On the contrary," I told him. "It's very helpful that they are both here. Have you gotten in touch with the former head of security, Miles Monroe?"

"Not yet. He appears to be on vacation. In Sydney, Australia. The time difference is enormous." It was a sixteen-hour difference, but there was nothing to be gained by telling Lapides that.

"Have you found someone to check the security system's wiring?"

"I have someone willing to do it, an expert the county prosecutor's Major Crimes Division uses, but Ackerman is refusing to let anyone into his secure facility." Lapides started to reach for his cigarettes, looked at me, and took his hand away from the pack.

"I will talk to him about it," I said. "What about Ms. Masters-Powell's ex-husband?"

"I don't want to wait until he can get on a plane," Lapides said. "But I want to see him, not just hear his voice over a phone. I think the eyes are the window to the soul."

That was an expression I'd heard before and it had been explained to me, so I did not try to picture a window in someone's face. But Lapides's use of the cliché reminded me of the Beatles song "It's All Too Much," a George Harrison composition from the *Yellow Submarine* soundtrack, which had a line about looking into a woman's eyes and seeing love there. It has always seemed an odd line to me; love is not something immediately visible. It is an emotion, and while I have spent long hours studying facial expressions for emotions like fear, elation, anger, and disapproval, I have never recognized one that signaled love.

That thought wasn't helping. "See if Mr. Powell has a computer with a video call feature like Skype," I said. "You—and, if you would permit me, I—would be able to see his expression and hear his tone of voice at the same time."

Lapides's face brightened. "I'll get an officer on that right away. Thank you, Mr. Hoenig."

"Not at all. May I question the Masters family members when you have completed your interrogation?" I asked.

"I'm almost done. Just give me a few minutes." Lapides nodded, then walked back to the table where Arthur and Laverne Masters were seated.

Ms. Washburn, who had given Lapides and me space while we were talking, moved back to my side and spoke softly. "What have you found out?" she asked.

"That Lapides might have some potential as a detective, but he's going to need a great deal of help," I answered very quietly. I have learned about voice modulation. If I had said that in a normal tone, Lapides would have heard me, and he probably would have been offended, although it was actually a compliment, given that I had previously thought him hopeless in his chosen field.

"What's our next move?" Ms. Washburn asked.

Lapides was speaking to the younger man and leaning on the table at which he sat, palms down. If he was trying to look like an intimidating interrogator, the effect was less than he might have hoped. By a considerable amount. If Lapides was attempting the "good cop" technique, trying to ingratiate himself with the subject of the interrogation, the expression on Arthur Masters's face indicated he was being no more successful.

"When Lapides is done with the Masterses, we will have our own chance to ask them questions," I said. "And based on what I'm seeing, we will probably have a greater degree of success."

"I don't see how we could do worse," Ms. Washburn mumbled. She was being a little cruel, perhaps, but certainly accurate.

Across the room, I saw Lapides stand fully erect, taking his hands off the table and staring down at the seated Arthur Masters. "You're going to have to explain all this *sometime*," he insisted loudly.

The uniformed officer standing near Lapides looked, if I was reading his face correctly, embarrassed.

"Go on, you're done," Lapides told his charges. "Mr. Hoenig has some further questions for you."

"I don't understand," said the woman, whom Lapides had identified as Laverne Masters. "Are we finished, or are there further questions?" It was a good point—even I had been somewhat confused by Lapides's statement, and I already knew what the plan was supposed to be.

"Mr. Hoenig is not with the police department, but he is conducting an investigation for the institute," Lapides explained. "You're not obligated to talk to him, but we would all appreciate it if you would."

"I don't see any reason we should submit to more of this badgering when we've clearly done nothing wrong," Laverne told him. She stood and held up her hands, apparently anticipating her son helping her on with her coat, which was draped over a nearby chair.

But Arthur Masters did not come to his mother's aid immediately. "Who is this Mr. Hoenig?" he asked.

I took the opportunity to walk over and extend my hand. "Allow me to introduce myself," I told him. "I am Samuel Hoenig."

Arthur stood up but did not take my hand, which was actually something of a relief to me. "And what is your capacity here, Mr. Hoenig?" he asked. "Do you think we killed someone, too?"

"I most certainly do not," I answered, because I saw no possible explanation that could put Arthur or Laverne inside the institute facility at the time of the murder. "But I think your knowledge of the situation and your information on your sister's dealings with the institute could be instrumental in discovering exactly what happened, both to her remains and to Dr. Springer."

"So you want to talk to us as witnesses, not suspects." Arthur appeared to need clarification, although that was precisely what I had just said.

I decided not to overstate the obvious. "Yes," I said.

Arthur looked at his mother. She raised her eyebrows, a gesture I'd always interpreted as a sign of surprise, then nodded quickly. Arthur looked back at me. "All right, Mr. Hoenig. Ask your questions."

Laverne sat down, and Arthur was about to do the same when I interrupted. "I am not using this space for my interviews," I told them. "Please come with me down to—" I stopped, because Ms. Washburn, coming up on my side, was shaking her head rather violently. She drew near enough that we could speak without being heard by the Masterses.

"We're not going back to that conference room," Ms. Washburn said with a determined tone. "I've been in that room all day, and it's a windowless, airless box. No more."

"But that is where I have set up my center of operations," I protested.

"*I'm* your center of operations," she answered, "and I'm saying no. Besides, you start jogging around the room and waving your arms in the air every twenty minutes. It scares the people you're interrogating, and you're due for another jog around the room in five minutes."

That was at least technically true—it was actually seven minutes—but since I had resumed my regimen of exercise, the answers coming from witnesses had been unusually terse, and sometimes took a long time coming. Sometimes I had gotten the impression that the subjects were not listening to the questions so much as counting the moments until they could leave. It was odd how a man trying to elevate his heart rate could so disturb fully grown adults, but it was unmistakable.

"What do you suggest?" I asked Ms. Washburn.

She smiled. "I have just the place," she said.

SEVENTEEN

"WHEN DID YOUR DAUGHTER first mention her desire to be preserved in cryogenic freeze?" I asked Laverne Masters. Admittedly, the question was punctuated by gaps caused by my breathing rather heavily.

Ms. Washburn had suggested we move our interview headquarters to the institute's employee fitness center, which was currently closed off during the police investigation. We had cleared the plan with Lapides, who was thrilled to cooperate with me in any way he could, so now I was conducting the interrogation while walking on a treadmill at four miles per hour. To get in my accustomed amount of exercise, I would continue walking another six minutes at this pace. I could not increase my heart rate by raising my arms at this pace, uphill at a six-degree angle, because I was holding tightly to the side rails, which I had made sure had been cleaned and disinfected. I decided to do extra work on my arms tomorrow.

"She told us only a month or so before she died," Laverne replied. "She hadn't even informed us of her diagnosis, and then she was telling us that she had terminal cancer *and* instead of having a proper funeral when she died, she was going to be decapitated and frozen. You can imagine how I felt." She seemed less upset that her daughter had died, and more that she had not done so in a manner Laverne would have deemed dignified.

"Did you know she was ill?" I asked Arthur.

He shook his head. "We weren't especially close after Rita's marriage," he answered. "I think she believed I didn't approve of her husband, and she stopped talking to me before I could even express an opinion. She cut me out of her life without even asking first."

Another five minutes and I would be finished. "*Did* you approve of her choice of husband?" I asked.

Arthur did not answer immediately; it seemed he was trying to decide. "It wasn't my place to approve or disapprove," he said. "I was her brother, not her father. But if you're asking me whether I liked Bill Powell, I'd say no. He is an unimpressive little man, almost without a personality at all. I never understood what Rita saw in him."

I realized that it would have been better to have brought a bottle of water with me onto the treadmill, but then it occurred to me that drinking from it would have required my removing one hand from the side rail, and I wasn't about to do that. There was a fear—which might have been somewhat irrational, but was nonetheless real— that the change in exercise routine, coupled with the concentration in another area, might cause me to slip and fall. Perhaps one of the elliptical trainers would have been a more efficient choice, with more calories burned per minute. I would consider that for my next exercise session.

"How long ago were they divorced?" I asked. Ackerman had given me an estimate; I wondered if either Arthur or Laverne could be more precise.

"Three years ago," Laverne said. "I remember the exact date, it was April the twenty-seventh, three years ago. Every year I had to fight the urge to send Rita a card of congratulations on the date. Smartest thing she ever did."

"Was Mr. Powell cheating on your daughter?" I suggested. So many marriages end because one party is unfaithful, it seemed logical to start there.

Arthur chuckled. "Bill isn't interesting enough to have an affair," he answered with a sneer.

"Then, was Ms. Masters-Powell cheating on her husband?" I asked.

Laverne looked as if I'd suggested her daughter had suddenly become a giraffe. "I should say not!" she exclaimed. "Rita would never even consider such a thing! Arthur, we don't have to submit to these indignities. Let's go." But her son did not move from his chair, which was set up like his mother's next to the treadmill, where I had only three minutes left to go. I set the control for a three-mile-per-hour pace to begin the cool-down process.

"Excuse me if I expressed myself in an inappropriate manner," I said. "I have Asperger's Syndrome, and sometimes I do not say things the way other people expect to hear them." I did not believe I had said anything wrong—in fact, I was sure I hadn't—but sometimes mentioning a "disorder" with which people are not intimately familiar can have its uses.

As it did this time—Laverne flattened her mouth but remained silent.

"What was the reason for Ms. Masters-Powell's divorce?" I asked.

"I suppose she finally got bored," Arthur replied. "Like I said, we weren't speaking by that point, so I really haven't any idea. Did she say anything to you, Mother?"

"Your daughter was speaking to you, Mrs. Masters?" I said.

She sniffed. "Of course. A daughter talks to her mother. But all she said about the divorce was that she had grown tired of her husband, they had drifted apart, and she was leaving."

"She was leaving?" Ms. Washburn asked. "Isn't it more common for the husband to leave than the wife?"

The Masterses looked at Ms. Washburn with two completely different expressions: Arthur appeared to be finding her attractive, if my analysis was accurate. It was as if he had not looked at Ms. Washburn before and was pleasantly surprised by what he saw.

Laverne Masters, however, considered Ms. Washburn as if she were an especially lowly employee who'd had the temerity to question an order. "Rita left because she wanted to leave," she said with an icy tone. "What was *common* was never a consideration."

"My apologies if I said something to offend you," Ms. Washburn said. "I didn't mean to."

"Oh, you didn't offend me," Arthur Masters said before his mother could comment. "Don't worry."

Ms. Washburn nodded, and I noticed she made a point of brushing back her hair with her left hand—the one with the wedding ring on the third finger—slowly, so Arthur could see it. I assumed that meant she had noticed his interest and was trying to dampen it.

"Mrs. Masters," I continued, "were you with your daughter when she died?" I had not yet seen Rita Masters-Powell's death certificate and did not know if there was a police report, which would be the case if she died alone.

It was difficult for me to understand the dynamic between them, but that was not the issue at the moment. The treadmill program ended, and I stepped off. Ms. Washburn reached over with a bottle of water, and I took it and thanked her. I hadn't noticed she'd brought it into the fitness center when we'd entered, and I had no idea where she might have found it.

Laverne Masters shook her head. "The night she passed away, Rita had been moved to a hospice without my knowledge," she said. "They said she hadn't been there more than a few hours before she was no longer conscious, and she did not live long after that."

"And the hospice didn't call you?" Ms. Washburn asked. "That's usually the . . . typical procedure."

"They did not," Laverne assured her, not taking exception with the use of the word *typical*. "We had already agreed to pay the monthly fee this ghoulish place charges, despite my utter disbelief in this voodoo system of theirs, and when the time came, I was not even notified. Rita, apparently, had not listed me as a person to contact. She had provided them with only two names."

"What names were those?" I asked.

"Her ex-husband and Dr. Rebecca Springer," Arthur said.

When Laverne and her son were preparing to leave, I walked over to Arthur and spoke to him quietly, out of his mother's earshot. "Some of what you just told us was a lie," I said.

He stopped and regarded me as one would a servant who had been impertinent. "I beg your pardon?"

"I'm told that *you* initiated the contact with the institute on your sister's behalf, and that you knew her condition was terminal long before she told your mother. Rita never even visited the institute personally before she died, did she?"

Arthur sniffed the air as if something had fouled it. "You were *told* incorrectly," he said. "The only thing I did was set up the fund to pay these charlatans through my family's personal accounts, not the company's, *after* Rita was dead." He turned on his heel, took his mother's arm, and left the conference room.

I nodded. That had gone exactly as I'd anticipated.

EIGHTEEN

"I CAN'T AND WON'T allow some police functionary to crawl through our security systems and pull out intricate wiring and computer hardware, some of which is based on proprietary designs," Marshall Ackerman said.

We had returned to Ackerman's office after I concluded my questioning of the Masterses. Facts—or at least, reported interpretations of facts—were coming at me rapidly now, and while they added possibilities, they were not helping by eliminating others. This led to an abundance of possible explanations to the questions of the stolen head and the murder of Dr. Springer, but I needed to narrow the competing theories in my mind, not expand them. Still, it is a mistake to eliminate explanations strictly because they make it more difficult to answer the question; I would have to be vigilant and wait for a clear pattern to emerge.

I had communicated Lapides's request that Ackerman allow a security technology expert in the employ of the police department to review the institute's systems, which had clearly failed twice at crucial moments. And his refusal to do so was, frankly, baffling.

"I don't understand," I told him. "The police are trying to determine what went wrong with your equipment. Why would you not want that to happen?"

"Actually, initially I was all for the idea," Ackerman replied, "but Commander Johnson convinced me that allowing an outsider access to all of our security measures would present a more serious threat to the stable environment we provide here, and I have seen his point. There will be no further discussion on that matter."

I shook my head. "There will be further discussion when Detective Lapides obtains a search warrant from a judge," I told Ackerman. "Then you will have no legal recourse but to allow the examination. Why go through that ritual when it isn't necessary? A very serious theft of property you want back and an even more serious murder have taken place here. Refusing help when it is offered makes no sense."

"It's after five," Ackerman said. "Lapides won't be able to get in touch with a judge before tomorrow. Besides, I've talked to our brilliant police detective. I doubt he'll think of getting a warrant all by himself. And I forbid you to suggest it to him, Mr. Hoenig."

I raised an eyebrow. "Forbid?" I said.

"You are an independent contractor hired by this institute," Ackerman said, as if I were unaware of the situation. "As such, you are temporarily an employee of this institute. And that makes me your boss. I'm specifically instructing you not to tell Detective Lapides to seek a search warrant that would compromise our security."

"That would be considered withholding evidence, and I am not interested in violating the law," I replied. "I *am* an independent contractor under your employ, and you have every right in the world to dismiss me if you are displeased with the service I provide."

That statement might have been a bit hasty, given that I still had to pay the rent on my office and its utilities, along with other expenses for Questions Answered. It would not necessarily be a crushing blow if Ackerman discontinued my services, but I had already come up with a number of ways to spend the inflated fee Ms. Washburn had negotiated on my behalf, including paying her a salary and asking her to stay with the company indefinitely.

So I took a deep breath, as I had been coached to do in social skills sessions throughout my teens and twenties, and said, "I will not suggest a warrant to Detective Lapides."

Ackerman smiled in a way I have seen villains smile in James Bond motion pictures. "That's playing ball, Mr. Hoenig," he said.

I glanced quickly at Ms. Washburn, who was situated in a corner behind Ackerman's desk so she could see the computer screen. She shook her head—no, Ackerman did not mean we were playing baseball. I filed the expression away mentally.

There was no further time to discuss the matter, since Detective Lapides, followed by Commander Johnson and Amelia Johnson, walked into the office. Lapides wasted no time. "We've set up the video link with William Powell," he said.

"I think that unlikely," I said, thinking I was making a joke. I knew William Powell as the motion picture star of the Thin Man series and other classics. But no one in the room laughed, and Lapides looked strangely at me.

"No, we definitely have," he said.

"Never mind," Ms. Washburn told me before I could explain my comment.

We all maneuvered behind Ackerman's desk to get a view of his computer screen, which luckily was quite large and tilted upward. Commander Johnson made some adjustments to the program, called up the video conference function, and there, seated behind what appeared to be a kitchen table, was Rita Masters-Powell's ex-husband, Bill.

He appeared haggard and pale; it was possible he had not slept much recently. And he was thin, but it was equally possible he'd always been of a slight build. His eyes, if I were reading them correctly, betrayed a very deep pain.

"Can you see me?" he asked.

"Yes, Mr. Powell," Lapides answered. "This is Detective Lapides. I am taking the liberty of recording this conversation, with your permission."

"Yes, all right."

Lapides nodded to Commander Johnson, who performed various functions on the keyboard again, and a small indicator appeared in the top left hand corner of the screen, signaling that Powell's side of the call was being recorded on the computer's hard drive. I assumed there was a wireless feed to a laptop Lapides was using to record it for the police department's purposes.

"Thank you, Mr. Powell. Now, you understand that in addition to the … misplacement of your ex-wife's remains, there has also been a homicide here at the institute today."

Powell seemed a little groggy; he might have been on antidepressant medication. "I wasn't there," he said.

"No, we're aware of that," Lapides assured him. "But any information you have might be useful in both investigations, all right?"

"I suppose so. But I don't know anything."

"Well, we'll see about that," Lapides answered. "Now, can you tell me the circumstances under which you and your wife separated?"

"I don't know."

That was cryptic, certainly. A look of confusion passed around the room. "You don't know why you got a divorce?" Lapides reiterated.

"Not really. Rita came home one day and said I was boring and she wanted a divorce. She really didn't explain it any more than that."

Lapides looked at me with something like desperation in his eyes. So I leaned over toward the monitor and said, "Mr. Powell, allow me to introduce myself. I am Samuel Hoenig. The institute has hired me to answer the question of what happened to your ex-wife's remains."

"Answer the question? What does that mean?" Powell seemed almost disoriented. My suspicion about him being on some sort of medication became stronger.

"I am investigating the theft," I said. "Do we understand you correctly? There was no problem in your marriage until your wife announced her intention to seek a divorce?"

"That's right. She came home from work one evening and told me we were through. I tried to argue with her about it, tell her I wasn't boring, but I guess that's the sort of thing each person gets to decide for themselves, and she wouldn't hear it. She called her lawyer the next morning."

There had to be more to it than that; I don't know much about marital relationships, but it seemed odd for a wife to decide to end the marriage simply because her husband seems suddenly dull to her. "How long had you been married, Mr. Powell?" I asked.

His eyes rolled up toward the left side of his head; he was trying to remember. "Three years? Or four? No. Three. It would have been four, but the divorce came through a week before our wedding anniversary. Three years. Why?"

It was a legitimate question. "I'm trying to establish a timeline, Mr. Powell. How did you meet Rita Masters?"

"I used to work at the country club," he said, as if that explained it.

"What country club is that?" I asked.

Powell looked at me as if I'd challenged him on the theory of gravity. "The Woodline Meadows Country Club, in Mendham," he said with an air of obviousness. "The whole Masters family used to come by, and I was working there."

"In what capacity?"

"I was a busboy."

It seemed the wrong time to comment on the inherent cliché in the situation of a country club busboy meeting the wealthy daughter of the club's prominent family, so I did not, but I saw Ackerman stifle a chuckle. Amelia Johnson rolled her eyes heavenward.

"How did the two of you become friendly?" I asked. It was the most diplomatic term I could conjure.

"Rita told me later she always had an eye for me when she'd come to eat at the club," Powell said with a touch of pride in his voice—highly incongruous for him. "I didn't realize it at the time; it never occurred to me she'd be interested."

"Were you interested in her?" I asked.

"I didn't notice her especially at the beginning," he said. "I was mostly paying attention to my tables. You know, they really don't like it if you don't fill a half-empty water glass, or refold a napkin when someone leaves their seat for a moment. I didn't want to get fired, so I just watched my tables.

"But this one night, after my shift was over, I walked out the back way—you know, the staff entrance—and there's Rita, waiting for me. She asks if I'd walk her back to her car, and I say sure. I mean, it was probably a longer walk for her to go all the way around the building to get to the staff entrance than it would have been to go straight to her car, so I figure there's no way I can tell her no. I'd have gotten fired if she complained."

"You didn't *want* to walk with her to the car?" Lapides asked. I thought it was a legitimate question.

"They didn't like seeing staff—you know, male staff—with women members," Powell explained. "You heard about it all the time. But I couldn't tell her no, either. I guess there was some attraction from the beginning."

But the walk to the car had become something much larger, and I asked Powell how that had developed. As I spoke, I noticed Ms. Washburn watching the screen intently. She wrote something in her notebook.

"She said she'd been watching me in the dining room, and she wanted to know what it was like to work for all the rich people in the club," Powell explained. "I told her I really liked the job, even though I didn't, because I figured I'd get fired if she told my boss I'd complained. We got to talking, and she sort of maneuvered me into asking her to a movie on my next day off."

"And that's when you started seeing her socially," I said. Lapides furrowed his brow at the phrasing, and I wondered if I had somehow used it incorrectly.

"Yeah, we dated for a few months, and then Rita told me she was pregnant," Powell said.

The impact of that statement was palpable in the room. Ackerman actually rocked back on his heels a bit, and Commander Johnson looked at his shoes, something I had not seen him do at any other time that day.

"I thought you did not have any children," I said to Powell.

"Oh, we didn't," he answered. "That was something she told me so I'd marry her. And it worked. We got married a week later, as soon as we'd had blood tests and everything, in the courthouse in Morristown. We didn't tell Rita's mother or my parents until after, because we didn't want them to try and talk us out of it."

While this tale was interesting, it was not providing facts that would help answer either of the questions involved in the recent incidents at the institute. So I jumped far ahead. "Did your wife keep in touch after the divorce?" I asked.

Powell looked confused. "You mean, did she call or something?" he asked.

"Yes."

"After the papers were signed, I never heard Rita's voice again."

That did not seem to add up. "How did you learn of your ex-wife's death?" I asked Powell.

For once, the man's face showed some emotion, and he seemed to shake the haze of medication or depression that had been his most noticeable characteristic. He looked angry.

"I read about it in the newspaper," he snarled. "No call from her family, no letter of condolence, nothing from anybody. Just a five-paragraph obituary. I didn't even get mentioned under 'surviving.' It was humiliating." He slurred the word *humiliating* a bit, and I began to wonder if Powell was intoxicated.

"Did you know that she had decided to be preserved here at Garden State Cryonics?" Ackerman asked. He clenched his teeth, no doubt bracing himself against the answer causing him either insurance or legal difficulties.

"She had started talking about that right before we got divorced," Powell responded, and Ackerman visibly relaxed, letting out a large breath. "Came home with a brochure, said something about how she could come back to life if they ever found out how to cure whatever was going to kill her. I thought it was nuts, frankly. I mean, suppose you get run over by a bus. They gonna find a cure for that?"

Ackerman opened his mouth to reply, then apparently thought better of it. I asked, "So your ex-wife was already discussing cryonics with you three years ago, before you separated?"

"Yeah, that's right. I never gave it much thought. I mean, we were both in our thirties and it seemed like we had plenty of time to worry about what was going to happen when we got old. Maybe they'd find the cure *before* we got sick, and there'd be no reason to think about this freezing stuff. But we never really got the chance to discuss the whole thing before Rita decided she didn't want to live with me anymore."

Lapides had told me earlier that Powell was "shocked" when the detective had called with news of the theft at GSCI. I asked Powell, who appeared to be getting sleepy, whether he'd contacted his ex-wife's family after her death.

"I didn't want to have anything to do with them," he said. "You ask me, they're the reason Rita decided to get a divorce."

"Did she mention something about her family?" Ms. Washburn asked.

"No. But they didn't like me from the beginning. Her mother always looked at me like I needed a shower. And her brother pretended to be my pal, but you could see he wished I'd go away."

That seemed to contradict what Arthur Masters had told us. "Your ex-wife was in touch with her brother while you were married?" I asked.

"Sure. Called him once, maybe twice a week. They were thick as thieves."

I looked at Ms. Washburn, who seemed as baffled as I felt. It was Lapides who pressed the issue, however. "Arthur Masters said she never spoke to him after you were married," he told Powell.

"Then he's lying."

"You're sure you're remembering right?" Lapides tried. "Rita spoke to her brother at least twice a week?"

Powell nodded. "Every week. They got together for lunch every once in a while, too. The mother wouldn't give her any money—that's why Rita got the job at the bank—but her brother used to slip her something every once in a while over lunch. I never wanted to … to take it, but Rita said it was family money, and she was entitled to it."

"Where did you wife work?" I asked him. There wasn't going to be much more time. Powell's speech was slowing, and he would not be especially helpful as a witness for much longer.

"At the United Station Bank in Morristown," he answered. "She was an officer in the bank by the time she quit working and left me."

"She stopped working at the same time she filed for divorce?" That didn't seem to make sense—Rita certainly would have expected less money, not more, when leaving her husband.

Powell nodded too enthusiastically, like an alcoholic trying to be sincere. "Stopped working the day she moved out of the house. Got herself an apartment in Madison. Started going to the country club again. My friends who still work there told me."

I estimated, based on the tone of Powell's voice and his half-closed eyes, that only one more question would be answered coherently. "Did you wife ever mention Dr. Rebecca Springer?" I asked him.

"Becky?" Powell said. "Becky Springer? They went to high school together."

NINETEEN

I WAS CORRECT ABOUT Powell—after he made that rather amazing statement, he was no longer a credible witness. His responses to questions tended to be off-topic, mostly concerning how much he had come to love his ex-wife and how stupefied he was when she left him. Beyond that, we got very little from him, so Lapides terminated the interview less than five minutes later.

"This question continues to become more perplexing the more we discover," I told the assembled group. Lapides had checked with his Information Technology expert to be assured that the interview had been saved to a hard drive and a disk for later use. Now the Johnsons, Lapides, and Ackerman stayed behind Ackerman's desk, while Ms. Washburn joined me in the larger part of the room. I paced; Ms. Washburn stood with her notebook and watched.

"Rita Masters-Powell and Rebecca Springer went to high school together?" Ackerman said. "Does that even mean anything?"

"Not necessarily." Lapides, doing his best to be the detective in charge of the investigation, stood fully straight and made a great effort to appear confident. "Sometimes things really are just coincidences."

"I don't believe that is the case here," I broke in. "Two women involved in these two crimes, that closely bound, and they had a previous relationship that went back decades. Ms. Masters-Powell knew Dr. Springer well enough in her adulthood that her ex-husband knows the name without having to check, even in what was clearly an impeded state of mind."

"What about that?" Commander Johnson asked. "Isn't is possible that Powell was just answering with what he thought you wanted to hear? By that point in the interview, he clearly was not completely awake and alert."

I checked my watch. It was 5:07 p.m., which meant I no longer had to exercise every twenty minutes. That regimen is observed only from eight a.m. to five p.m., my normal hours at Questions Answered, in order to work most efficiently.

"If he had merely said that his ex-wife knew the doctor, that might have been his intention," I answered. "But he added the context, that they knew each other since high school. That was not something he could have taken from my question; it was a detail he volunteered on the spot. I believe it to be true, but I imagine that your employee records on Dr. Springer will bear me out, won't they, Dr. Ackerman?"

Ackerman sat back down at his computer station and readjusted the flat-screen monitor to face him in a seated position. He began to work the keyboard, and in less than a minute, stopped and scrolled down a page on his screen.

"Rebecca attended West Morris Mendham High School," he confirmed. "I can check the educational records on Ms. Masters-Powell, but they probably show the same school during the same years."

"Please do confirm it, though," I said. "We want to be sure of our facts."

Ackerman began the task, but Amelia Johnson was not willing to wait. "So they went to high school together," she said. "I went to high school with Queen Latifah. Doesn't mean we're tied together in any way, shape, or form. She was just Dana Owens then, anyway."

"We have some evidence, strictly on the word of Ms. Masters-Powell's ex-husband, that they saw each other more recently than high school," I reminded her. "Did Dr. Springer have any family?" I asked Ackerman.

"I told you," Lapides broke in. "She was divorced and had no children, remember?"

"Yes, but did she have parents, siblings, someone in the area who might have known about her friends? Ackerman?"

"She did go to West Morris Mendham High School, and she was there for two years with Rita Masters," Ackerman said, answering a question from a few minutes before. "Let me scroll up to her family records…"

"Where is this getting you?" Amelia demanded. "It's not helping to clear my husband's name."

"Mrs. Johnson, our goal here is to arrive at the truth," I informed her. "If we try to apply the facts to a theory, rather than collect facts and see where they lead us, we will no doubt arrive at an incorrect answer to the question."

"What does that mean?" Amelia asked.

"We are not trying to vindicate the commander," I explained. "We're trying to find out what happened."

Amelia's eyes flashed anger, which startled me. It had never been my mission to advocate for the commander; it made no sense that she should expect me to do so. If her husband had indeed participated in either of the crimes being investigated—and there had been no conclusive evidence for either position on that question as yet—I would indeed be foolish to spend my time trying to prove his innocence. It would be like attempting to prove that the Boston Red Sox have won more World Series than the New York Yankees—no matter how much a dedicated Boston fan would like that proposition to be true, the facts clearly prove it otherwise.

But before Amelia could voice her indignation, Ackerman pointed to his screen. "Rebecca didn't have any siblings, but her father is still living in Mendham," he said, sounding proud of himself for his ability to look up his business's own personnel records. "Has he been notified, detective?"

Lapides picked up a clipboard he had placed on a side table and began leafing through the pages clipped to it. After a moment, he said, "Yes. He was advised of the loss this morning."

"Call him and ask if his daughter was close to Rita Masters-Powell," I suggested.

Ms. Washburn coughed, which I interpreted as a way of getting my attention. "Maybe we could find a classmate, or a current friend, to ask," she said. "I think Dr. Springer's father might be a little upset today."

I almost protested, thinking that Dr. Springer's father would benefit from our discovering who had murdered his daughter, but it occurred to me that Ms. Washburn might be applying an emotional context that I may not have considered. Mother often does the same thing for me in certain situations. I have found it best to defer to her judgment in such situations.

"Perhaps so," I agreed with Ms. Washburn. "Detective, have you found any close friends of Dr. Springer's?"

Lapides went back to his clipboard. "There's an Amy Fitzgerald," he said. "She knew the doctor from medical school; she was an instructor there. I'll have a uniform get in touch with her."

"Maybe you could see to it yourself," I urged. "It would be helpful for you to talk face-to-face to Ms. Fitzgerald, to gauge her reactions, her comfort level answering the questions."

Commander Johnson's eyes widened. "Lapides?"

"Yes?" the detective responded.

"No, I just meant … I'm saying, reading a person's face, getting a feel for whether they're lying …" The commander seemed to be backpedaling from something he had wanted to say. "It doesn't seem like those are your best things."

As soon as the commander began speaking, I turned my attention to Detective Lapides's face. I've made it a priority to learn as much as I can about facial expressions. Their interpretation does not come naturally to me, so a great deal of practice has been necessary—and helpful—for me to read faces. I'm still not an expert, and perhaps not even as proficient as a person without Asperger's Syndrome, but I have come far from where I began.

In this case, it occurred to me from Commander Johnson's tone that he was going to say something derogatory about Lapides, and as his speech progressed, that became more and more evident. Seeing how the detective reacted facially would tell me much about the situation, and about Detective Lapides.

At first, he looked merely surprised. But as the commander continued, the detective's expression took on an air of sadness—he appeared to concur with Commander Johnson's assessment of his interrogation technique, and was unhappy about what he saw as a major shortcoming. But by the time Commander Johnson finished speaking, Lapides's expression had changed.

Now, he appeared purely angry.

"I can handle it," Lapides said through clenched teeth. "Don't you worry."

Since I had seen the detective in action only when he was questioning Ms. Washburn and myself, my experience was limited, and my assessment incomplete. It was entirely possible that Commander Johnson's expression of contempt was merited, but I could not be certain of that now. Again, it was Ms. Washburn who stepped in diplomatically to defuse the situation.

"Maybe you should bring Ms. Fitzgerald here, so that we can all see how well you do," she suggested to Lapides. "I'll bet you can prove Commander Johnson wrong."

"That seems to be what everybody around here wants to do," Amelia Johnson muttered.

Lapides took the bait, not having heard Amelia's comment. "I'll do just that," he said.

With a new expression of determination on his face, Lapides turned to leave the room. But before he began walking, I noticed Ms. Washburn trying to catch my eye. She signaled toward Lapides with her eyes, and I nodded. I hoped the intent of the message was the same on both our parts; having worked with Ms. Washburn for just one day, I couldn't be sure, but every instance so far had shown a rapport that I would have considered extremely unlikely after such a short acquaintance.

She intercepted Lapides on his way out of the room and spoke very quietly to him for just a moment. He nodded and walked out.

"What was that all about?" Ackerman asked when Lapides had left.

"I was encouraging him," Ms. Washburn answered. "I thought what Commander Johnson said to him was mean and unfair."

Amelia Johnson gasped at the impudence of it all and turned to leave the room. "The depth of this conspiracy is unbelievable!" she shouted as she left.

Her husband made no move to stop her. He actually seemed to exhale after she was out of the room.

"This squabbling isn't getting us anywhere," Ackerman said, mopping his brow with a handkerchief. "How much time do we have left before Rita's remains are no longer viable?" He looked at his watch, something he'd done frequently since we'd come into his office.

"There are too many variables to answer that question," I responded. "We do not know who has the material, or what equipment they have to preserve it. In theory, someone could keep the cranium frozen indefinitely, in which case we have nothing to worry about in terms of time.

"But if there is no means of preservation at the site where the thieves have taken Ms. Masters-Powell's remains, we have probably already lost any possibility of recovering them safely," I continued. "And since Ms. Masters-Powell's family is already aware of the situation and we have still had no communication with the thieves, I suggest that it is best for us to assume the cranium is being preserved properly, since we have no recourse if it is not."

Ackerman's mouth flapped open twice, but he said nothing. He seemed stunned.

Commander Johnson, arms folded behind Ackerman's desk, appeared completely unaffected by my analysis. His interest was the facility's security, nothing else. Whether or not a Masters family fund continued to pay a somewhat upscale monthly fee was not his concern.

"We should be spending this time trying to track down the thieves," he said. "If the head is still usable or not, they still broke into this facility and stole secured property."

"An excellent point," I agreed. "How do you think we should proceed from here?" I have found, after a good deal of trial and error, that appealing to most people's egos usually has the effect of increasing the flow of information and avoiding uncomfortable scenes. Mother tends to believe this is strictly a male trait, but I have seen it work with women as well.

Sure enough, Commander Johnson's chest seemed to swell as he took an even more erect stance and very visibly considered the question. "What you've been doing so far has been ineffective," he began. Social skills training would have benefitted the commander, as criticism is rarely the best conversation starter. "It's not your fault; you are not experienced in security and criminal justice."

"What do you suggest?" I reiterated. There was no sense in debating who might be at fault when the theft and the murder took place under the commander's watch, before I was consulted at all.

"Physical evidence," he answered. "Interviewing witnesses can only take the investigation so far. What is the physical evidence present at the crime scene?"

"Detective Lapides has gathered the evidence so far," I said, and did not react when the commander rolled his eyes at the mention of Lapides's name. There was no time now for this juvenile turf war. "But what I saw consisted of the receptacle for Ms. Masters-Powell's remains, which had been removed from its storage site, behind Dr. Springer's body, which was face down on the floor, blocking the door to the chamber. There was a bullet hole in the receptacle, but not in Dr. Springer. The rest of the receptacles were undisturbed, or at least appeared so to the naked eye. There was no blood on the floor, as Dr. Springer was not shot, but suffocated. In the outer chamber, there was no sign of a struggle, nor was the alarm system activated. Is there anything I am leaving out, Ms. Washburn?"

She seemed startled at my addressing her. "Not that I saw, Samuel," she said.

I turned to face the commander and waited for his assessment. It was not long in coming.

"Very good," he pronounced my report. "But another examination of the scene, by a trained eye, couldn't possibly hurt."

I was about to agree with him but to avoid noting that his eye was no more trained than most, when Lapides opened the door to Ackerman's office and walked back inside. He was wearing a most unfortunately smug grin on his face.

Lapides strode directly to Ackerman's desk and pulled a paper from his inside jacket pocket. "There!" he said. "A warrant signed by a judge that gives my technology expert access to your video surveillance system." He slapped the paper down onto Ackerman's desk with a theatrical flair. "He'll be here inside of an hour."

Then the detective did something so ill advised that I questioned his social skills as well. He looked at me, winked, and gave me a thumbs-up gesture. He turned back toward Ackerman. "And I will be interrogating Dr. Springer's friend Amy in the conference room very soon. Be sure to come in and see how I do."

Ackerman, taking notice of this, narrowed his eyes and positively scowled.

At me.

Lapides, not noticing the damage he had just caused, turned on his heel, no doubt having rehearsed the move, and left Ackerman's office.

I avoided the urge to look at Ms. Washburn.

Ackerman stood up, his face a picture of rage, turning redder as he rose, and pointed his index finger at me. "You!" he shouted. "You told him to get that warrant!"

"I did not," I said. "We had an agreement that I would not recommend a warrant to the detective, and I did not violate that agreement, even though I believed it was the right thing to do."

"I don't believe you," Commander Johnson insisted. "Lapides never would have thought of that himself. I'm surprised he thought to tie his shoes this morning. You had to have suggested it to him."

"I did not," I insisted.

"There was no one else who could have," Ackerman told me.

Ms. Washburn walked to the front of his desk. "There was someone else," she said. "There was me."

Ackerman, who had spent the day mostly acting as if Ms. Washburn were not even in the room, looked positively astonished. His eyes widened and his nostrils flared. His mouth opened, but no sound came out. Even a person with Asperger's Syndrome without social skills training could tell that he was furious.

Commander Johnson, unlike Ackerman, was having no trouble finding his voice. "You!" he shouted at Ms. Washburn. "You have betrayed this facility and breached our security!"

"Oh, I did not," she answered, her voice confident. "I'm helping the police in the investigation of a theft and a murder. Isn't that what citizens are supposed to do?"

Ackerman worked his jaw for a moment, just opening and closing his mouth, and then he looked not at Ms. Washburn, but at me. It's an eerie feeling for a person with an autism-spectrum condition. Even when we have a decent inkling of the other person's intent, we know we are at a disadvantage, because we have to take the extra time to extrapolate facial expressions and tones of voice at the same time.

So having Ackerman stare me directly in the face was a somewhat unnerving experience.

When he could get his voice under control, he breathed out at me, "She does your bidding. You asked her to do this."

His anger did not make sense to me. "I do not understand your position," I told him. "There is no reason to oppose an examination of the wiring in the closed-circuit system. Allow it to happen, and we will answer your question sooner and more accurately."

Ackerman bit his lip hard. I was surprised it did not draw blood.

"You're not going to answer anything," he hissed. "I want you and her"—he pointed at Ms. Washburn—"out of here immediately. You're fired."

There are times when someone like me is lost for a response, and this was one. I have a difficult time dealing with irrational emotion. Even when I have what my mother still refers to as a "moment," there is thought behind it, not just blind rage. So when Ackerman turned so heatedly and made me that uncomfortable, I was taken by surprise and could not find the appropriate answer to his statement.

"I…I…I…"

Ms. Washburn took my arm and started to lead me away from the desk, but my feet did not respond to my command.

I had never been fired before.

"You heard him," Commander Johnson said. He stepped out from behind the desk, perhaps in an attempt to appear physically threatening. I wasn't sure.

I tried to think more clearly and took a deep breath, as I have been trained to for years. "I don't think you have a clear view of the situation," I said to Ackerman.

"He didn't ask me to do anything," Ms. Washburn said. "We didn't discuss it. I'll leave, but Mr. Hoenig should stay. He didn't do anything wrong."

Ackerman narrowed his eyes and looked at me. "Is that true, Hoenig?" he asked.

I shook my head. "No," I said. "Ms. Washburn did exactly what I wanted her to do."

He nodded, a short, swift motion. "Then you are still fired. Leave immediately."

Perhaps he was simply misinterpreting my intentions, which were obviously to answer his question efficiently. "Dr. Ackerman," I began.

"Get. Out."

We got out. There was nothing left to say.

I saw some advantage to the situation, however—now I would not be late for dinner.

TWENTY

"You didn't have to do that."

Ms. Washburn, sitting in the driver's seat of her car, did not look at me because she was concentrating on the road. And her inflection was difficult for me to read. I hadn't done anything; I was sitting quietly in the passenger's seat, mentally going over the last meeting with Ackerman and trying to understand what had happened.

"Do what?" I asked.

"Tell Ackerman that I did what you wanted me to do. I could have taken the heat for what happened, and you would have been able to go on trying to find the answer to the question."

My eyes were tired, and I rubbed them with my thumb and index finger. "What I said was true," I told Ms. Washburn. "You did do what I wanted you to do. There was no point in denying it."

"Sure there was. You could have kept the job." She made a turn onto US Highway 1 heading north. We would be back at my home in fourteen minutes at this speed.

"I wouldn't have had a ride home," I pointed out. "And you wouldn't have been able to continue on the question."

"You don't need me. I just signed on for the day, remember?"

That seemed like a long time ago. I had gained a good deal of admiration for Ms. Washburn in the time we had worked together and did not want her to leave Questions Answered, even if we were not working for Ackerman and his institute any longer.

"Would you like to continue on with the company?" I asked her. "I'd like you to stay."

Ms. Washburn's lips puffed out a bit. I wasn't familiar with that expression and did not have time to ask her what it meant before she said, "I don't think I can, Samuel. You know how my husband feels about this."

In fact, Ms. Washburn had taken another call from her husband on her cell phone while we walked from the GSCI building to her car through the parking lot. I tried not to eavesdrop, but Mr. Taylor's voice was quite piercing, and he seemed quite displeased with his wife's absence. He also mentioned something about "working with that retarded guy," which drew an acidic response from Ms. Washburn that I would not care to repeat.

"How do *you* feel about it, Ms. Washburn?" I asked.

She paused for what seemed like a long time but was really only eight seconds. "Samuel, my marriage has been a little … troubled for a while now. I don't want to give up on it, and my working with you seems to be a sore point for my husband right now. I'm sorry, but I have to make that a higher priority than Questions Answered. Do you understand that?"

"Of course I understand. I am not ... that is, I have an IQ of one hundred thirty-seven, Ms. Washburn."

Ms. Washburn smiled, but it did not seem a happy smile. "I know. And you can call me Janet."

"Thank you, but I don't think I will." She just seemed like Ms. Washburn to me, and I do not especially care for change, particularly change in the way I think.

"Why do you think Ackerman is so dead set against someone looking into his closed-circuit system?" Ms. Washburn asked, skillfully changing the subject after what I perceived was an awkward moment. "Do you think he's involved in the theft, or Dr. Springer's murder?"

"I do not have enough facts to form an opinion yet," I reminded her. "But it would seem illogical for Ackerman to participate in the crime, then hire me to investigate the crime and answer the question. And he would have no motive to steal Ms. Masters-Powell's remains. He couldn't ransom them from himself."

"Maybe the theft was just a distraction. A red herring set up to provide cover for the murder of Dr. Springer," Ms. Washburn suggested.

There was a high-pitched chirping sound, which I had come to realize was the ringing of Ms. Washburn's cellular phone. She pulled it out of her pocket and extended it toward me.

"I don't want to take my eyes off the road," she said. "Who does it say is calling? Because if it's my husband, he can wait until I get home."

I did not take the phone from her because I prefer not to handle other people's personal belongings unless it is necessary, but I could read the writing on the screen. "It appears to be a call from Detective Lapides," I reported.

"Oh, go ahead and take it," Ms. Washburn said. Again, the phone was pushed in my direction.

It would have been rude to have taken a handkerchief from my pocket to handle the phone. Mother has told me that, and I have found her word to be reliable under similar circumstances. If the phone had been a stranger's, I doubt I would have touched it. But Ms. Washburn was, I had come to believe, a friend, and I did not want to insult her. Still, the idea of the microbes and microorganisms existing on that telephone was daunting. I don't understand why people think it a good idea—or, more to the point, don't think about it at all—to exchange such items freely. I am not technically germaphobic; that is not part of my Asperger's Syndrome. But it seems like simply good common sense to protect oneself.

I decided, therefore, to touch the phone as little as possible. "Just touch that button for speakerphone, and talk," Ms. Washburn said. "That way we both can hear. Go ahead, Samuel." She held out her hand far enough that I became concerned about her ability to make turns accurately.

Gingerly, I took the phone from her hand and held in between my thumb and index finger, mentally resolving to wash my hands immediately upon getting home. I pressed the button Ms. Washburn had indicated, and heard the familiar static sound often associated with a speakerphone call.

"Yes, Detective Lapides?" I said. "This is Samuel Hoenig."

There was a brief delay. No doubt my voice on Ms. Washburn's phone had confused the detective. "Hoenig," he said. "Where are you?"

It seemed an irrelevant question, but since I did not know the reason for Lapides's call, it was impossible to know what was relevant. But that thought had taken longer than it would for someone without Asperger's Syndrome to reply, so Ms. Washburn said, "We're in my car, detective. What can we do for you?"

"You can come the hell back is what you can do," Lapides said. He sounded irritated. Someone at GSCI must have done something to annoy him, I assumed. "I got the warrant for my tech guy to come in and search through the video surveillance system, and now I don't know what to tell him he's looking for. Why aren't you here, anyway?"

"We have been dismissed from the investigation," I told Lapides. "Ackerman fired us."

"What? Why?"

"For recommending that you seek the warrant," I answered. "So there is no point in your asking for my advice on your case. I am no longer involved."

"How can you not be involved?" the detective lamented. "I've got Amy Fitzgerald walking in here in two minutes to be interrogated, I told that Johnson asshole that I'd really show him when I interviewed her, and I don't even know what to ask. I need you back here."

"I'm sorry, detective," I reiterated. "I have no client. I have no question to answer. You are a professional police officer. This is your job; I'm sure you can conduct a very effective interview."

"No, I can't," Lapides argued. "I'm no genius, Hoenig, but I know my own shortcomings. It took me years to be promoted to plain clothes, and I had to take every test six times, but I did it. I'm persistent, not insightful. I'm going to botch this interrogation and that Johnson asshole will be able to laugh at me again." In such ways does the criminal justice system operate.

My patience and my willingness to handle Ms. Washburn's cellular phone any longer had reached an end. "It's simple, detective," I said. "All you need to do is establish whether Dr. Springer was a close friend of Rita Masters-Powell, and how often they saw each other. What the basis of their relationship might have been. And while you have Ms. Fitzgerald there, you'll probably want to know whether Ms. Masters-Powell had talked to her about her motivation to seek a divorce, and her decision to be cryogenically preserved at the time of her death. Are there other detectives you work with?"

"There's one other in the department," Lapides answered.

"Record your interview with your laptop and play it back for the other detective. Is that detective male or female?"

"Female," Lapides said.

"Ask her to look at the interview. See if there is anything you have left out or missed. See if there should be a follow-up session with Ms. Fitzgerald. And by all means, get that technical expert in to examine the GSCI video surveillance system as quickly as you can."

"Why?" Lapides asked.

"Because Ackerman doesn't want you to," I told him. "I am no longer involved with your case, but I wish you good luck, detective. Good-bye." I disconnected the phone and placed it in a console cup holder before Lapides could protest.

"So we really are off the investigation," Ms. Washburn said.

"Yes," I agreed. "We really are." I sat back, and while I did not close my eyes, I did allow myself a moment of relaxation. Not pondering the GSCI questions seemed like a strange sort of relief.

We rode in silence until Ms. Washburn pulled the car into the parking space in front of my house. "This is the right house, isn't it?" she asked.

"Yes, you arrived here quite accurately," I said. It wasn't exactly what I meant, but the right phrase had not presented itself to me in time.

"Well, thank you for the day's work, Samuel," she said. "It was very interesting."

I was reaching for the door release, but I stopped. "You're not coming in?" I asked. "Mother will be very disappointed to have missed you."

"I'm sorry. I'm late for home already."

I nodded. Her family responsibilities did have to come first. "But you should come in so I can pay you," I said. "You have more than earned your wages for the day."

She smiled. "You can mail me a check. You have my business card."

I did have it, so there was no point in arguing. "Thank you, Ms. Washburn," I said. I got out of the car, but before I closed the door, I looked inside once more.

"You're sure, then? About not staying on?" I closed the door, but the window was still open.

She just shook her head.

That move confused me, because when people shake their heads, it usually means no. That could mean Ms. Washburn was not sure, and that she might want to continue working with me at Questions Answered. But before I could ask Ms. Washburn any further questions, she put the transmission into drive and the car moved down the street.

I stood there for a moment, trying to discern what that might have meant, but I was at a loss to explain it. I decided to ask Mother about it, so I turned and walked around the back of the house and inside through the mudroom.

She was not immediately visible when I entered through the back door. That was unusual, but not terribly so. Mother is usually in the kitchen when my friend Mike, who drives a taxicab, drops me off in the evening, and therefore in the sight line of the back door, but this was seventeen minutes later than my usual homecoming, I'd called Mike to tell him no ride would be necessary, and Mother's routine was surely disrupted.

Sure enough, she emerged from the direction of the living room as I entered the kitchen. She was carrying a platter, the one she usually uses for roast chicken dinners, and seemed a little startled when she noticed me near the door.

"Samuel!" she said. "You're a little bit late."

I walked over and took the platter out of her hands, then gave her a small kiss on the cheek. I know Mother values that sort of thing, although it does not have a great deal of emotional value for me. I do sometimes like the sensation of a tight embrace, particularly when I feel tense or overwhelmed with sensory input, but a "peck on the cheek," as Mother calls it, is simply a gesture I make to please her.

"Were you worried?" I asked.

"No, not really. I knew you were out of the office today, so there was no way of knowing if your usual schedule still applied. Are you hungry?"

"Of course. It is past seven o'clock."

For those of us with Asperger's Syndrome, meals can be very stressful occasions. Generally speaking, our culinary preferences are rather narrow compared to those of other people, and the idea of being presented with a new food produces anxiety. It is less the idea that we will dislike the offered item so much as the feeling that others are watching and judging our choices that produces the tension.

That is what makes rituals such as dinner with Mother so important to someone like me. I'm confident that Mother will not introduce an unfamiliar item without advance notice, if at all. And I am fairly certain that if she does try something new, she will not think less of me if I dislike it, and will have a comforting standard on hand as a backup.

Tonight was no exception. Mother had indeed roasted a chicken, and once we had sat down to eat, she offered me a plate with two chicken legs on it. Another small plate held steamed broccoli, and a small dish of brown rice (which I'll admit is a concession to Mother, as I prefer white) was on the side.

"Thank you for making dinner, Mother," I said, as I do every evening.

"You're more than welcome," was her usual, and current, response. "Now, tell me about your day."

It took much longer than usual to recount the events of the day, even though I had seen Mother at lunch less than seven hours previously. She listened attentively and asked questions as points came up. She seemed especially concerned about Dr. Springer's father, whom she said Ms. Washburn was correct in "sparing any extra sorrow" on the day his daughter had died.

When I reached the end of my account, I told Mother about Ms. Washburn's decision not to continue with Questions Answered, and about the way she had shaken her head when I'd asked if she were sure about that choice.

"I'm confused," I told Mother. "Her action was unclear. Did that mean she does not want to work for the company anymore, or that she was not sure and needs more time to think the question through?"

"I think it means she's torn, Samuel," she answered. "I think she'd like to keep working with you, but she doesn't want to make the situation with her husband any worse than it already is. She doesn't know what to do."

That did not help me understand. "It seems like a very easy decision to make," I said. "Ms. Washburn's husband is being unreasonable about her professional situation. Neither of them has a job at the moment, and that means no income for the family. Why he should object to his wife having a paying position is a question I really cannot answer. Ms. Washburn should come and work at Questions Answered, and she should realize that."

Mother's eyes took on a look she calls "melancholy," although the dictionary definition of that word is somewhat imprecise, so my understanding of the emotion is incomplete. "She's a married woman, Samuel," she said.

"Ms. Washburn? I'm fully aware of that. Why do you bring it up?"

"I saw a different manner from you when you were with her than with anyone else you've ever known," Mother said. "And I understand it, but you have to remember she's another man's wife."

That baffled me. "I was not under the impression she is my wife, Mother."

"Don't be obtuse; you know what I mean. You might have ideas about Ms. Washburn, but you can't act on them. She's not available." And Mother gave me a significant look.

I made sure to make eye contact with her. "I have not known Ms. Washburn long enough to say whether she can become a friend," I told Mother. I'm aware Mother is concerned about me in social situations; it's natural when talking about a person with Asperger's Syndrome. Others often fail to understand us and think we are emotionless. We are not. But we are often at a loss to adapt to a situation that focuses on emotion rather than facts.

"I'm not suggesting you were behaving inappropriately, Samuel. I'm just wondering if you recognize all the feelings you've been having today."

For a long time after that, neither of us spoke. We cleared the table and put the dishes in the dishwasher but did not run it, as it was not sufficiently full. While we performed those tasks, I thought about what Mother had said about Ms. Washburn, but no matter how much thought I put into the question, I could not come up with a verifiable answer, and that irritated me.

The New York Yankees were playing a game against the Chicago White Sox at US Cellular Field in Chicago that night, so the telecast of the game began at eight o'clock rather than the usual seven o'clock.

I sat down in time for the opening sequence, during which announcers described the night's contest as "pivotal" and provided information about the starting pitcher for each team.

Mother, who does not care much for baseball, came in a few minutes later and sat down to read. Once the game began, I pressed the mute button on the television remote. I never listen to a baseball telecast—the loud and unpredictable sounds of the crowd, in addition to the constant chatter of the announcers, disturbs me. I understand the game well enough to appreciate it without those distractions.

It wasn't an especially interesting game, although that is almost a contradiction in terms. As a sport, baseball is the most cerebral and interesting of games; it is a series of situations, each of which arises from the one before it and leads to the one that will follow. It is an excellent mental tool to use when planning strategy or analyzing probabilities and human differences. Style is important, and statistics are a constant in baseball, but in order for a player or a team to be successful, the two must meet in a relevant fashion.

During the top of the seventh inning—with the New York Yankees at bat, trailing by one run and creating a situation that I thought indicated they would at least tie the score—Mother said it was late and she was going upstairs to her bedroom. She kissed me on the cheek and left the den.

I fought the urge to go into the kitchen for a snack. I had not been as physically active today as I would have preferred, and I did not wish to gain weight. The situation of the game became more compelling, as the Chicago White Sox pitcher managed to extricate himself from the inning without allowing a run, and the score remained the same. Sometimes probability does not accurately predict real events.

In the bottom of the ninth inning, with the New York Yankees now leading by one run and trying to end the game with their new closer—a pitcher trusted to get the final outs—I was intent on the screen and was not concentrating on anything else.

That is why I did not hear the telephone ring.

Mother called down from her bedroom, and I heard her voice. I make sure to be aware if she calls, because Mother has had some health problems and could need me for help, especially during the night. So when she called my name, my focus left the baseball game, and I walked to the foot of the stairs.

"Are you all right?" I called up to her.

"I'm fine," Mother answered. "There is a phone call for you. Dr. Ackerman from the institute."

That was surprising. Ackerman had fired me less than five hours earlier. Perhaps he was calling to renegotiate my fee, but I did not intend to charge him, since I had not answered his question. I thanked Mother and heard her return to her bedroom. It wasn't until then that it occurred to me I ought to apologize for missing the call and requiring her to get out of bed to notify me. Perhaps later.

Now I needed to take the call from Ackerman, so I walked into the kitchen, where there is a wall phone. I picked it up to hear Ackerman, obviously speaking to someone else, saying, "There just isn't time for that."

I alerted him to my presence on the line, adding, "I have no intention of charging you for my services because I did not answer your question."

"What? I don't care about that," Ackerman said. "There's been a development, and I need you back here immediately."

"It's ten forty-three at night," I told him. "I'm glad you have reconsidered employing my company, but I don't usually work this late unless there is an emergency."

"There *is* an emergency," Ackerman replied. "We've been contacted by the people who stole the specimen from our facility. They have ransom demands."

"I'll be on my way shortly," I said and hung up the phone. It wasn't until a moment later that I realized I had not said good-bye, but I believed that Ackerman would not be offended by that breach of social protocol.

Clearly, however, I had not been thinking the situation through. Ackerman needed me back at the facility in North Brunswick, a nineteen-minute drive from my home. But I did not feel confident driving there at this time of night, and I felt it would be unreasonable to ask Mother for a ride after she had gone to bed twice.

I reached into my pocket for Ms. Washburn's business card.

TWENTY-ONE

"I CAN'T BELIEVE YOU talked me into this," Ms. Washburn said as she steered her car into the parking lot of the Garden State Cryonics Institute. "My husband is going to kill me." Before I could react, she held up her right hand and said, "It's an expression."

"Was he very upset that you were leaving?" I asked. "It didn't occur to me that this question would cause difficulty in your marriage."

She maneuvered the car into a parking space near the front entrance and let out a breath. "No more difficulty than there already was," she said. "Don't worry. I could have said no and told you to call a taxi. Ackerman would have paid for it. But the fact is, I want to see this job through, I liked working with you, and my husband is just going to have to understand that. You're not going to cause my divorce, Samuel."

"I certainly hope not."

We got out of the car and walked to the front entrance, where Commander Johnson opened the door and checked us through the security desk. We stayed on the main floor and entered a conference room that bore a number of photographs on the walls, mostly of the facilities we had already seen downstairs, looking considerably warmer and more welcoming than clinical, which was not really the case.

Inside were Ackerman, Detective Lapides, and a woman I had not met before, who introduced herself as Captain Harris of the county prosecutor's Major Crimes unit. She said she was there to supervise the negotiations with, as she put it, "the perpetrators of the crime or crimes."

Charlotte Selby was also present, looking strangely satisfied. I could not construct a scenario that required her presence, but I assumed that would be explained. Amelia Johnson, I was told, had gone home, no doubt in a fury over her husband's mistreatment.

"I assume this means Ms. Washburn and I are rehired," I said to Ackerman when the introductions had been completed.

Commander Johnson scowled.

"Yes," Ackerman responded. "The same conditions and the same rate. Your non-disclosure statements are still valid."

"Has there been a report from the technology expert the police have commissioned to look at your security system?" I asked.

Ackerman looked sour but shook his head. "There's supposed to be one at any minute. Damned waste of time," he muttered.

"I think not, but we will see," I told him.

"I'd have to agree," Captain Harris said to me. "The report could be very useful in discovering if someone who works here in the institute had a hand in this murder."

Commander Johnson almost choked on the gum he was chewing. "A hand in the murder!" he said. "I absolutely reject that notion. I have personally checked the background of every employee in this facility, and..."

"*And*, in the past twenty-four hours, there has been the theft of a person's remains and the murder of a member of the medical staff," the captain broke in. "That's some great background check you did."

The commander raised his index finger in protest but was unable to come up with a proper rejoinder.

"How was the ransom demand communicated?" I asked.

Ackerman opened his mouth, but Charlotte got there first. "I got it in an e-mail," she said. "It said that I should get in touch with the institute and tell them it would take seventeen million dollars to get back Rita Masters-Powell's head."

I looked at Lapides. "Have you had anyone try to trace the sending e-mail address?" I asked.

The detective nodded. "It was a public site from which it was sent," he said. "A Barnes and Noble here in North Brunswick that has Wi-Fi. The address is obviously one that was commandeered by the sender, taken over, and hijacked."

"It's called phishing," I informed him. "How do you know the e-mail address was phished?"

Lapides looked uncomfortable. "It was mine," he said.

There was a long silence during which Lapides seemed embarrassed, Ackerman seemed angry, and Commander Johnson looked amused. "That's very interesting," I said. "It tells us something valuable about the people who are behind this theft."

Ackerman made a confused face as Charlotte took a notepad from her purse. "What does it tell you?" Ackerman asked.

"The fact that these people know Detective Lapides is assigned to this case is useful," I explained. "It means one of two things: either the thieves are people who have been here sometime today and met the detective..." I paused to contemplate what I was about to say.

"Or what?" Captain Harris asked. The fact that it was the captain making the inquiry made the answer that much more difficult. It was not my intention to denigrate Lapides in front of someone who could be identified as his superior officer.

"Or the thieves have a source of information somewhere in the police department," I said. "I'm afraid we have to at least explore that possibility."

Captain Harris raised an eyebrow in surprise. Lapides looked like his stomach did not feel well.

"I'll talk to someone at Internal Affairs," Captain Harris said. "I don't like to think it could be happening, but I can't ignore it, either."

"I agree," I said. "Although I think the former scenario more likely than the latter. We have been questioning employees of the institute all day, and it is not at all unlikely that one or more of them could be involved in the theft of the cranium."

"And Dr. Springer's murder," Ms. Washburn added.

"It would be an enormous coincidence if those two crimes were unrelated," I agreed. "Ms. Selby, what else did the e-mail say?"

"We have printed out a copy," Commander Johnson noted, and handed me a sheet of paper.

It read: *We have taken possession of Rita Masters-Powell. If you want what we have back again, you will pay us $17 million. It is in good condition, and we can keep it that way indefinitely. We know you have already called the police, but you must not tell them about this communication. Gather the money in cash, bills no larger than $100, non-consecutive serial numbers, and await further instructions. They will not come through this e-mail address, so don't bother to monitor outgoing messages. You will be contacted.*

"This does not tell us much," I said after reading the note. "I am not able to garner a great deal from reading it."

"If it were up to me, you wouldn't be reading it at all," Commander Johnson replied. "I was against calling you back here."

Ms. Washburn looked shocked at the commander's words, but they were not surprising to me. He had appeared to consider me a threat from the moment we first met, and there was no reason to think the situation had changed.

"Indeed," I said. "What can you learn from this communication, commander?"

He widened his eyes for a short moment, then he snatched the paper from my hand. "They want seventeen million dollars, and they can keep the head frozen as long as they want. They'll get in touch again, but they don't say when, and they won't use the same e-mail address."

"Something that *isn't* stated directly in the e-mail, commander," I suggested.

"What can you see other than what's stated on the paper?" Charlotte asked me.

"Not very much," I admitted. "There is no way of knowing whether the person writing the e-mail is telling the truth. We must operate on the assumption that Ms. Masters-Powell's remains are indeed being kept in the proper condition, because any other circumstance would leave us with no positive options. So even if we have no evidence to that effect, we will begin from that premise.

"The ransom demand for seventeen million dollars is interesting," I continued. "I wonder how they arrived at the figure. How much money would you say was available to the Masters family in cash, Dr. Ackerman?"

Ackerman looked startled, as if he had been expecting me to address someone else in the room about the Masterses' finances. "How would I know that?" he asked.

"You would know because you would run a financial check on anyone paying a perpetual fee on a monthly basis. You would check it before the contracts were signed, and you would be certain that there would be no difficulty in obtaining the money. I would assume you'd have the family members sign a contract guaranteeing the payment of the fee in perpetuity. The only way any finance company would agree to such terms would be if a thorough analysis of the family's assets was made and verified, again, *before* you agreed to store Ms. Masters-Powell's remains. So I'll ask again, Ackerman, how much money does the Masters family have available to it that it could convert to cash on an emergency basis?"

Ackerman, properly chastised, did not even have to look up the records on his computer. He simply looked at me and said, "Just about seventeen million dollars."

I began to pace around the room. "So the thieves know exactly how much money they can expect, and they have no intention of asking for more, because it would slow down the process. Exactly what they don't want to do."

"Why not?" Ms. Washburn asked. "If they can keep the … remains preserved indefinitely, why would time be an issue for them?"

"This isn't the kind of thing that can be done in your freezer at home," Ackerman answered. "You need special equipment, special power sources, a sterile environment. Those things take up a lot of space, and in a residential area, for example, would attract a lot of attention. It shouldn't be hard to find these people."

I nodded. "That would mean they'll want to get rid of Ms. Masters-Powell's remains as soon as possible. In turn, that should mean we will be hearing from the thieves again shortly with further instructions. Have you contacted the Masters family?" I asked Ackerman.

He looked very uncomfortable. "Yes," he said. "They're in the process of deciding what step they want to take next. Arthur told me he and his mother are divided on whether or not they should invest that kind of money into what Laverne called a lost cause." He seemed disgusted with the idea that a dead woman's severed head could be considered anything less than a shining possibility for continued life.

"How soon before they get back to us with an answer?" I asked him.

Ackerman sat down behind his desk and looked unbearably tired. "Soon," he answered. "They know that time is a factor here."

"Are you prepared to pay the ransom if the family decides against it?" I asked.

His face went white and he took in a deep breath. "I couldn't," he said. "That would bankrupt us. I can't allow the entire business to be brought down over one guest's misfortune."

It was an emotional argument, but not a factually based one. "You might be just as badly damaged by inaction," I pointed out. "The institute's reputation would be severely diminished once news of this incident was made public, and you can be assured it would become public knowledge the minute Detective Lapides were to file his report, which he is obligated to do. The next newspaper reporter to read through the police blotter would find it almost immediately."

Ackerman sat back in his chair as if shot. He bit his lips.

"That does not even account for the lawsuit the Masters family would no doubt file against the institute, which could easily result in damages larger than the amount the thieves are demanding," I added. "Given that the theft took place under the watch of your security personnel, you could certainly be held liable. I think it would be a legal probability, in fact."

Commander Johnson stepped in front of Ackerman, his eyes wide and sweat visible on his brow. "You know it wasn't my fault," he hissed at me. "You know that."

"I know nothing of the kind," I answered. "Until the security technology expert hired by the police finishes his investigation, I have very few facts about the way the theft was executed, and therefore it is impossible to assign blame. But since you are in charge of security and the theft did take place under your watch, it would not be unreasonable to assume that in some way, you did fail at your job."

"I knew it!" Johnson said, turning toward Ackerman to make his case. "He's been vying for my job all day!"

I think I actually laughed. "I have no interest in your job, commander," I said. "I'm merely pointing out that you have not done very good work, if the facts are examined rationally."

The commander had no time to answer, because the phone on the table near Ackerman's seat rang. Ackerman picked it up and said, "Yes." He listened for a few seconds, said, "Yes," again, and hung up. "Laverne and Arthur Masters are here," he told us.

Charlotte Selby closed her reporter's notebook and placed it inside her purse, which was quite large and enveloped the notebook immediately. I doubted she would be able to find it again easily. "This is a private moment for the family," she said. "I'll step out for this one." That seemed like highly uncharacteristic behavior for a reporter of any kind, but she left just as she said she would, and quickly.

Ackerman nodded his head, looking like a man trying to think quickly. "We should be ready with a plan," he said.

"Yes, you should," I agreed.

Ackerman's head turned quickly and he said, "What do you mean—" But he was cut off when he caught a glimpse of the Masterses through the glass wall to the conference room. He stood and walked to the door to open it for Laverne Masters.

She entered ahead of her son and hobbled a bit to the seat closest to the door. She seemed a bit winded after having done so, and it occurred to me that she must have had arthritis or some other condition that limited her mobility.

Arthur, for his part, looked haggard. Clearly, both of them had been called after they were asleep, but that fact was not visible in Laverne's case. She was dressed exactly as she had been earlier in the day, and she wore makeup. Arthur was in a sweatshirt and sweatpants and had a growth of beard.

"I won't beat around the bush," Laverne said when she could catch her breath. "We think that you've mishandled this entire affair from the beginning."

Ackerman, to his credit, did not look wounded or say anything to contradict Laverne. Commander Johnson, however, straightened his neck and looked as if the top of his head might blow off.

"I'm sorry you feel that way," Ackerman said. "The institute has always done everything possible to ensure the security of its guests. This regrettable incident—"

"Spare me the boilerplate you give to those unfortunate types you dupe into spending all their money on this science fiction fantasy of yours," Laverne said. "I'm not interested in the kind words of sympathy you've rehearsed so thoroughly. What I want to know is exactly what's being done to return what's left of my daughter to where she should be. And keep in mind once that happens, I fully intend to remove her from your custody and have her remains disposed of in a proper fashion. Is that clear?"

Ackerman's expression changed from his professional one of concern and empathy to another, colder and more calculating. "Crystal clear," he said with an edge of hostility in his voice. "Detective Lapides here has already begun using the new information to root out the kidnappers, and as you insisted, we have re-commissioned Mr. Hoenig and his assistant here to aid in the investigation."

So that was the truth about the sudden change in GSCI policy concerning Questions Answered. Ackerman had (probably very reluctantly) contacted the Masterses with the news of a ransom demand, and they—or more likely, Laverne—had demanded that Questions Answered once again join in the hunt. That certainly made more sense than the idea of Ackerman suddenly changing his mind.

I decided to use this newfound influence to move the proceedings forward more quickly. "Well then, Mrs. Masters," I said, bypassing Ackerman and going directly to the center of attention in the room. "Have you decided if you will pay the ransom being demanded for your daughter's remains?"

Ackerman shook a little, as if trying to restrain himself from taking violent action against me. Commander Johnson simply stared in a way that brought to mind the phrase, *If looks could kill.*

"We have decided," Arthur Masters interjected, "to negotiate with the kidnappers the next time they make contact."

Negotiate? Ms. Washburn looked at me with a question on her face, and I was wondering the same thing.

"Do you think that is wise?" I asked Arthur. "These people have broken through considerable security precautions and stolen something very valuable to you. They are most likely implicated in a murder that occurred here this morning. This is a carefully planned crime perpetrated by thieves who are very probably willing to use violence as a tool. Haggling over price now is not apt to bring a positive resolution to this situation."

Ackerman, I noted, was nodding his head vigorously, but that probably had as much to do with his reluctance to risk the institute's money as it did with my calculated analysis of the situation.

"We think that we have a unique bargaining position here," Arthur answered. "They have something they want to sell, but it isn't of value to anyone but us. If they don't sell it to my mother and me, they will receive no return whatsoever on their investment. So we can offer them, perhaps, two million dollars, and they have to be satisfied with what they can get, or get nothing." He looked in Ms. Washburn's direction, as if anticipating her approval. She was not looking at him.

"I would advise you against that strategy," I said directly to Laverne Masters. "This is not a business negotiation; it is a hostage negotiation. If they do not see this situation ending the way they want it to, I doubt that you will receive your daughter's remains again, and I would be concerned about your personal safety."

"Arthur has decided," Laverne replied. "Quite frankly, I said we should tell these people to go screw themselves, but he thinks it's important we at least make the gesture. If it were entirely up to me, I wouldn't give them a dime."

Before Ackerman or I could argue against that stance, the sound of a cellular phone chirp was clear in the room. Ackerman reached into his pocket after a moment and pulled out his phone. He glanced at the screen, presumably to see if the caller was a familiar one, and his eyebrows dropped precipitously. He pushed a button on the phone and said, "Yes?"

It took only a moment before his eyes widened and he paled. He mouthed toward Commander Johnson, "It's them."

I reached for a pad and pencil on the table—there was one at each seat, presumably left for those who attended meetings to take notes—and wrote quickly on it in all capitals, *SPEAKERPHONE*. I held it up for Ackerman to see. It took him a moment, as my handwriting is not especially legible, and then he nodded and pushed another button on his phone.

Lapides immediately moved away from the phone to speak into his communications link, no doubt to order a trace on the call, not realizing that Ackerman's cellular phone had not been prepared for such an event, so it would be impossible to configure such a thing quickly enough.

The voice that came through the tiny speaker was filtered, probably with a mechanical device (the handkerchief over the mouthpiece often seen in motion pictures really does not do much to change the sound of a person's voice). Whoever called was in midsentence when Ackerman pushed the speaker button, so what we heard first was, "... no deviation from the instructions I am about to give you."

"Wait," Ackerman interrupted. "I need to find paper and a pencil to write down your instructions."

"Don't insult my intelligence," the caller responded. "You're trying to keep me on the phone long enough for the police to triangulate my position. That won't be possible; I won't stay on long enough for that."

Perhaps the thief believed the call to Ackerman's cellular phone had been anticipated, and therefore the phone itself would be set up for a trace. It was the first mistake the perpetrators had made, and that was interesting, although not immediately useful.

"I wouldn't try to insult you," said Ackerman, pulling a tissue from a box on the table to wipe his brow. The tissue was not sufficient to the task; it almost immediately shredded into pieces while Ackerman continued to perspire. "But we're having trouble raising the amount of money you requested, and—"

"The Masters family would not have even a little difficulty coming up with seventeen million dollars," the voice insisted. "And if they refuse, I'm sure your institute would be more than willing to pay. Your reputation mustn't be damaged so badly, wouldn't you say, Ackerman?"

He began to answer but was shouted down by Arthur Masters, who immediately identified himself. "We have no intention of paying that much money for an ... object you can sell to only one buyer," he said. "We will make you a counteroffer, but you must be reasonable."

"We have no intention of lowering our price," the voice replied. "You will put the seventeen million in non-sequential bills into five separate briefcases and leave the cases beneath the high-tension wires in the Rutgers Village housing development between East Brunswick and New Brunswick immediately off Route Eighteen going north. You have two hours."

Laverne Masters looked at her son, but I could not read her expression. Arthur stared straight ahead and did not so much as consider his mother.

"We will not pay seventeen million," Arthur repeated.

The caller did not react to that statement. "If you need more incentive, Ackerman, keep in mind that we know where you live and we can get inside when we like. I wouldn't want to be your wife if you were foolish enough to take us anything but seriously. Deadly seriously."

Before anyone could react, the caller disconnected.

Ackerman sat motionless in his chair. "My wife," he said. "Were they threatening my wife?"

I thought it more likely the caller had been making the point that Ackerman's wife could be made very unhappy—that Ackerman *himself* was being threatened—but I was unsure about the social speech the caller had been using, so I chose not to express an opinion.

"Don't worry," Ms. Washburn said. "I'm sure Mr. Masters and his mother will pay the ransom now that negotiations have broken down." She turned toward the Masterses. "Won't you?"

Neither of them spoke. Indeed, neither moved a facial muscle. But for the first time, Arthur looked his mother in the eye. She did nothing.

"Detective Lapides," I said. "Perhaps it would make sense to assign a patrol car to the area of Dr. Ackerman's home for the rest of the night."

Ackerman blinked twice. I am not certain he had heard everything that had just been said—and more specifically, what Laverne and Arthur Masters had *not* said.

"I'll get right on it," Lapides answered. He picked up the phone at the far end of the conference room and started to punch numbers.

"Much of what just happened is odd," I said. "Perhaps it would be a good idea to review the phone call."

"Is there time for that right now?" Ms. Washburn said. "We've only been given two hours, and the money has to be collected somehow." She was looking at the two Masters family members, neither of whom had moved or spoken since the phone call had ended.

"I don't know where I can get that kind of money," Ackerman said. He was speaking very quickly and breathing in and out quite deeply. "I'd have to get all the members of the board to sign off on it, and I just don't think there's time..."

Lapides got off the phone and walked back to the group gathered at the head of the table. "There'll be a car near your house all night, Ackerman," he said. "What's the status of the ransom?"

Something was wrong, and I couldn't quite discern what it could be. "You got the call on your cellular phone," I said to Ackerman. "I thought they did not work in this building because of the security system you have in place."

Ackerman seemed distracted, then snapped his head toward me quickly. "What?" he asked. I repeated my concern. "They don't work on the lower levels," he explained. "Cell phones will work on the street level. So will the police communication links."

"And why would the thieves threaten you or your wife?" I asked. "Why wouldn't they threaten Mr. or Mrs. Masters if they thought the ransom money was being withheld?"

Ms. Washburn walked up to me and forced eye contact. "Samuel," she said. "These are legitimate questions, but this is not the time for that. Right now, we have to figure out what we're going to do to resolve this situation in the next two hours."

Captain Harris stood straight behind Ackerman and clasped her hands together. "She's right," the captain said, indicating Ms. Washburn. "It's time to get organized." She turned toward Arthur and

Laverne. "I take it you are adamant in offering no money for the ransom."

Arthur Masters folded his arms across his chest and shook his head. "We didn't say that. What we said was that seventeen million was excessive. We're willing to pay two."

"Two million dollars?" I asked.

"Yes. We had that much cash organized, and brought it here with us. It is under armed guard downstairs." Then he smiled grimly and added, "For whatever *that's* worth."

"All right," the captain said. "Ackerman, how much do you think you can get here in the next hour, in cash?"

Ackerman was the very picture of a man overwhelmed. I have been incapacitated by loud sounds and social situations that I found difficult, but I have never been *completely* unable to think. Sitting stock still in his leather bound chair, that was the very impression the head of the institute was now presenting.

"Ackerman," Captain Harris repeated.

"I'm not authorized," he finally answered. "The board would have to be contacted. I can't get more than two hundred thousand dollars in cash without that kind of approval."

"Get the two hundred thousand," the captain told him. "We're going to have to do the best we can."

It took Ackerman a moment, but he finally picked up the phone.

TWENTY-TWO

In the end, Ackerman was able to contact a majority of the institute's board and arrange another million dollars, making the total that would be offered in ransom three million. I have no idea how that much cash was found at this late an hour of the night, but it appeared promptly enough. It wouldn't be nearly enough to satisfy the thieves, but Captain Harris believed that if the briefcases were lined deeply with real cash, and then stuffed internally with blank paper, the amount might be enough to fool them.

I disagreed but was shouted down. And when the shouting began, I reacted to the volume of the words, not their meaning, and did not offer much resistance. I could not think strategically over all the noise in the room.

The thieves made contact once again twenty-eight minutes later, sending a text message to Detective Lapides, perhaps just to remind us that they could. The instructions for dropping off the money were detailed in the text, which was quite lengthy for such a thing.

Within minutes, we were headed to the parking lot for a trip to the drop-off point in three separate vehicles: Lapides, Captain Harris, and Ackerman would ride in a Sport Utility Vehicle provided by the county prosecutor's office; Laverne Masters would ride in her own car with an officer driving; and Ms. Washburn was to drive her car with me in the passenger seat. Commander Johnson, much to his chagrin, was being left behind to assure that no further breaches of security occurred at the institute, and to convey any messages the thieves might send to that location. Arthur Masters flatly refused to go along, saying he thought the exchange was destined to be a failure because the total amount demanded was not being paid. He felt he was more valuable at the institute monitoring with Commander Johnson, and had unsuccessfully lobbied his mother to stay behind as well, citing her health. She did not answer him.

Before we reached our respective rides, however (Laverne Masters waiting at the institute door for the officer to pull the car closer), Ackerman stopped dead in his tracks. "Charlotte Selby," he said. "Did anyone see Charlotte Selby as we left?" He looked quite anxious.

"She was not anywhere we might have seen her," I said, because I would have noticed if Charlotte been anywhere in the path we'd taken.

Ackerman picked up his cellular phone and pushed a button. "Johnson," he said after a moment. "Is Charlotte Selby in the building?" He waited for a response, and his mouth dropped open for him to take in larger gulps of air. He put the phone back into his pocket without another word. I know that some sort of acknowledgment that the conversation has ended, such as *good-bye*, is expected in such situations, but Ackerman did not seem concerned about having ignored such an obvious social custom.

"She wasn't there," he said, seemingly to no one in particular. "She signed out only a few minutes after she left the conference room."

I walked over to talk to Ackerman, Ms. Washburn just behind me. "I don't understand," I said. "Why are you so concerned about Ms. Selby's whereabouts?"

Ackerman's eyes flashed and moved to one side, then the other, very quickly. He looked like a man who was thinking about something other than what was being asked of him. "Don't you see," he said after a moment, "Charlotte is a blogger trying to make a name for herself in this field. She was privy to enough information to damage this company irrevocably. If she decides to go public with it before there's a resolution to this problem, the institute could be finished no matter what happens tonight."

I thought about that and nodded. "It is possible," I said. "But I think it unlikely. I doubt Ms. Selby would want to trumpet her knowledge before the whole story is told. It would attract too many competitors who might have sources in more places than she does. The only way she manages to distinguish herself with this story is to tell the *whole* story."

Ackerman again appeared to be only half-listening. "I hope you're right," he said. Then he turned toward Lapides. "Have you heard from the patrol car at my house yet?" he asked the detective. "I'm concerned about Eleanor."

"Eleanor?" Lapides asked.

"My wife." Ackerman's voice had an edge that indicated he thought Lapides something other than an intelligent police detective.

"I checked in a couple of minutes ago," Lapides answered, with no indication he was at all aware of the tone in Ackerman's voice. "They're there, and your lights are out. Only one car in the driveway. Your wife is safe."

Ackerman mopped his brow, although it was cool outside. "Thank you," he said to Lapides.

"Did the officers check with Mrs. Ackerman?" I asked. "It is possible someone got into the house before the patrol car arrived." Ackerman once again looked perplexed.

"It's standard procedure," Lapides told me. "They rang the bell, despite the late hour, and checked with Mrs. Ackerman. Everything was clear in the house."

I nodded at Lapides, and so did Ackerman. There was very little extra time left, so we all got into our vehicles and let the police SUV lead the way.

Ms. Washburn was unusually quiet as she drove, making sure to keep Laverne Masters's car visible, but at a reasonable distance. At 2:37 in the morning, there was very little traffic, even on the well-traveled US Highway 1. The drive could not have been difficult.

"You are very quiet," I said after eight minutes and fourteen seconds. "Is something troubling you?"

Ms. Washburn shook her head. "I wouldn't say *troubling* me," she replied. "I've been thinking about the case."

"The *question*," I corrected.

She nodded. "The question. I think you're right; there are a lot of things that don't add up."

It would be interesting to see if Ms. Washburn had been struck by the same contradictions and incongruities as I had. "Please tell me," I said. "What does not add up for you?"

"Well, you mentioned two things. It doesn't make sense to threaten Ackerman's wife. He's not the one refusing to pay. It would seem a lot more effective to threaten Arthur Masters or his mother."

"Laverne seemed somewhat unmovable on the subject," I suggested. "Perhaps the thieves think they have a better chance of swaying Ackerman, or they know about a source of money that he has not yet tapped, nor told us about."

"I guess so, but the voice sounded so much more personal about it, like whoever it was wanted to hurt Ackerman, to scare him as much as they possibly could. I realize that's not a fact; it's an impression I got from the tone of voice, even though it was filtered."

"That's exactly the kind of thing I need to have pointed out to me," I told her. "You are an invaluable member of the Questions Answered team."

"You and I are the whole team so far," Ms. Washburn reminded me, "and I'm not even really working there."

"You could be," I answered, but that sounded unlike what I was trying to communicate. I decided to move on with the questions we were trying to answer. "What else bothered you? Something I didn't mention."

She thought for seventy-six seconds. "I can't figure out the dynamic between Arthur and Laverne Masters," she said. "Sometimes he seems to be completely under his mother's thumb, and other times…"

"Other times, he's flirting with you," I pointed out.

Ms. Washburn gritted her teeth a little but nodded. "But that's not what I'm talking about. They walked into that room with a ransom figure in mind, and it was my impression that there had been an argument about it between them, and Arthur lost. And when the kidnapper on the phone said that there could be consequences and they wouldn't see what's left of Rita again, Arthur looked at Laverne, almost like he was asking her to be flexible, but she never so much as blinked. But Arthur is supposed to be the one clearly in charge of the business."

"It is not unusual in a family dynamic for one person to be considered the authority in a certain area, even if that is not his customary role," I pointed out. "My mother often defers to my judgment on the brands of products she buys at the supermarket, largely because she knows I research the advantages and disadvantages of each."

Ms. Washburn took a quick glance at me, as if deciding whether she should voice a thought she was having.

"Go on," I said. "You won't insult me."

"Why do you still live with your mother?" she said quickly. "You are—if you don't mind the expression—high-functioning enough to have your own apartment. Why not do that?"

I frowned. For one thing, the term *high-functioning* is somewhat insulting, although I was sure Ms. Washburn used it because she did not know a more accurate one. But my more immediate concern was that she seemed to be seeing me as something I was not, and I wanted to explain my situation precisely.

"My Asperger's Syndrome is not the reason I still live in my mother's house," I said after a moment. "There are, in fact, a number of reasons. For one thing, Questions Answered is not yet profitable enough for me to pay rent on an apartment in this area, and I am not inclined to move far away where rents are lower. Part of that is because of my Asperger's; I am uncomfortable in unfamiliar surroundings.

"But I also have some concerns about my mother," I continued. "Her health has been a little precarious for the past two years since she retired. There was a heart incident that required the implantation of a stent in one artery. And her legs are not strong. She has some difficulty walking, although not as much as Mrs. Masters, so you might not have noticed when you met her yesterday afternoon.

"And I will admit, Ms. Washburn, that there are few people with whom I can comfortably and enjoyably spend an extended period of time. My mother happens to be one of those few. Not many people find my company enjoyable; she does. Not many people's conversation interests me; hers does. So you see, I live with my mother chiefly because I like her."

Ms. Washburn turned off US Highway 1 onto the right-lane ramp (called a "jug handle" in New Jersey) that led to Rutgers Village, a development of single-family homes, almost all in the Cape Cod style, built on the border of New Brunswick and East Brunswick. The development was meant mostly as a haven for New Brunswick city police and fire employees when it was built, because there was a residency requirement for such personnel at the time and no suburban settings in the New Brunswick city limits for those with young children. It is a small section carved out of two large municipalities to accommodate those who served one. Living there, separated from the urban reality that the old city of New Brunswick represented, it seemed out of place.

We followed Laverne Masters's car into the development, and then Ms. Washburn said to me, "I didn't mean to insult you."

"You did not insult me," I answered. "I wanted to be sure you understood."

Ms. Washburn nodded but did not respond.

We drove up Tunison Road into Rutgers Village and made a right turn past the homes, which were old enough now that they had been individually renovated and were no longer identical. Since the 1950s, when they were built, owners had come and gone and left their specific fingerprints on each structure: Some had additions on one side, others had full second floors with the dormers expanded for second or third bedrooms. A few were meticulously landscaped in the front yards, and others had stockade fences that blocked our view of any back yard at all.

At the top of a small hill there was one area of open space separating Rutgers Village from Edgewood, its slightly more upscale sister community. The local utility had installed towers of high-tension electrical wiring through the open field, and they ran the length of the development and past it as far as the eye could see. We stopped the three cars at the opening to that field, and all of us except Laverne Masters got out of our vehicles and gathered at the entrance to the open space. A small fence—really just a piece of metal placed as a barrier less than two feet from the ground across the opening—was meant to delineate the space, but it could not possibly have been considered a deterrent to anyone who might want to enter. It was probably an insurance precaution, because a sign reading HIGH-TENSION—DO NOT ENTER had been hung on the fence. It was difficult to read the sign in this light.

"This is where we're supposed to leave the briefcases," Lapides said. "Actually, over there." He pointed to the middle of the field, where the towers bearing the electrical wires 50 feet above stood. "Next to the second high-tension tower. At the base of the northeast leg." He started, suddenly, and drew a deep breath. "Did anybody bring a compass?" he asked.

I pointed at the utility towers. "On the right side, nearest us," I said. "The position of the stars indicates the directions perfectly."

Captain Harris took a long look at me then nodded. "Of course it does," she said. "Well, let's go."

Ackerman held up a hand to stop her. "The text message said I was to go alone, and when I was done, we were all to drive away. Whoever these people are, they're going to be watching, and if they don't like what they see, a lot of money is going away and nothing is coming back." I found it interesting that he did not mention his wife or her safety.

"How will the remains be returned?" I asked.

"Once they've seen us leave, I'll get another text message telling me where to go for the specimen," Ackerman answered. "But when they find out all the money they asked for isn't there..."

No one responded to that, so Ackerman took a breath, stepped over the low barrier at the opening, and started walking toward the tower. He was not an especially athletic man, and more than fifty years old, but it was a straight walk, and not dangerous. There was a slight decline from the road toward the utility towers, and carrying five briefcases could not have been easy for Ackerman. The grass had not been recently mowed, however, and was high, so the walk was especially difficult—I'm not sure I could have done it, thinking only about the many insects that must have been living in that foliage. Once, Ackerman stopped, looked at the bottom of his shoe, said something disparaging about people who walk their dogs in unpaved areas, and scraped it on the ground. Then he continued walking.

There had been some discussion on how he could carry five briefcases into the grassy area. With the money and the inside paper stuffing, the cases were not insignificant in terms of weight, but the thieves had been very specific about the number of cases, so consolidation was not a consideration.

He slipped one under each arm and carried the other three, one in his left hand and two in his right, by their handles. He continued his walk toward the high-tension towers, but he was slowing, and often shifted the weight of the case under his left arm. He also set down the cases and fidgeted with something in his pocket, moving it from one side to another; it turned out to be his cell phone, as I determined when he opened it to check the time and the screen glowed briefly.

"He looks so exposed out there," Ms. Washburn said quietly. "It seems dangerous, even though he's just walking."

"The instructions were for him to go alone from here," I reminded her. "Any other presence would have increased the danger, as we can assume the thieves are watching us every moment from somewhere in the area."

Captain Harris looked at me with an expression I could not read. "Don't be silly," she said. "I have snipers on either side of the field, and one on the roof of a house right near the second tower. We're not letting him walk out there alone."

I looked in the areas she had pointed out, and there were officers in all three sites. My mouth felt dry. "Don't you think the thieves can see those snipers just as well as we can?" I asked.

"Hardly," she said. "They don't want anything to happen to Ackerman. They just want their money. There's no reason to get violent, and I doubt they could even get into a position to see him without our knowing it. I think you're overestimating them."

At that moment, a low electronic chirp came from Captain Harris's belt. Her face registered surprise as she reached for her cell phone. When she read the message there, her eyes widened.

"My god," she rasped. She reached for her communications link and said clearly into it, "All sniper positions stand down immediately. Repeat, stand down."

I must have been staring at Captain Harris, because she looked at me and said, "Fine. You know more than I do about criminal nature."

"I sincerely doubt it," I said truthfully.

Captain Harris did not answer, but she held up her cell phone, which showed a text message: MOVE YOUR SNIPERS AWAY OR ACKERMAN DIES.

The timing of that message was especially unnerving. "Do you think they can hear us, as well?" I asked.

The captain shook her head. "I'm not even sure they're here. They could be watching from the comfort of their own homes with the right satellite link. But there's no sense in taking a chance on something like that. *We* can see Ackerman, and that's all that's necessary at the moment."

Surely enough, when I looked back at the rooftop and the trees looking down at Ackerman's position, the snipers were gone.

While this exchange had been taking place, Ackerman had reached the second tower, and after a slight hesitation during which he looked in our direction, he placed the briefcases on the ground next to the northeast leg. He stood and looked at the cases for a long moment, then began his walk back.

When he reached the point just past the first electrical tower, Ackerman seemed to hesitate, looking back at the cases as if they contained his own offspring, or something equally dear to him. Since all the cases contained was money—and none of it Ackerman's—the move seemed a little bit odd.

"I was planning on leaving some men behind to watch for the people who are going to pick up the money," Captain Harris said. "Now I'm worried they'll be seen."

"Is it possible to leave a camera or recording device?" I asked. "Positioned properly, that could make it possible for you to monitor the pickup, and be prepared to act on what you see."

The captain nodded and instructed her team to remove two video cameras from the SUV and set them up unobtrusively. We walked back to the car where Laverne Masters was sitting, door open, facing forward. "A good suggestion," the captain said. "I can see why the North Brunswick police called you in to consult."

That was not correct. "The North Brunswick police..." I began.

Detective Lapides cut off my sentence. "Now all that's left to do is go back to the institute, wait, and hope the thieves will accept a million dollars as their ransom."

One million dollars? "Three million, detective," I corrected him.

Lapides glanced at Captain Harris, who glanced at Laverne Masters. "I'm afraid not," Laverne said after a pause. "I insisted we

199

withdraw our funds. We believe these people should not be encouraged to play so malevolently with the loved ones of a deceased woman. We should not negotiate with terrorists."

It took a moment for that thought to sink in, during which I considered correcting Laverne on her definition of *terrorist*, and rejected that thought. "There's only one million in five cases?" I asked.

"Actually, the real money is all in one case, the one Ackerman left on top," Lapides answered. "I didn't think it was a good idea, but nobody listened to me." He spread his hands in a gesture of futility.

I turned immediately toward Ms. Washburn. "Let's go," I said. I started to walk away just as Ackerman's walk was coming to an end at the "fence" to the utility company's cordoned-off area.

Ms. Washburn fell in behind me as the others watched with blank stares. "Go? Go where, Samuel?"

"Ackerman's house. I only hope we're not too late."

TWENTY-THREE

"Do you really think someone's going to try to hurt Ackerman's wife?" Ms. Washburn asked as we drove—at a speed somewhat above the legal limit, I noted—to the Ackerman home, whose address Lapides had given us and Ms. Washburn had programmed into her GPS device, kept in her glove compartment and now mounted on her dashboard. It was estimated by the device that at our present speed, it would take twelve minutes to reach Ackerman's Spotswood home.

"They have done everything they said they would do so far," I noted. "While I will admit that they have not promised much, everything they have warned about has proven to be accurate. I think it would be a very serious error to underestimate their resolve now."

I felt the car speed up a little more. I did not say anything to Ms. Washburn about her driving, because I understood the urgency of the situation, but I did inwardly note it. I decided to concentrate on the fact that it was 3:24 in the morning, and there would be very little traffic on any road we would use.

"I still don't understand why they would target Mrs. Ackerman," Ms. Washburn went on. "She seems to be the person least involved in this whole business. Why punish her for something she probably doesn't even know about?"

That question had been bothering me as well. "Perhaps the idea is to prey on Ackerman's mind," I said. "Make him feel guilty about not following their instructions."

"I don't see how that helps them," Ms. Washburn said, shaking her head slightly. The speedometer showed the car traveling at a rate 25 miles over the speed limit. "What benefit is there to make Ackerman feel bad once they've already missed out on getting their money? And why not direct their anger at the Masters family? Aren't they the ones who should be paying off on this?"

"I agree, the selection of Mrs. Ackerman seems irrational," I said. "But criminals are not always the most logical of thinkers."

"You said it yourself," she answered. "It would be a very serious error to underestimate them."

I considered that for much of the ride. And as I sifted the pieces of the question in my mind, there appeared to be many contradictions involved in everything we had done since Ackerman appeared at the door of Questions Answered the previous morning. Many of the points were small; they didn't necessarily point to enormous incongruities. But the number of them was troublesome, particularly since I could not yet discern a pattern in the thought process behind them.

Ms. Washburn concentrated on getting us to the Ackerman home as quickly as possible. I had asked Ackerman if he wanted to come along, but Captain Harris had dissuaded him, saying there were police already guarding his house who would contact him if there were any disturbance. She and Lapides felt Ackerman would be more valuable at the GSCI facility, where the remote police cameras watching the drop-off point could be monitored and action taken after the briefcases were picked up.

Captain Harris probably believed there was little real danger to Mrs. Ackerman, and that if a threat did present itself, her husband should be elsewhere. At least, that is the way Ms. Washburn had interpreted the captain's position.

Ackerman had looked nervous, but he acceded to the advice the police officers gave him and got into the SUV for the trip back to the institute. Laverne Masters was also being returned to the institute facility in her car.

It seemed odd that Ms. Washburn and I were the only ones concerned about Eleanor Ackerman.

We were only 1.2 miles from our destination, according to the GPS system, when Ms. Washburn's cellular phone rang. Rather than try to drive and talk at the same time, she noted the incoming call, handed the phone to me, and said, "It's Lapides."

This time, I was prepared as soon as the phone rang, and took a handkerchief from my pocket to receive the phone. Ms. Washburn looked at it, then turned back to face the road and placed the phone in the handkerchief. I pushed the appropriate button and said, "Detective?"

"They came to pick up the money," Lapides reported immediately.

"How many people were there?" I asked.

"Just one, and it seemed to be a man. But the cameras couldn't zoom in close enough, and the lighting there was not great. They weren't night-vision cameras."

"What was the reaction when they discovered that the bulk of the money was counterfeit?" I asked Lapides.

"We don't know; they didn't check while they were there. That was about ten minutes ago. I'll keep you posted."

"Thank you, detective," I said and disconnected the call. I placed the phone in the cup holder between the two seats and folded the handkerchief to put back into my pocket.

"I'm not contagious, you know," Ms. Washburn said.

"I apologize if I offended you," I answered. "It was not personal. I would have done the same with any other person."

"Even your mother?" she asked.

I considered that. "Yes."

Ms. Washburn nodded. "All right, then."

We were driving up to the Ackerman home and could see the police cruiser in front of it, when Ms. Washburn asked, "Samuel, why don't you carry a cell phone yourself?"

I lowered my head for a moment. This was an embarrassing statement to make, but it was an honest question, and it merited an honest answer. "I tend to . . . lose things," I said softly. "I do not always pay attention to objects. So on those occasions when I have owned a cellular telephone, I have not been able to keep it with me. It is, as my mother would say, an Asperger's thing."

Ms. Washburn did not respond, and I was unsure what that might have signaled. She parked the car on the side of the street opposite the police cruiser, and we got out after I asked for and received the flashlight Ms. Washburn kept in the glove compartment. I walked to the cruiser, and the officer in the driver's seat lowered his window.

"Allow me to introduce myself," I told him. "I am Samuel Hoenig of Questions Answered. Detective Lapides and Captain Harris might have told you we would be on our way."

The officer, whose nametag read Sikowski, nodded. "They called a little while ago," he said. "It's been quiet, not a peep from the house."

"Has anyone approached the house?" I asked.

Sikowski shook his head. "At this time of the morning, this is about as quiet a street as you're going to find," he said. "We've been sitting here for more than an hour. We checked with the lady inside as soon as we arrived—woke her up and scared her, I'm afraid—and since then we haven't seen one person so much as walk or drive by."

"Have you done any foot patrol of the area?" I asked. "A sweep of the perimeter?"

"There's nothing in the back but woods," Sikowski said. "We took a look when we were first here, but there hasn't been a light or a sound, no reason to do it again since we arrived."

That was a little worrisome. "Do you mind if I take a look?" I asked.

He shrugged. "Knock yourself out."

I was not sure what to make of that. "Why would I do that?" I said.

Sikowski looked perplexed.

"It's an expression, Samuel," Ms. Washburn explained, taking my arm. "It means you should go ahead and check around the house."

"Oh. Good. I will, then." I nodded toward Sikowski. "Thank you, officer."

He raised the car window again without comment. I turned to walk toward the house, but something occurred to me, and I knocked on Sikowski's window, which he lowered and looked at me.

"Are there any pets in the house?" I asked. "A dog?"

Sikowski shook his head. "No, we asked that, too. Turns out Dr. Ackerman is allergic." And he raised the window again before I could thank him or ask another question.

As we crossed the street, I looked at Ms. Washburn. "Perhaps you should stay here," I told her. "If there is a problem back there, I don't want you exposed to it. Your husband is already concerned ..."

"Never mind about my husband," she insisted. "I'm here to help you. I can't do that sitting in the car. Let's go." And she started toward the house again, so I followed.

We made a cursory inspection of the front entrance, which was locked and had a keypad and a small sticker indicating there was an alarm system at work in the house. I did not jostle the door handle or lock enough to set it off, but did confirm that it was not the subject of any recent tampering.

There was no reason to favor one side of the house over the other, so I walked slowly toward the left side, where the driveway led to an attached garage. Again, the garage door was secure, so we walked around the side, careful not to disturb any of the tidily planted flowerbeds or trip over the garden hose, which was left unrolled behind the garage. I suppressed the urge to roll it onto the cart standing not ten feet away and proceeded toward the back of the house. There was no exterior door on this side.

While it had not rained recently, the garden hose indicated that there had been some watering done recently, and the grass was a bit damp, perhaps with dew this early in the morning. I instructed Ms. Washburn to be careful about where she stepped and to try to restrict herself to paved areas. I also asked her, although it was considered impolite, to let me walk ahead of her. She had no objections and actually seemed to welcome the suggestion.

When I turned the corner to glance at the back of the house, I stopped in my tracks and held up my hand to halt Ms. Washburn before she could make the turn. "Someone has been here," I said.

"Are you sure?" Ms. Washburn looked alarmed, which was sensible on her part.

"There are indications in the grass and muddy footprints leaving the house," I told her. I advanced twenty-five feet to take a closer look, and Ms. Washburn followed. "They are not old enough to be anything but signs of an intruder."

"The footprints are just leaving the house?" Ms. Washburn whispered. "None going in?"

I considered that. "No, and you're correct that it is notable. It might be that something alarmed Mrs. Ackerman, and she simply left the house. I'll check. Please call the police and tell them to alert the officers in the cruiser."

Ms. Washburn's responses were coming with a delay. She was breathing hard. She must have been frightened. "I can't. I think I left the phone in the car."

"Then go back and tell them," I said. "I will signal with the flashlight if there is a problem. If there is not, I'll simply turn on the lights in the front room, and you can come inside."

Again, there was an interval before Ms. Washburn answered me, and her voice was a little shaky. "I don't want to leave you here alone," she said, although her tone, if I was judging it correctly, was contradicting her words. It was confusing.

I pointed out the obvious. "I will not be alone," I told her. "Either Mrs. Ackerman, the intruder, or both will be inside the house."

"That doesn't make me feel better." Ms. Washburn turned and began to run back toward the street.

I assessed the situation and decided that if Mrs. Ackerman was in need of immediate help, there was no sense in waiting for the officers. I approached the back door of the house, noting that there appeared to be no signs of a forced entry, and that the security alarm was not sounding, despite the presence of a keypad at the back door entrance.

When I pushed on the door with my elbow (to avoid leaving fingerprints the police would find later), it opened without my turning the doorknob.

I did not consider that a good sign.

There was a mudroom immediately inside the entrance, and no signs of a disturbance there. A washer and dryer stood in one corner of the room, but there was no laundry hamper present. The laundry had been done. There was no blood on the floor or anywhere else in the room, and if the intruder had indeed come this way while exiting the house, that was clearly a positive sign. Unlike the person who had last left this room, I was careful to wipe any mud off my shoes on a mat by the door. Then I walked inside as quietly as I could manage.

I considered calling for Mrs. Ackerman, but if there were still an intruder in the house, that would be a most unfortunate alert. Better to search.

Given the time of night, it was obvious that the most likely place to find Mrs. Ackerman would be the master bedroom, which is most often located upstairs. I made my way through the kitchen, which appeared quite peaceful, and into the living room, where there was a carpeted stairway.

I thought that would give me an advantage, muffling my steps, but it was not to be—the third stair from the top creaked loudly, and I immediately heard a sound coming from a room to my left, no doubt the master bedroom. I had alerted someone that I was in the house.

Unarmed as I was, it crossed my mind that waiting for the police officers to arrive might still be a viable option, but they had not yet arrived in the house (at least as far as I could perceive), and there was still the very real possibility of danger to Mrs. Ackerman, the reason I had come here to begin with.

I stopped at the top of the stairs, considered my plan carefully, and moved as quietly as possible toward the open bedroom door on my left.

It did not take long to reach the doorway. Even forcing myself to look around the unlit hallway—my pupils having adjusted to the darkness—I could not find anything that could reliably be used as a defensive weapon. I am a second-degree black belt in tae kwon do, after years of training that my mother had insisted would help me socialize with others my age, and decided to rely upon that skill if the need arose. If my opponent was armed with a gun, however, tae kwon do would be a less effective option.

But it was the only one I had.

I stepped inside the bedroom, once again grateful for the sound-dampening effect of the wall-to-wall carpet. I stood absolutely still in the new atmosphere, letting my eyes adjust once again, then assessed the scene.

It was an upper-middle-class bedroom, with a king-sized bed in the center, a master bath to the right of the bed, and two dressers, one on each side of the room, which I'm sure were quite lovely but which I could not see clearly enough to confirm the suspicion. A full-length mirror on the left side of the bed gave me a start before I realized I was seeing my own reflection. There was almost no light coming in from any of the three windows in the room. A humidifier unit was turned on, so white noise hummed quietly as I stood.

The one unexpected feature of the room was that there was no one in the bed.

I walked slowly around the bed and looked inside the bathroom. There was no one visible there. A quick look inside the shower unit confirmed the absence of anyone inside. A second door led to a small sauna, but there was no one inside that room, either.

The sauna was the darkest room in the suite, with no windows, so my eyes were especially well adjusted when I walked back into the bedroom itself. And that meant I could see something I had not noticed before. Specifically, I examined a black hole running through the comforter and the sheets beneath it. A hole that bore the smell of something burning.

A bullet hole.

Had an intruder come in and shot at the bed, incorrectly believing someone was sleeping there? That seemed unlikely, because the bullet hole was at the foot of the bed. A person trying to kill someone sleeping in a bed would probably not first take aim at the toes.

I considered the noise I'd heard on the stairs, almost a high-pitched whimper, and dropped to my knees. I looked under the bed. There was a woman under there.

A live woman.

"Mrs. Ackerman?" I asked. But the woman did not respond; she merely stared at me and whimpered again. "Are you Eleanor Ackerman?" That question solicited only a more pitiable moan. It had not occurred to me before, but suddenly I understood that Mrs. Ackerman would not know who I was, or whether I was there to attempt to harm her, as someone else had clearly done shortly before.

Downstairs, I heard the front and back doors open at the same time. "Police!" came a cry from below.

"Mrs. Ackerman, I am Samuel Hoenig," I told the woman under the bed. "Your husband sent me here to see if you were all right. I mean you no harm, and I have no weapon. Are you injured?"

She shook her head; no, she was not injured.

There were footsteps on the level beneath us. It would be best to let the officers know we were not hostiles. "We're up here, officers!" I shouted. "No one is injured! No one is in the room with us. I can't be sure about any other rooms except the mudroom and the kitchen!"

"On our way up," I heard Officer Sikowski say. "Identify yourselves, please."

"Samuel Hoenig," I called. I gestured to Mrs. Ackerman that she should do the same. It seemed to distract her enough to compose herself.

"Eleanor Ackerman," she tried to shout, but she was lying on her stomach under the bed and could not generate much volume.

"What?" Sikowski called.

"Mrs. Ackerman is coming out from under the bed," I said. "She's all right."

Sikowski appeared at the door, weapon drawn but held with the barrel to the floor, as I helped Mrs. Ackerman out from under the bed. She coughed twice as Sikowski, making sure we hadn't been coerced by an unseen assailant, searched the room. He turned on the overhead track lighting when he was finished.

Eleanor Ackerman was a woman in her mid-forties, perhaps forty-six, standing five-foot-five. I did not estimate her weight, but she was neither underweight nor seriously overweight. Her disheveled hair was a light brown, and probably had been at least highlighted, if not dyed, professionally. She struggled to catch her breath. She was, clearly, terrified.

"I saw … a gun," she said finally, heaving between breaths.

"It's Officer Sikowski," I assured her. "You are in no danger."

Sikowski's partner appeared at the door, and Sikowski turned to him. "The house is clear," the other officer said, and Sikowski nodded.

"Wait for backup and watch the entrances, especially the back," he told the other officer, whose nametag I could now see read PATEL.

Officer Patel exited, and we could hear his footsteps on the stairs. They were muffled by the carpet and faded as he got farther away. Sikowski turned toward us again.

"I saw a gun," Eleanor repeated.

Sikowski's eyes narrowed. "You mean my weapon?" he asked.

Eleanor shook her head. "No. I mean when I was under the bed. I saw a gun in a hand. Then I heard the shot into the bed. It went right by my head." Of course, Eleanor would have hidden under the bed facing the door, so she could see the person invading her home when he or she entered the bedroom.

"Did you hear the intruder break in?" I asked. Sikowski frowned; he was not comfortable with someone other than a police officer asking the questions, but he had probably been alerted to my involvement in the case by his superiors, and so gave me leniency he likely would not have allowed another civilian.

"No," Eleanor answered. "After the two officers came and woke me, I was so nervous that I took an Ambien to get back to sleep. So I didn't hear anything until there were footsteps on the stairs. I didn't even have time to reach for the phone; I just dove under the bed."

"It probably saved your life," Sikowski observed. I had been thinking the same thing, but thought the suggestion might frighten Eleanor further and make her a less useful witness.

She did not seem upset, however. "I saw the feet, in black sneakers, you know, not like sports shoes, but the rubberized ones that make your steps quiet. And I saw a gun in the person's right hand."

"Was the intruder male or female?" Sikowski asked.

"I don't know. The lights were completely out, and I could just see shapes, and only from the waist down. If they were holding the gun up in the air, I wouldn't have seen it."

Perhaps there was another way to determine the gender of the intruder. "Were the shoes large or small?" I asked.

Eleanor narrowed her eyes in thought. "I really couldn't tell. They were dark and they were moving. Maybe smallish. Maybe not. I don't know."

"But they were not overly large," I pressed on.

Again, she thought. "No. I would have noticed if they were really big or really small."

"We've called your husband," Sikowski assured her. "He's on his way here."

Eleanor showed no outward emotion, but she said, "Good."

Sikowski spent the next eleven minutes questioning Eleanor about what she had seen and heard, and finding out not much more than we had already heard, but I understood the technique—the more you get the subject to think about the moment, the more they are likely to remember. Then, he spent three minutes examining the bullet hole in the mattress and the trajectory it had taken.

By that time, Marshall Ackerman had arrived, and his wife had gone into her master bathroom to change into exercise clothing. Ackerman burst through the door with a dramatic flair and shouted her name.

She walked to him and Ackerman embraced her, but Eleanor's arms did not rise to hold her husband close. She still appeared to be in a state of stunted emotion brought on by the shock she had experienced. Or she might have been a person with Asperger's Syndrome, although that seemed unlikely. Men are far more likely to be diagnosed with an autism spectrum "disorder." While it is estimated that one in every eighty-eight people has some such "disorder," males are diagnosed four times more often than females. So Mrs. Ackerman was probably just upset.

After being given a detailed report on the evening's events, and having voiced absolute despair at the account—particularly once he saw the bullet hole in the mattress—Ackerman suggested we go downstairs, "away from this horror," and continue the interview in the living room.

A crime scene team was arriving at the same time, so we retreated to another room off the living room, which Eleanor identified as the library. This was confusing, since I saw no books on any shelves in the room. But I did not voice my puzzlement, since I assumed it related to my perception as a person with Asperger's Syndrome. Officer Sikowski did not comment on it, and I made a mental note to ask Ms. Washburn when I saw her again. That led to me to ask Sikowski where she might be, and he replied that she had stayed outside to avoid any danger in the house.

As he asked Ackerman the same questions I had been asking all day—who might have a grudge against him or the institute, and why Eleanor might be a target—I excused myself and went outside the house to find Ms. Washburn. She was sitting in her car with the engine running and the heater turned on. The sky was just beginning to show signs of light in the east.

She made no gesture toward me, so I was not sure if I should sit in the passenger seat again, but that had been my assigned seat all day. I decided, then, that it would not be a breach of social protocol to open the unlocked passenger door and sit next to her in the car.

"I'm sorry," Ms. Washburn said before I could begin a conversation.

That was not what I had been expecting to hear. Ms. Washburn's face was unreadable; she had no expression, and her voice did not

215

betray an emotional state. I had no data to process about her at the moment. "Why are you sorry?" I asked.

"I didn't come in to help you," she said. "The cops told me to stay out here, and I did. I left you inside alone."

"That is what I expected you to do," I told her. "There was danger inside. The police were here to handle it. You had no reason to place yourself in harm's way."

She shook her head. "I did have a reason. You went in there yourself. You're not a police officer; you did it because you wanted to help Mrs. Ackerman."

"But the officers instructed you to stay outside," I reminded her.

"And I never so much as suggested otherwise," Ms. Washburn replied. A tear escaped her right eye, the one I could see, as she was staring straight out through the windshield. "I let you go in there and face the danger with no help at all because I was afraid."

Her position was not a sensible one. She had done the right thing by remaining out of the line of fire. It had eased some of the burden on my concentration not to have her in the house while I was searching for Eleanor. But no matter how many times I suggested these points to Ms. Washburn, she would not accept their validity.

"You were going in there alone, and I let you do it," she said. "I was afraid, and I let you down."

I thought she might begin to cry, and that made me anxious. I do not know how to react to emotional outbursts like that, so I try to defuse them before they can occur, and thereby prevent them from becoming something that will make me uncomfortable. It is not a technique I was taught in social skills training, where I was encouraged to embrace projections of emotion. I had developed this strategy on my own, particularly on those occasions when my mother would become upset over my father's absence or because I was a more difficult child to raise than most.

"You did nothing wrong," I assured Ms. Washburn. "You did exactly what I would have advised had I been here. Please don't cry."

Her head turned quickly, indicating that she might have been surprised. "I'm not crying," she said.

"I thought you might start."

Ms. Washburn smiled wanly. "It's late and I'm tired," she said. "I wasn't going to burst into tears. Don't worry, Samuel."

I was, of course, relieved to hear that. "In that case, would you please drive us back to the institute?"

She looked surprised. "We're going back?" she asked. "We're not done for the night?"

Done for the night? "The questions remain unanswered," I reminded her. "The remains of Ms. Masters-Powell are still in jeopardy, and there has been no progress in the investigation of Dr. Springer's murder. Until there is no longer any urgency in those matters, we must remain at work."

Ms. Washburn nodded slowly and started the engine.

We did not speak for the nineteen minutes it took to drive from Ackerman's home to the Garden State Cryonics Institute. Ms. Washburn appeared preoccupied, to the extent that I had to point out the proper entrance onto US Highway 1 when it was looming. She nodded and made the turn but continued to present the appearance of a person thinking about something else, a circumstance that makes me anxious when riding with someone.

217

Still, we arrived at GSCI safely and without incident. Once there, I got out of the car, but Ms. Washburn did not turn off its engine. I waited next to the vehicle for forty-seven seconds, but there was no indication that she intended to exit immediately. So I walked to the driver's side, and when she saw me, Ms. Washburn lowered her window.

Before I could speak, she said, "I'm not going in, Samuel. I'm going home."

"I do not understand."

She nodded. "I know you don't," she said. "But this whole day—and night—has exhausted me and frightened me. I'm worried that I'm doing you more harm than good. And I think it's best for both of us that I leave now."

We had already gone through this conversation, so it occurred to me that there were unspoken issues and motivations at work in her decision. "I understand that your husband is upset with the kind of work we do, but—"

"Let's not make this about my marriage, okay, Samuel?" Ms. Washburn asked. "I'm very serious about what I'm saying. If I will abandon you at the most crucial moments, it's best that you find someone else, or go on by yourself. You were doing fine as a one-man operation until this morning. Just continue on as if I'd never been here."

That was difficult to imagine. "But you have been here," I said. I was about to add, *and you have been an invaluable associate*. I was about to add that she was in fact referring to *yesterday* morning, but Ms. Washburn spoke before I could continue.

"I know, but I want you to pretend I wasn't. Just go ahead and do what you do so well. Answer the questions. I'll come by your office tomorrow, and you can tell me how it went. But please, Samuel, don't ask me to go back into that building and talk to those people anymore. I think someone there killed Dr. Springer and tried to kill Mrs. Ackerman. And I don't want either one of us to be the next target."

I felt it was best not to mention that I agreed with her assessment and was starting to form a theory as to which of the people we had met today was involved in the murder. Ms. Washburn was already agitated. Confirming that we were probably less than fifty yards from a killer would not calm her nerves.

The knowledge certainly did very little to calm mine.

"I will not ask you to do something that frightens you so deeply," I told her. "Please accept my thanks for your work today, and please consider coming back to work with Questions Answered tomorrow. Believe me, we almost never deal with violent criminals. In fact, this is the first time for me as well."

Ms. Washburn smiled. "I'll think about it, Samuel. I promise." She reached over to the console between the front seats of her car, and picked up her cellular phone. "Do me a favor and take this, okay?" She extended her hand, holding the phone, toward me.

"I do not understand," I said. "That is your cellular phone."

"I'm not saying take it forever," she answered. "Just in case you have to go out somewhere else again on this question, I would feel better if you'd have a means of communication with you at all times. Okay? To make me feel better?"

The phone was still extended out the window. Clearly, she wanted me to take it, but I was still apprehensive. "I've explained my history with such objects," I reminded her. "I am not necessarily the most reliable person with whom to trust such a valuable piece of equipment, something you'll need."

"I'm going home to sleep," she said. "I intend to sleep quite late, hopefully long past the amount of time it will take you to answer these two questions. I'll come by in the afternoon and pick it up. So I won't need it the whole time you have it. Okay?"

With another gesture, she extended the phone again. "But I might lose it," I protested.

Ms. Washburn made sure she held my gaze when she said, "I trust you."

The discussion was completed. I took the phone, and Ms. Washburn drove away.

TWENTY-FOUR

THE FIRST THING DETECTIVE Lapides asked me when I walked into the GSCI lobby was, "Where's your assistant?"

I was tempted to correct his terminology and point out that Ms. Washburn was my associate and not my assistant, but instead I merely said, "Ms. Washburn has gone home for the day," and left it at that. I was struggling to understand the change that had just taken place and was not yet ready to discuss it in detail. For someone like me, a surprise is not a pleasant experience; we prefer to know as much about an experience in advance as we possibly can.

"Come on in," Lapides said, waving me through the security checkpoint at the entrance. "We have a lot to talk about."

We walked into the same conference room where we'd seen Ackerman receive the messages from the thieves. Inside were Laverne and Arthur Masters, Commander Johnson, and Captain Harris. Neither Mrs. Johnson, Charlotte Selby, nor, of course, Marshall Ackerman were present.

"Where's your assistant?" Arthur Masters asked, looking especially disappointed. I began to think that it was possible I did not like Arthur, but I told him the same thing I had told Lapides. When Arthur began to ask another question, Captain Harris cut him off.

"Things have escalated since you left, Mr. Hoenig," she said. "I appreciate your help at the scene. We might not have the limited video footage we have if not for you, and your instinct regarding Mrs. Ackerman might very well have saved her life."

"It was not an instinct," I corrected her. "It was a conclusion reasoned through use of the facts."

The captain waved a hand as if to dismiss the difference as irrelevant. I knew it was not, but I did not offer an argument. "As you've been told, the kidnappers have rejected the ransom that was offered and are now threatening to destroy the remains they have with them. But Mr. and Mrs. Masters are now saying they will pay the full ransom requested under the right conditions."

That statement came as something of a shock. Laverne especially had been so adamant about not paying for her daughter's head that her acquiescence on the subject of ransom seemed completely out of character. Changes in behavior that dramatic are sometimes the sign of an ulterior motive, and that did not coincide with the theory I had been developing on the question of the missing head.

I looked in Arthur's direction, and he was looking at a picture on the wall above Captain Harris's head. "Exactly," he said. "Under the right conditions."

"What would constitute the right conditions?" I asked. Unlike many such circumstances, when one would ask a question in anticipation of a certain response, I had no idea what Arthur's answer might be.

"We need to see Rita's remains, in person, before the money is transferred into a numbered account," he said. "No actual cash will change hands."

"Other than the one million that the institute has already lost, apparently," I pointed out.

Laverne shook her head. "That's not our concern," she said. "We advised against paying anything to people who hadn't even proved they have what they say they have."

A small, thin man of about forty, showing signs of male pattern baldness, opened the door just enough to enter the conference room. He seemed barely strong enough to bear the weight of the door, and came close to becoming wedged in before he managed to achieve entry. He did not say anything, and no one seemed to notice his entrance, but he walked to Captain Harris's side and stood there.

"Have your conditions been communicated to the thieves?" I asked the Masterses. I took Ms. Washburn's cellular phone out of my pocket to assure myself that I still had possession of it. The phone was there but was not receiving a signal.

"We sent a text message to the number that had sent the last demands to Ackerman," Commander Johnson said. "We're still waiting for the reply."

There was a silent moment at that point, and the thin man cleared his throat, which, even for someone like me who is more sensitive to sounds than most, was almost inaudible. But he was close enough to Captain Harris that she turned to face him.

"Oh, what is it, Epstein?" she asked. The man mumbled a reply, and the captain, leaning toward him to hear, appeared irritated. "Speak up," she commanded.

"You had asked for a report on the security system," Epstein said, his voice barely registering above the hum of the climate control system in the room.

"Yes, hours ago," the captain answered.

"I've been waiting in the storage chamber to make my report, but no one came down to hear it," Epstein explained. "Would you like the report now?"

There was an embarrassed silence, as everyone in the room including me looked elsewhere, having forgotten about the report that might explain how the crimes at GSCI had been committed.

"Yes, of course, man," Captain Harris finally responded. She addressed the rest of us. "This is Jerome Epstein, the technological consultant we commissioned to examine the video security system here at Garden State."

Commander Johnson snarled and said something I could not understand under his breath.

Epstein cleared his throat again, presumably for theatrical purposes to indicate that everyone in the room should pay attention. "Will you all join me in the security station?" he requested. "I believe I can show you exactly what happened."

———

"Well, maybe I overstated it," Jerome Epstein said.

We had eagerly adjourned the meeting to the security station to hear Epstein's report. The station, on the first level down from the ground level, was a rather small room, and it was difficult for the five of us to fit inside. Laverne Masters, having determined that the walk might be far, had chosen to stay in the conference room upstairs.

"I can't show you what happened," Epstein continued. "But I can certainly show you exactly what *didn't* happen."

Captain Harris looked perplexed. "You brought us here to show us something that didn't happen?" she asked.

"In a way, yes." Epstein turned toward an electronic console in front of him that, in a downsized fashion, approximated what one might see in the control room of a television studio. He turned a dial and nodded toward an overhead flat-screen monitor. "Take a look at that screen," he said. "This is the data that was recorded at the approximate time Dr. Springer was murdered, as close as we can estimate from the preliminary report of the medical examiner."

Everyone in the room immediately directed his or her attention to the monitor. After four seconds, it flickered to life, and we saw a very clear, full-color view of the specimen storage chamber, taken from inside the inner chamber door. It showed the left side of the room, with five full-body preservation units and eight for the preservation of the brain or full head.

Nothing disturbed the picture. I noted the time and date etched at the bottom of the screen, and they were as accurate as I could estimate. There was sound being recorded, since I could hear the hum of the cooling units, but nothing else appeared on screen or made an audible sound while we watched.

That trend continued for ninety-seven seconds before Captain Harris asked, "How long before we see something?"

"You're seeing it now," Epstein replied. "This is what the security system recorded."

"I don't understand," the captain said.

"Are you saying that no one came in and stole my sister's remains?" Arthur Masters demanded. "That no one killed a woman who is quite clearly dead? Are you trying to cover for the institute?"

Epstein shook his head. "Nothing of the sort," he said. "I didn't say this is what happened. I said this is what the security system recorded."

Detective Lapides took on a very stern look. "Don't try to fool us," he told Epstein. Lapides then looked at me, perhaps recalling that it was my recommendation to employ an expert that led to Epstein's presence in the room.

"What you're seeing is the same recording that you looked at earlier today," Epstein said. "And the fact is, the security system was told to record this image at the time of the theft, and at the time Dr. Springer died. But it is not the image the system should have been recording."

I began to understand what Epstein was trying to say. Like many scientists and technical experts, he was not especially adept at conveying his thoughts in anything but the technical jargon of his profession, so when he attempted to do so, he could be misleading or appear obtuse. It was a difficulty I understood quite well.

"So something has been done to the security system to make it record the wrong image," I said, attempting to clarify for Epstein.

He nodded with enthusiasm and pointed his index finger at me. "Exactly," he said. "Someone has tampered with the system. This is actually a recording of Preservation Room B, when it should be a recording of Preservation Room D."

That explained a great deal—how thieves could steal into the storage chamber without being detected, why the security system was not activated, why the previous security data we had examined had shown nothing. "What about the other cameras mounted in Preservation Room D?" Lapides asked. "There have to be at least four cameras in each room."

"There are six," I told him. Lapides gave me a look that was not as appreciative as I had expected.

"All of the security detection devices—cameras, microphones, and motion sensors—in Room D were switched off externally and rerouted to Room B at specific times," Epstein explained. "So all of the data we got from the security system shows an empty room, interrupted only when a technician comes in to do a routine check during the night. And we have checked with the technician and her work log; she was indeed in Room B at the time this record shows her in Room D. Three other security personnel verify her account."

"Was this rerouting of the data done automatically or manually?" I asked.

"Now, that's very interesting," Epstein replied. "The first time, when the remains of Rita Masters-Powell were stolen, was done automatically, and set up in advance. But when Dr. Springer was murdered later in the day, the system was breached manually, from inside the facility, only a minute or two before we can assume the assault on Dr. Springer took place."

"Is there any way of restoring the correct security record?" Captain Harris asked.

I knew the answer, but I felt it was better to let Epstein explain. He shook his head. "There's nothing to restore," he said. "The footage was never taken. It's like trying to replace a photograph when the lens cap was on the whole time."

Lapides raised his arms in what I took to be frustration. "Then there's nothing we can do," he said. "We'll never know who stole the head, or who killed the doctor."

"There is a great deal we can do, now that we know how the perpetrators managed to commit their crimes undetected," I argued. "Commander Johnson, how many people in your security crew would have the expertise and the access to the system to be able to reroute the security devices the way Mr. Epstein has described?"

The commander put his hand to his chin and lowered his eyebrows, then turned his head abruptly and looked at me. "Wait a minute," he said. As always when someone says such a thing to me, my mind noted that this is an imprecise and inaccurate phrase to use. If we had waited a full minute, he would not have been able to make his following point until we had stood still for sixty seconds. But I was sure Ms. Washburn would have advised me to let that point remain unexpressed, so I listened. "Are you suggesting that I had something to do with these crimes?" Commander Johnson asked loudly.

"I am not suggesting anything," I replied as calmly as he had spoken emotionally. "I am asking a question that is designed to help us uncover the truth."

"Answer the question, please, commander," Captain Harris said quietly. Her face was without expression and her eyes did not blink as she watched him reply.

He stood straight at attention, as I'd noticed he always did when performing a task he clearly did not consider a pleasant one. "My-self," he said, then his eyes surveyed the room for reactions, which were not very noticeable, or which I missed. "Dr. Ackerman. My second-in-command, Jose Feliz, but only on those occasions when I am not present."

"Why would Mr. Feliz have access only when you're not here?" the captain asked.

"Because he would need a key card," I said. Commander Johnson looked sharply at me. "I assume that the commander relin-quishes the key card that sets and unsets the security system in the storage rooms only when he is not present, and that there is not a duplicate key for Mr. Feliz."

Commander Johnson barely moved his lips when he said, "That is correct. There is a second key, but I keep both of them and give Feliz his only when it is necessary."

"But you weren't here when the remains were stolen," I reminded the commander. "You said you received the call at home. Did you question Jose Feliz, Detective Lapides?"

"Yes!" Lapides snapped. It was becoming quite crowded for my taste in the tiny room, and I began to wonder if Epstein's presenta-tion had concluded, so we could vacate to more comfortable quar-ters. "He had someone with him through the entire shift, and his movements during the questionable times were verified on the video records."

"Are we finished here?" I asked. Arthur Masters's breath on the back of my neck was hot and unpleasant.

"Just one thing," Lapides responded, while I pondered exactly how long I could tolerate the close quarters. Lapides turned toward Epstein. "How would someone rig this up to *automatically* switch from one storage room to another? Wouldn't that show up on the video record?" Looking at Commander Johnson, he added, "Don't you have someone monitoring at all times?"

"Of course we do," the commander answered before Epstein, who tended to consider and draw breath before speaking, could. "But the blip from one empty room to another empty room would be almost imperceptible. The personnel monitoring would almost have to be watching for it."

"I intend to sue this facility whether we retrieve my sister's remains or not," Arthur said behind me, spraying the *s* on the word *sue* and again on *sister's*. I reached for my handkerchief and wiped the back of my neck.

Instinctively, I also checked for Ms. Washburn's cellular phone. It was safe in my pocket but still was not receiving a usable signal.

"What it indicates," said Epstein, answering the question Lapides had asked, "is that the person or people who configured the video system to switch over had to have a very close working knowledge of the security procedures here. It is possible that if they were technically proficient enough, the whole thing could be done from outside the facility, but that would require some very sophisticated equipment that, quite frankly, would cost so much money it would no longer make the ransom seem like a very big haul."

"How does that help?" Lapides asked. It didn't occur to me to look, but I noticed everyone in the room suddenly seemed to be looking in my direction, so I concluded that Lapides's question was directed at me.

"It narrows the list of suspects a bit, because it means the thief has to be someone who at least knows an employee of the institute very well," I answered. "And since at some point a key card to the security system had to be used, it is clear that one of two things is true: Commander Johnson or Dr. Ackerman is involved in the theft and possibly the murder, or someone has stolen the duplicate key card that exists for Mr. Feliz's use."

"There's another key," Commander Johnson said. "Ackerman has a spare, I'm sure. He said it helped increase security because he could never be without the proper key card."

It was becoming more difficult to think in this small room crowded with people. "Mr. Epstein," I asked, "is there any reason for us to stay at this station?"

Epstein shook his head. Everyone else in the room seemed to exhale at the same time, and Arthur opened the door, which allowed some welcome cool air inside as we began to file out.

Marshall Ackerman was already walking toward us as we headed in the direction of the conference room. The cooler air in the hall-way—and the lack of saliva on the back of my neck—made it easier to think. But I was not properly prepared for what Ackerman said when we reached him.

I asked about his wife, and Ackerman said she was doing well and had gone to a hotel for the rest of the night, which would not be long; it was already close to five in the morning. But the police were watching her, he said, more closely now that an attempt had been made on her life by what Ackerman called "an unbalanced mind."

Ballistics tests were being made on the bullet found in Ackerman's box spring.

Something sounded wrong, but speech patterns often sound unusual to me, and I missed the counsel of my mother or Ms. Washburn. There was no time to dwell on it, however, because Ackerman's cellular phone chirped, and he reached into his jacket for it. I considered the time: In another three hours, if the question was still unsolved, I would have to ask for use of the fitness center again to exercise every twenty minutes.

His eyes widened when he saw the incoming number. "It's the kidnappers," he said, and opened the phone to read a text message. "They're accepting the terms you laid out, Arthur. They'll produce your sister's remains in three hours if you can show them you are prepared to transfer the money to a numbered account they will specify."

Arthur Masters didn't look happy, but he nodded. "I'll need to talk to my mother," he said and headed back to the conference room. The others followed, but I stayed behind.

As Epstein passed, I was tempted to reach out and hold his arm, to get him to stop, but I am not given to touching strangers, so I said as quietly as I could, "Mr. Epstein."

Luckily he heard me and stopped walking.

"Are you familiar with the aspect of the security system that makes it difficult to receive a cellular phone signal in this building?" I asked him.

Epstein shook his head from side to side while tilting it, indicating that he was somewhat familiar with it, but not an expert on the subject. "Sort of," he said. "What do you need to know?"

"Is it possible for one phone to receive a signal, while another does not?"

Epstein clenched his teeth as he thought about that. "It's possible, I guess," he said. "But I would consider it extremely unlikely. Why?"

He had confirmed what I had already believed. "Because I think one of the thieves, probably one involved in Dr. Springer's murder, is in this facility right now," I told him.

TWENTY-FIVE

It was not an easy task to isolate Det. Glendon Lapides from the crowd. He was standing in the conference room, hunched over a table, which I supposed was used for a dais when panels or meetings were held here. Lapides was surrounded by Captain Harris, Commander Johnson, Ackerman, and Arthur Masters, who had left his mother sitting at the table. And he was not looking out into the hallway, where Epstein and I stood.

Not wanting to alert the others to our conversation and unsure whether it would be possible to call or text Lapides on his cellular phone, I instructed Epstein, who had a talent for not being noticed, to walk into the room and inform the detective—very quietly—that I had an important matter to discuss with him in the hallway.

The gambit did not go as smoothly as I'd hoped. Epstein was able to enter the conference room unnoticed and did whisper to Lapides, but apparently the detective had a hearing problem on his right side or the technician was whispering too quietly, because

Lapides asked "What?" at least three times, the last so loud I could hear him outside the room. I managed to hide behind a potted plant to avoid the looks of the gathered group, but I did see Epstein pull Lapides aside and the others return their attention to a legal pad upon which Ackerman was writing something.

Lapides did finally walk out to meet me, and the rest of the group in the conference room did not seem to notice.

"What do you mean, the killer's in this building?" Lapides said after I had told him the reason for the clandestine conversation. It baffled me momentarily that he did not seem the grasp the meaning of a simple declarative sentence, until I realized it was a way of asking why I thought the facts supported my conclusion.

"The cellular phones prove the point," I explained. "I was not able to get a signal on Ms. Washburn's cellular phone. Are you able to call out on yours?"

Lapides reached into his pocket and pulled out his cellular phone, which he opened. He shook his head. "But Ackerman said they would work on this level," he said, seemingly baffled.

"That is what he said, but the facts do not support it," I told him. "Mr. Epstein here says it is unlikely such a selective system could be put in place. If the institute does not want cellular communications to be possible on the lower levels for security reasons, the cost of that provision is that such signals would not be possible anywhere in the building."

"But Ackerman received messages from the thieves, and so did I," the detective noted. "I know I wasn't pretending to get a text; was Ackerman?"

I told him I thought not.

"I suppose text messages could be sent through the institute's Wi-Fi signal, which probably wouldn't accommodate voice communication," Epstein said. "I've seen it done. It's similar to an intercom system, a closed system, all kept within the building, but more flexible. Places that need special security within their walls, like a company that prints lottery tickets, for example, would use such a system. This one is more sophisticated and can be made to work with cell phones, even if they're not receiving signal from a tower or satellite."

I had never done research on that kind of technology, but what Epstein told Lapides and me appeared to make sense. With a security operation as sophisticated as the one at GSCI, proprietary technologies would no doubt have to be developed, and Ackerman had alluded to that earlier. It was probably one of the reasons that Ackerman and Commander Johnson had been so adamant about Epstein staying away from their system—it was entirely possible that some regulations had not been completely obeyed.

"Does this mean that Ackerman is in on the theft?" Lapides asked. "How does it make sense that he would steal from his own institute?"

"We must not jump to conclusions until we have all the facts," I told him. "Ackerman might be legitimately ignorant of the technology. It is possible that he has never tried to use his cellular phone in the building, especially if he was told it would not work. During the day here, I saw him use a land line whenever he had to make or receive a phone call."

"What other explanation is there?" Lapides asked.

"There are many. If Commander Johnson has lied to Ackerman about the limitations of the security system and communications, it is possible the commander is one of the thieves, or that he or his wife was the person who picked up the briefcases at Rutgers Village or attacked Mrs. Ackerman in her home."

"You think Commander Johnson was involved?" Lapides looked shaken.

"I did not say that. I said it was possible. It is equally possible that the commander is trying to do his job well and has not been successful. We don't know enough yet to make a determination."

My mind was racing with possibilities. Surely the next question would be how to proceed, and there were far too many options to sift through before I made a decision. I trusted that Detective Lapides was honest, but his problem-solving skills did not appear to be on a very high-functioning level. I did not know Captain Harris well enough to judge her abilities and felt that I was without the benefit of a person I could use as a sounding board. I wished again that Ms. Washburn had not left.

"If at least one of the thieves is in the building, what should we do?" Lapides asked.

I would have to trust my own judgment, something I am not naturally inclined to do. "How many uniformed officers do you have in the building?" I asked the detective.

"Only two," he answered. "We sent the rest home hours ago."

"And how many levels are there in the building?" I knew the answer to this one but was buying myself time to think.

"Six," Lapides answered.

"Very well. Excuse yourself from the conference room, and alert your uniformed officers. Each of you will be responsible for three levels. Ask for every cell phone from each person you find, and check the outgoing text messages. That might be a place to start. Would such texts be traceable, Mr. Epstein?"

Epstein thought and said, "I've never dealt with a system exactly like this one before, but I'm guessing they would be. The problem is that if the thieves are smart, and so far they have been ..."

"Then they will have undoubtedly deleted the outgoing texts in question, I know," I said. "But if Detective Lapides, in his proper role as lead investigator, were to confiscate any cellular phones he finds, the thieves would be deprived of a way to communicate their further conditions and demands. Anything that might force a rash move should be encouraged; the less time they have to plan, the better off we are. Right now, we have the element of surprise—they think we are still unaware of their presence here. Mr. Epstein, in your examination of the security system, could you find the avenues through which intercom communication might have gone?"

Epstein nodded. "It's possible that an electronic log is kept of any communication that goes through that system, and that would be the most obvious place to look for this kind of text. I'll double back and check. But keep that commander guy off my back. I don't like the way he looks at me."

"He looks at everyone like that," Lapides said.

"If you start now, he'll be engrossed in the conference inside and won't even notice you're gone," I said. "Go."

The two of them went off on their respective tasks, and I gathered myself, checked on the presence of Ms. Washburn's cellular phone again, and walked into the conference room.

Ackerman looked up from his work, which appeared to be almost finished. Commander Johnson had broken away from the group and was at the other side of the room, pacing and looking displeased. Captain Harris, holding the yellow legal pad, was reading and nodding.

Arthur Masters was at the conference table, leaning over and talking to his mother, who appeared—for her—quite animated. She gestured with her left hand at her son.

"I'm not staying here another minute," she was insisting as I entered. "I've had enough talk about remains and craniums and ransoms. That was my daughter, and whether we get back what's left of her or not, she's dead. No matter what Dr. Ackerman thinks, she's going to stay dead forever. You run the business, Arthur. If you want to spend millions and get back nothing, be my guest. I'm old, and it's numbers on a ledger to me. I don't care, truly. But I'm not going to stay and watch it done; this place depresses me." With that, she struggled to her feet, grabbed her cane from the section of the table on which it had been resting, and began to hobble toward the conference room door.

"Mother, we've made the offer," Arthur pleaded. "We can't renege on it now."

"I'm not suggesting that you should," Laverne answered him. "Go ahead and give away our money. It honestly doesn't matter to me. But I'm tired and disgusted, and I'm going home. I'm perfectly capable of driving my own vehicle. I will see you later."

Arthur looked at Ackerman and Commander Johnson in a gesture of embarrassment and what I perceived as frustration. Once Laverne had made it through the conference room door, he said, "I can't let her try to navigate home in the dark; I'll follow her in my car, then go home to oversee the transfer of funds from my house.

Keep in close touch with me." Before either of the other men could protest, Arthur had left. I saw him through the glass wall, catching up to his mother and taking hold of her arm.

"What caused that change of heart?" I asked.

Ackerman shook his head. "I don't know," he said. "Maybe she's tired. Maybe she's annoyed. No matter what, they're planning on suing the institute, and I've already lost a million dollars tonight. What can I do for you, Mr. Hoenig?"

"How is your wife?" I asked.

He lowered his head a little. "I didn't thank you properly for that, did I?" he said. "I apologize. You might very well have saved her life. I owe you a great debt."

"That does not answer my question."

As he often did, Ackerman hesitated one second before replying to me. "She's doing well," he said. "A little shook up, but she'll be all right."

"We're on the clock," Commander Johnson interrupted. "There's no time for this. The thieves will be contacting us at any second with the final instructions. What are we going to tell them without Arthur and Laverne here?"

I wondered when the commander had reached a comfort level with the Masterses at which he could refer to them by their first names, but this was not the time to ask about that. "What is the current status?" I asked the commander.

"We are awaiting the final delivery instructions from the thieves," he answered. "They should be arriving via cell phone any moment."

I wondered about that, if Lapides and his officers were truly confiscating every cellular phone they found in the building. It was possible a hidden one would still be usable, or that they had not reached the right phone in time. But I kept my musings to myself and instead asked, "How are they going to comply with the demand to verify the remains before the ransom is paid?"

Captain Harris brought over the legal pad on which Ackerman had been writing when I'd looked in earlier. "We've made our demands to the disposable cell phone number we traced before," she said. "This is what we sent." She put the pad down on the table where I could read what Ackerman had written.

It read: *Visual confirmation of remains by GSCI staff; mutually agreeable location—B&N lot; meeting before banks open; A. Masters on hand to verify.*

"What does 'B&N lot' mean?" I asked.

"We proposed the parking lot of the Barnes and Noble store on Route One as the meeting point," the captain said. "We can control that environment, and if the meeting takes place early enough—which we're insisting on so they can't demand the money before we see the remains—there won't be anyone there at the time."

There were numerous tactical problems with the location, but the rest of the plan appeared sound. I felt that since the message had already been transmitted, there was no point in alerting the police to the flaws in their plan—the huge number of cars driving by at any hour that could cause difficulties; the other stores in the strip mall that might open much earlier, for example—and moved on to the next point.

"I wish you hadn't allowed Laverne and Arthur Masters to leave," I told the captain. "Do you not consider them suspects in the crimes you are investigating?"

"I don't see how they could have stolen the remains," Captain Harris said. "And they were definitely not in the building when that happened or when Dr. Springer was murdered. The security logs show they have never actually visited this building before Detective Lapides summoned them here today."

"I consider it unlikely they are involved," I said, "but it would be best to have all the suspects in one place."

Before the captain could answer, the conference room door swung open and Charlotte Selby entered, looking angry. "What's going on?" she demanded. "How come you sent that bozo Lapides to take away my cell phone?" She advanced on Captain Harris, who looked understandably confused.

I was more interested in the reactions the two other men in the room exhibited. Commander Johnson looked at Charlotte and narrowed his eyes. "Where'd you come from?" he snarled quietly.

Marshall Ackerman, however, did not seem annoyed or confused by Charlotte's sudden reappearance. I am not very expert when reading the facial expressions of people I do not know well, but even I was practiced enough to have no doubt about Ackerman's face.

He saw Charlotte, and he was terrified.

"What are you talking about?" Captain Harris asked. "I didn't send Lapides anywhere to do anything."

"The detective was responding to a suggestion I made," I said. Every eye in the room turned toward me. "I thought it was best to know where every cellular phone in the building was when the next message from the thieves was received."

"What?" the captain exclaimed. "Why?" Then she thought for a moment. "You think the perpetrators are in the building?"

"I see no reason to assume otherwise," I told her. Then I turned toward Charlotte. "Where have you been the past few hours, Ms. Selby?" I asked.

"Are you saying I'm a suspect?" Charlotte responded angrily.

"Until I know definitively who is guilty, I assume everyone involved is a suspect," I told her. "I imagine Captain Harris and Commander Johnson would agree."

Just then, Lapides appeared around the corner outside the conference room, carrying a small bag in which, I gathered, the collected cellular phones had been stored. He walked into the conference room with a satisfied look on his face. "Eighteen people in the building, eighteen phones," he said. Then he noticed Charlotte. "You'd be amazed how angry people get when you take away their cell phones," he said, looking directly at her.

I checked to make sure Ms. Washburn's phone was still in my pocket. It was.

Charlotte's face registered irritation. "Well, I didn't steal anything and I didn't kill anybody," she said. "Can I have my phone back now?"

I looked at Captain Harris, who said, "No. You can't."

"Why not?" Charlotte uncrossed her arms and put her left hand in the hip pocket of her jeans.

"Because we haven't heard back from the thieves yet," the captain explained. "Until then, no phones will be returned to their owners."

In motion pictures, events often occur in a fashion much more convenient to a screenwriter's desires than to a depiction of reality.

So it was with some astonishment that I noted the moment, just then, that Ackerman's cellular phone chirped. He looked at the phone and said, "Who?" But then he nodded. It was another text message.

The thieves were responding.

TWENTY-SIX

THE COMMUNICATION WAS BRIEF: It read simply, CONDITIONS AC-
CEPTED.

That left approximately three hours before the exchange would
take place in the bookstore parking lot. Captain Harris and Lapides
left to coordinate the police presence at the drop. I assumed their
plan was to survey the scene at which the remains would be presented for inspection and either follow the representative of the
thieves who appeared or attach some sort of GPS device on the person or his or her vehicle to better track the area where the thieves
were based. I hoped there was no intention of making an arrest at the
exchange point, because any chance of finding Dr. Springer's murderer and the thieves of Ms. Masters-Powell's remains would be lost.
But the officers were gone before I could ask any further questions.

I asked Ackerman if it would be possible to examine the scene of
Dr. Springer's murder one more time.

"I think you've done enough," he said, in a tone I think he meant to sound kind. "Let the police handle it. Get some rest."

"I do not need rest," I told him. "And I have been contracted to answer the question of Dr. Springer's murder. Is it possible?"

Ackerman's face suddenly looked angry. "I don't want any more people down there," he snapped. "I have to think about the rest of the guests we have in that chamber now. Any more tampering down there could mean the end of this institute, whether we get Rita's cranium back or not."

"I have disturbed nothing, and will disturb nothing," I persisted. "You have seen that my work is precise and my intentions are the same as your own. You have no reason to deny me a few minutes of access now, Mr. Ackerman." I realized immediately that Ms. Washburn would no doubt have informed me that addressing him as Dr. Ackerman would have probably have shown more respect, and be more likely to elicit a positive response.

Still, he managed through clenched teeth to say, "Ten minutes. You have ten minutes. If you're still there in ten minutes and one second, I'll have you forcibly removed. Is that clear?"

I did not answer his question, as I was already heading for the door. I did not want to waste any time. Then, it occurred to me that I had a question for Ackerman. I stopped abruptly and turned to face him.

"Is that ten minutes from now, or from the time I arrive at the chamber?" I asked.

"Just go," he croaked, and I decided to start counting at that moment.

The elevator trip to the chamber level seemed slower than before, but I knew it had to take the same amount of time as each trip I had taken previously. The time limit on my visit was preying on my mind, and I knew I needed to concentrate on what I saw in the chamber.

I raced down the corridor to the chamber and almost knocked over Epstein, who was heading back to the elevator to find me, he said. "I checked the voice communication units," he reported. "There is a way to trace the electronic signatures of any intercom or wireless communications that went on, but it'll take some time, at least eight hours."

I had only eight minutes and seventeen seconds before Ackerman was to have me ejected from the building. "Was Dr. Springer's computer confiscated from the office, and any laptop or home computers taken by the police?" I asked Epstein quickly.

He did not have to think about it, which was a relief. "Yes, and we should be getting a report on what they found on the hard drives soon. Probably right after nine o'clock."

"Too late," I said, continuing toward the chamber door. "They're making the exchange at eight."

I did not hear Epstein's reply because I was entering Preservation Room D's outer area, having been cleared by the security officer inside on orders from Ackerman.

Inside, the officer nodded at me, continued to watch the monitor on his console, and paid me no more attention. I was grateful for that, because there were only seven minutes and thirty-three seconds left for me to make my evaluation.

I had been in the chamber a number of times in the past nineteen hours, so a basic examination was not necessary. I was there to answer three questions to my own satisfaction, and time was short. I could not think about the people who had used the protective suit before me as I put it on once again and entered the inner chamber.

The security cameras, no doubt activated by perceived motion, were turning to follow me as I walked through the door and evaluated the room. The police had left pieces of wire indicating the trajectory of the bullet that had been fired in the room, and that was helpful. It indicated that the person holding the gun had been just inside the door, which told me that he or she knew the security cameras were taking the feed from another room so there was no need to try to find a less-visible firing point.

A bullet had clearly been lodged in the storage receptacle that had once held the remains of Rita Masters-Powell, but Dr. Springer was murdered after the remains had been stolen. Why would the shooter choose that receptacle to rupture, releasing the liquid nitrogen that would remove the oxygen from the room and suffocate Dr. Springer?

The trajectory did not show any other points of deflection, so the bullet was shot directly at the Masters-Powell receptacle.

Five minutes and four seconds left.

It was possible the answer to that question was not to be found in this chamber, so I moved on to the second. Why would Dr. Springer have entered the inner chamber without the protective clothing I was wearing, and why would she even consider handling the frozen receptacle without gloves, which must have been extremely painful and dangerous?

Of course, it was possible Dr. Springer had done so only because someone with a gun was forcing her to act against her will. But it would be necessary to explore any other options as well. The floor in the inner chamber was a smooth surface of rolled linoleum. That might have made it easier for Dr. Springer to lose her balance and fall if the floor had been wet. But the release of the liquid nitrogen, reducing the concentration of oxygen in the sealed and enclosed chamber, would have removed the oxygen from any liquid as well. I checked the floor for any sign of a suspicious powder that might have resulted from such an event, and found none.

Dr. Springer, then, probably fell to the floor as she asphyxiated, blacking out almost instantly. But if that were the case, why wouldn't the shooter have asphyxiated as well? And how did the shooter get out of the room before the oxygen content dropped enough to cause unconsciousness and death? Why was I still feeling the effects when I'd made my initial examination, long after the liquid nitrogen should have evaporated?

There were two possible answers to those questions, and neither one was very likely: Either the person who killed Dr. Springer had been pushed out through the chamber door by the release of the liquid nitrogen when the bullet penetrated the preservation receptacle, which would have let more oxygen into the chamber and prevented Dr. Springer from asphyxiating; or the shot was fired somehow from outside the chamber.

Three minutes and twenty-two seconds left.

The fact that the receptacle had been found behind Dr. Springer's body indicated that it had been torn from her hands when the bullet entered it. But the doctor's hands had shown no sign of the "burns" or frostbite that would occur if she had handled the extremely cold cylinder without protective gloves.

A theory began to germinate in my mind, but I thought it less than certain and very difficult to prove if true—at least until the complete medical examiner's report was released.

I had felt a very slight effect of the decreased oxygen level in the chamber when we had initially discovered Dr. Springer's body. Given the size of the room and the size of the receptacle that had been damaged, it was unusual that the effect would last that long. The chamber was sealed more completely than the average room would have been, but with an available access point—the door—could not be completely sealed. The liquid nitrogen should have dissipated much more quickly.

The most logical explanation for this phenomenon was one I could test quickly, and with only two minutes and seven seconds remaining, I would have to do just that. I walked briskly to the larger containment chambers, where entire bodies could be preserved in cryogenic freeze. There were fifteen available, but only six in use.

Above each preservation chamber was a monitor, which would echo the data the security officer and any personnel in the outer chamber could see on their computer screens. Among the statistics offered was the level of liquid nitrogen in each receptacle and its temperature.

I took note of each receptacle's nitrogen level, and noticed that the one farthest from the door had a much lower level than the rest. There was no specimen in the chamber, which raised the question of why an idle receptacle would be frozen. It was possible the chamber needed to have each receptacle at a certain temperature to maintain the proper level for those already in use.

But the last cylinder's level was 63 percent lower than the one nearest to its volume. And that was curious.

With only one minute and eighteen seconds left, I quickly left the chamber and removed the protective suit for what I hoped would be the last time. Then I walked to the security officer and looked at his computer screen, which showed the inner chamber, now empty.

"Can you view the data on each cylinder from here?" I asked.

"Sure," he said. "Which ones do you want to see?"

I indicated the left side of the room and said, "The six farthest from the door."

The security man punched his keyboard, and the statistics were revealed. "These?" he asked. I nodded.

I looked at the screen, and the six cylinder outputs were virtually identical. The last one, whose liquid nitrogen level had been less than half of the others, showed up as having almost a full tank.

The answer was starting to take shape. The murderer had left one tank slightly opened—not breached or broken, but not completely sealed—so liquid nitrogen had continued to leak very slowly after Dr. Springer had died. That would mean the murderer was trying to disguise the crime as something it was not. If I had time to get back into the chamber, I could confirm my suspicion and solve the theft and the murder.

But the chamber door flew open, and two strong-looking security officers rushed in. "That's it," one shouted, seemingly to me. "Dr. Ackerman says you have to leave."

"No," I protested. "Dr. Ackerman would want me to—"

Each of the officers who had just entered took one of my arms, and before I could protest further, my feet were lifted off the floor. They maneuvered me toward the door. "You're going to leave the building and not come back," the second security man said. "Dr. Ackerman's orders."

"You don't understand," I pleaded. "I'm so close."

We were already at the door, and no matter how hard I squirmed and struggled, I had no chance against these two. I had not used my martial arts knowledge in time, and it had cost me.

"You can't do this!" I shouted. "I still have twenty-two seconds!"

TWENTY-SEVEN

I was not allowed to plead my case to Ackerman or Commander Johnson, and both Captain Harris and Detective Lapides had already left. There was nothing to do but ask for a ride home, which a security officer named Davis—I never found out whether it was his first name or his last—provided in a GSCI car.

During the sixteen-minute ride, I did my best to explain to him why it was important that I be brought back to the facility, that I could save the Masters family millions of dollars and put Dr. Springer's murderer behind bars, but Davis never said a word as he drove. I was frustrated, but I admired his ability to focus on his driving.

He only nominally stopped the car when he dropped me off, and was driving again almost before the door closed securely behind me. I watched him drive off, then walked into the house through the back door.

The sun had risen now, and no doubt Mother would be awake and wondering about the remainder of my night. While I was extremely tired, I am unable to sleep in daylight, so I sought her out in the kitchen, but found her in the living room, listening to the morning news on National Public Radio.

When I walked in, Mother looked up, concern showing in her eyes, and turned off the radio. "I'm glad to see you," she said, walking over to embrace me, which I allowed. "You weren't in the house when I woke up. I was worried."

"There was no reason to be concerned," I said when she let go after what seemed like a long time but was actually only eight seconds. "I was never in any danger." That was technically true, although when I entered Ackerman's house after the intruder, I was unaware that there was no peril to be faced.

Mother said down in her armchair, her favorite place to hear stories and think. "Tell me what has happened," she said.

I opted against sitting down, concerned that my fatigue would escalate if I were seated. I told Mother of the events since I had been home last, which was only about eight hours earlier but felt strangely as if it had been days before. As I spoke, I had the opportunity to reconsider some of the facts as they had happened, and while some seemed contradictory, a pattern was, I believed, beginning to emerge.

Understanding what that pattern meant was going to be the challenging part.

"You lied when you said there was no danger," Mother said when I had finished.

"I did not lie. As it happened, I was never in any danger."

She shook her head slightly and smiled. "You have an interesting way of interpreting things, Samuel," she said.

"It's what makes me the man I am," I told her. It is a private joke of ours.

"It's a very baffling question," Mother went on. She stood and led me toward the kitchen. "How do you think you will answer it?"

"The only thing to do is to interpret the facts," I told her. When we got to the kitchen, Mother gestured toward a chair.

"Sit down," she said. "You haven't eaten in a long time."

"I'm not hungry."

"Sit down."

I sat down. Mother went to the refrigerator and came out with turkey bacon, milk, and margarine. She was, I realized, about to prepare some bacon and pancakes, a specialty of hers usually reserved for very special occasions or Sundays.

"Is there a reason we are commemorating the day?" I asked.

"You've worked hard and you need to work even harder," Mother answered. "That might not be special, but it's worth taking notice of." She began cooking, and I sat back to think about the questions at hand. "What is bothering you about this question?" she asked.

"There are too many seeming contradictions," I said after a moment. "The thieves, who appear to have at least had some knowledge of Dr. Springer's murder, have been very precise in their preparation. But their logic is questionable. When trying to extort money from the Masters family, they threatened the life of Eleanor Ackerman, who has no connection to the Masterses. They were adamant about not deviating from their original instructions, and appeared to have actually sent someone to harm Mrs. Ackerman, while at the same time they were capitulating on many of the points they had refused to even consider negotiable only hours before. It does not seem to make sense."

Mother turned from the stove for a moment, hesitated, and then said, "People don't always make sense when they act on emotion rather than reason, Samuel. Maybe the thieves are scared, or anxious."

"Because Detective Lapides is closing in on them?" I asked. "I hardly think so. But they do seem to be operating in something of a panic mode."

"Maybe the equipment they're using to keep the head preserved is starting to falter, and they don't think they can keep it going much longer," Mother suggested.

"I doubt that is the case at all," I said, although I did not say why, because I was not yet certain of my facts.

Mother used a spatula to place pancakes and bacon on a plate and brought it to the table for me. "Try not to think about the questions while you're eating," she said. "Taking a break is a good way to cleanse your brain. Concentrate on the Beatles or the Yankees for a while."

"It would be rude of me to ignore you while I eat," I said.

"Tell me about the *Rubber Soul* recording sessions," she suggested. "You know that one's my favorite." Mother has excellent taste in music.

I regaled her with my knowledge of that period in the band's history, about how George Harrison was first experimenting with sitar after having encountered one on the set of the motion picture *Help!* (which is widely underappreciated). I mentioned that Paul McCartney was trying to stay away from an electric guitar sound, hence songs such as "I'm Looking Through You" and "I've Just Seen a Face," and how John Lennon especially was finding more mature themes in his lyrics, with the most obvious example being "In My Life."

Twenty-two minutes had gone by since I'd started eating and talking, and I realized suddenly that I had actually stopped considering the questions of the theft and Dr. Springer's murder. And when those two topics reentered my conscious thoughts, I was much more certain of my theory than I had been before. But I needed physical evidence to prove my points. And most of my best research equipment was elsewhere.

"May I have the keys to the car?" I asked Mother. "I need to go to the office."

"Your office?" she asked. "At Questions Answered?"

"Yes. May I have the keys, please?"

Mother picked up the keys from the table next to the kitchen door and put them in her pocket. "No, you may not," she said. "You've been up for twenty-four hours and you haven't driven in months. I'll take you to your office."

"I don't know how long I'll be there, and I don't want to be without transportation if I need to go to the exchange at the bookstore," I reminded her.

She shook her head. "You're too tired to drive, and what do you know—I have nothing planned for today. I can stay as long as you like. Let's go." And she picked up a jacket from one of the kitchen chairs. She began to put it on.

There was no arguing with Mother when she became this determined. I decided to let her drop me off at the office and take a taxi later if I needed transportation elsewhere. We got into the car, and I was asleep in seconds. I hadn't expected that.

The trip to Questions Answered probably took about eleven minutes. I am not entirely sure, since I was asleep and did not check Ms. Washburn's cellular phone for the time when I awoke in the parking lot, although I did make sure it was still in my pocket.

"I was going to let you sleep," Mother said. "You need it."

"I don't," I countered. "I need facts, so I can reach answers, and then I will be able to sleep."

We walked to the storefront, and I unlocked and opened the front door to Questions Answered. "Thank you for the ride," I told Mother. "I'll call a taxi if I need to go elsewhere."

She stepped into the office in front of me. "Don't be silly," she said. "I'm not going anywhere if I can be of help." Sometimes, there really is no arguing with Mother.

It felt like weeks since I had been in my office, though it had been less than a full day. I turned on the lights and went, out of habit, directly to the computer to turn it on, then to the vending machine to buy a bottle of spring water. There weren't many bottles left; Les would probably be by to restock the machine in a day or two. I have learned to accept his erratic schedule, though it is not the way I would choose to run a business.

Before I could return to my desk to research the three questions I had, the office telephone rang. I checked the Caller ID, which indicated the caller was *Epstein, J.* I picked up the receiver.

"Mr. Epstein," I said. "Has anything of interest been found on Dr. Springer's hard drive?"

"As a matter of fact, there has," Epstein answered. "I thought you'd want to know. First of all, I've been banished from the institute by Ackerman himself. Something about breaching security, and without the captain or Lapides here, it's hard for me to assert my authority. I'm in the parking lot trying to decide if I should head back to the police station or try to get back inside."

That information was interesting but not relevant to my question. "The hard drive," I reminded Epstein.

"Yes. In the three days before she died, Rebecca Springer was exchanging e-mails pretty frequently with two people we've met—Arthur Masters and Charlotte Selby."

Now, *that* was interesting—I'd only been expecting one of those names. Out of the corner of my eye, I noticed Mother straightening up my bookshelf and taking a roll of paper towel out of a cabinet. "Charlotte Selby?" I asked. "Have you read the e-mails?"

"I've seen them, and they're pretty innocuous, about meeting one day or another, until the name 'Rita' comes up. Dr. Springer makes a statement about how things can't go on as they have been, and then suddenly Charlotte says not to discuss that in any traceable forum and stops the exchange."

I tried to process that information. Why would Dr. Springer be e-mailing to Charlotte Selby about Rita Masters-Powell? Why would Dr. Springer be communicating with Charlotte Selby at all? "What about the e-mails to Arthur Masters?" I asked.

"They were much less chatty," Epstein answered. "Arthur appeared to be helping the doc invest some money. They were discussing safe mutual funds and retirement accounts."

I sat down at my desk and looked at the computer screen. Left where I'd been looking when Marshall Ackerman had come in the day before was the project involving Yankee Stadium and the video clips Ms. Washburn had taken of me in front of the floor-to-ceiling window of Questions Answered, her camera facing toward the parking lot, me holding a baseball bat to demonstrate an uppercut swing.

Then I saw something in the background of that video that made me catch my breath. And all the contradictions that had presented themselves in answering these questions seemed to fall into place, and to no longer be contradictions.

Behind me in the video, as I swung the bat once, twice, three times, nothing moved. But on the fourth swing, there was movement outside the storefront that I had not noticed before, having focused on the quality of my swings to use in the presentation to my client, Mr. Teradino.

"Did you hear me?" Epstein asked. "Samuel?"

"Yes," I said. "Hold on for one moment, please." I slowed the speed of the video during the last two swings I took with the baseball bat, and this time watched the background instead of the image of myself. Mother had found a spray bottle of ammonia-based cleaner and was making herself busy on the windows.

Behind me (in the video), a car drove up in the parking lot and parked next to Ms. Washburn's car. I recognized the car now as Marshall Ackerman's. Since he had walked into the office only moments later, that was not surprising.

But Ms. Washburn and I had spent time loading the video onto my Mac Pro and were about to compare them when Ackerman walked through the door. Examination of the video indicated that he had clearly been in his car for some time before entering the office. What had he been doing?

"Samuel," Mother said, "why aren't you talking to whoever that is on the phone?"

"I am answering the questions," I told her. "I believe I will have an answer in a few minutes."

"Really?" Epstein asked through the phone. "What's going on?"

"Just a moment, please," I told both of them.

The gap in Ackerman's time could be explained when the video was examined closely, with an eye toward the background. After pulling into the parking space, Ackerman sat back, composed himself, and straightened his tie. Then he looked over into the passenger's seat and spoke.

There was a woman sitting next to him, and it was not his wife. I had to watch the video of the last two swings four more times before I could make a positive identification.

The woman seated next to him, blond and constantly talking, was Charlotte Selby. And if I could verify one last suspicion I had, I believed I could unravel the entire mystery and answer both questions for which I had been given responsibility.

Then, just before exiting the car, Ackerman leaned over and kissed Charlotte.

My excitement was palpable; I had never answered a question quite this momentous before. I took a deep breath and put the telephone receiver closer to my mouth. "Mr. Epstein," I said, "how much clearance have you been given in the police investigation of Dr. Springer's murder?"

"I have pretty much full clearance," he answered. "Why?"

"Have you seen a photograph of Rita Masters-Powell?" I asked him, having realized just moments before that I had no visual image of Ms. Masters-Powell to recall.

Epstein thought a moment. "You know, now that you bring it up, I don't think I have."

"Can you find one?" In the interim, I had searched Google Images, and had found nothing at all useful under "Rita Masters-Powell," "Rita Masters" (aside from some images of a woman at least twenty years older than the one in question), or "Rita Powell."

"I'll call you back," Epstein said.

"Quickly, please," I responded and placed the receiver back on the telephone base.

Mother had stopped cleaning, seeing my excitement, and walked over to the desk. "What's going on, Samuel?" she asked.

"Things are beginning to move fast," I told her. "What time is it?" I pulled Ms. Washburn's cellular phone out of my pocket to check the time.

At that moment, it rang.

Since no one would expect me to have Ms. Washburn's cellular phone, it was sensible to assume that the caller was hoping to speak to her. But the screen showed the call was coming from *Home*. It was possible Ms. Washburn was calling me from her home to get an updated report on the questions and our progress.

I moved to answer the call. "Should you?" Mother asked. I shrugged.

"Hello?" I said into the phone.

A man's voice, startled, responded, "Hello? Who is this?"

"This is Samuel Hoenig," I answered, since there was no denying it now. "Who is calling? Why aren't you Ms. Washburn?"

"Where's Janet?" the man asked in response.

"I will not answer until you identify yourself," I told him. "I am Ms. Washburn's employer. Who are you?"

"Her husband," the caller said with a definite edge of resentment in his voice. "Where is Janet?"

"She went home a few hours ago to rest," I said. "She had worked late into the night."

"No, she didn't," her husband said. "I just woke up, and she's not here."

At that moment, the e-mail program on my Mac Pro made the sound that indicated I had received an e-mail. I clicked on the program and saw the communication was from Jerome Epstein, who must have gotten my address from one of the business cards I had given the police.

"Perhaps she went out for something," I told Ms. Washburn's husband. "I'm sure there's no need for concern, Mr. Washburn."

"The name is Taylor," he corrected me, and I recalled that Ms. Washburn had told me that when we'd met. "And she hasn't been here at all. She left to go drive you someplace or another, and she never came back."

I opened Epstein's e-mail. He had typed in the message, *The picture you requested*. Beneath his words was a photograph of Rita Masters-Powell.

"Now, where is she?" Ms. Washburn's husband demanded.

But I was mesmerized by the image before me. The woman in the photograph, smiling gamely but without joy, if I was reading her expression correctly, was blond and brown-eyed. Her face was almost diamond-shaped, and her lips were thin and withdrawn. She was attractive, but not beautiful, because she looked like she could not be pleased by anything under any circumstances.

"I'm sorry?" I asked Mr. Taylor.

"Where. Is. My. Wife?" he reiterated.

And that was when it came together for me. But with the realization that I had solved the mystery and answered the questions came a very cold, hollow feeling in the pit of my stomach. "I will have to call you back when I'm sure," I said and heard Ms. Washburn's husband start to yell an obscenity at me before I disconnected the call.

Immediately, I found the number Epstein was calling from and called it. "Get back into the institute immediately," I told him. "Don't take no for an answer, and get some officers to help you. We have very little time to lose."

Mother leaned over my desk looking very concerned. "Samuel—" she began.

"I need the car, Mother," I told her. "I must go and save Ms. Washburn's life."

TWENTY-EIGHT

IN THE END, OF course, Mother refused to be left behind. The same arguments as before—my lack of sleep, her insistence on being helpful—were compounded by the lack of time and her deep concern, which I shared, for Ms. Washburn.

Luckily, Ms. Washburn's phone had also received a call from Lapides earlier in the post-midnight hours, and I used that call to redial the detective's cellular phone. I immediately explained the situation to him.

"I'll send some uniforms to the institute right away," Lapides assured me. "But I'm supposed to be leaving for the exchange in less than an hour."

"If we can save Ms. Washburn," I told him, "there isn't going to be an exchange. It's her head they're going to try to trade for the money."

Mother's attention, which had been riveted to the road in front of us, was caught by that remark, and she turned her head sharply toward me. I pointed to the windshield, and Mother turned back, but she looked positively mortified.

"What the hell do you mean, *her head*?" Lapides demanded. I have never understood the expression *what the hell*, since it refers to a mythological place with an article and does not actually seem to have an independent meaning, but I had no time to question it now. "Why wouldn't they just bring Rita Masters-Powell's head?"

"Because they never had it," I told him. "Don't you see? The reason that Dr. Springer was killed was that she was going to inform the authorities about the scam that Ackerman and Charlotte Selby were perpetrating on Laverne Masters."

"Scam? What scam?" Lapides sounded absolutely baffled.

"There is no time," I said. "Get to the institute as quickly as possible, and bring as many officers as you can arrange. Now!" I disconnected the phone and placed it gently back in my pocket. I fully intended to deliver it to its rightful owner as soon as possible.

"What's going on?" Mother asked as she stared ahead. "We're only a few minutes away. Tell me what you know."

"I am not able to explain everything yet," I said. "But suffice it to say that Marshall Ackerman and Charlotte Selby are behind the ransom demands, and I think at least one of them had a hand in the murder of Dr. Springer."

"But that doesn't seem to make sense." Mother shook her head slightly, trying to make sense of the situation. "Dr. Ackerman hired you to answer the question about what happened to the missing remains. Why would he do that if he were behind the theft himself?"

"He underestimated me," I told her. "He said he'd been recommended to me by Ellen Crenshaw. You remember Ms. Crenshaw, Mother. She was the one who had the missing Boa constrictor."

Mother nodded her head vigorously. "Oh, I remember."

"You'll also recall that Ms. Crenshaw was somewhat disappointed because I actually located the snake and did not tell her insurance company that it was irretrievably lost. She wanted to collect on her policy, not regain the animal. But she was pleased enough to recommend me, and probably told Ackerman the entire story, perhaps at a social occasion where alcohol was served. Ms. Crenshaw likes to talk."

Mother nodded. "I remember. So what makes you think that Ackerman is trying to do the same thing, but on a larger scale? Why would he try to extort money from the family of a client?"

"Because I believe that Ackerman is having an affair outside his marriage. I observed the way his wife greeted him after the traumatic evening she had experienced, and they were barely civil to each other," I told her. "Also, I have video of Ackerman kissing a woman who is clearly not his wife."

"Charlotte Selby," Mother guessed. Mother has a very perceptive and logical mind.

"Yes," I told her. "And that was what threw me off for a while. But once I started to piece things together, I realized that in all likelihood, Ackerman and the institute had never been in possession of Ms. Masters-Powell's remains. He and Charlotte were trying to extort Laverne Masters out of seventeen million dollars by selling her back nothing."

We drove in silence for twenty-one seconds, until the now-familiar Garden State Cryonics Institute facility came into view on our right. As

Mother steered the car into the driveway and then the parking lot, she asked, "How does that add up to Janet's life being in danger?"

"The thieves had been adamant about receiving the money before they produced the missing remains, which they claimed they had preserved properly somewhere close enough to the institute that it could be transported without difficulty," I explained. Mother turned off the engine and looked at me. "Then once the initial plan did not produce the payday they had anticipated, they suddenly agreed to show the cranium in question to the police and Arthur Masters."

"But if you're right, they never had the remains at all," Mother said.

"Precisely," I answered, getting out of the car. We had to get inside quickly, and Mother does not walk as fast as I do. I started for the entrance. "That's why they need a replacement head to show off in less than an hour," I called behind me as I started to run.

I looked back and saw Mother's hand go to her mouth.

There were five North Brunswick police vehicles in the parking lot, I noted as I rushed to the front entrance, and Lapides's car was also parked in back. The usual coterie of security personnel was missing from the reception area, leaving only a dazed-looking receptionist at the desk in front. As I ran past her, she called after me, "Welcome to Garden State Cryonics Institute," and I believe that as I made it to the elevator, she continued, "How may I help you?" Perhaps Mother would explain when she reached the area.

A quick look at the schematic of the building mounted near the elevator reminded me that the fourth level down contained what the literature issued by GSCI euphemistically called the "guest preparation area," where the bodies of those who had chosen to be preserved would be drained of blood and readied for the freezing process. Family members and other loved ones would not be allowed in the guest preparation area.

It was also the section where those who had opted for cranial preservation only would have their heads removed from their bodies.

Once Ackerman had seen to it that I was removed from the facility, he had somehow banished the police officers who had been left behind and insisted that Epstein be ejected from the building as well. Clearly, there was something about to happen that Ackerman didn't want anyone else to see.

I was hoping desperately that it had still not happened.

Two uniformed police officers were in the elevator when the doors opened, but I was already rushing toward the stairway, which was considerably faster. I heard one of the officers call out asking for my name, and I yelled back behind me, "Allow me to introduce myself; I am Samuel Hoenig." The officers did not follow me, so I assumed that was sufficient.

I raced down the stairs, not encountering another officer on the way, and reached for the door to the fourth level. But the knob would not turn; the door was locked. I had failed to consider that not every level would be unlocked with this kind of search going on throughout the building.

Now I was trapped. In all likelihood, the other access points from this stairway would be locked, as well. Ms. Washburn's cellular phone, still in my trouser pocket, was useless in the facility. But then I recalled that Ackerman had received a text message from inside the building. I was not sure if it would be successful, but I sent texts to

Epstein and Lapides reading LOCKED IN FOURTH LEVEL STAIRWAY. OPEN THE DOOR.

Then I waited, but not without trying to determine if I could remove the hinges from the locked door with the Swiss Army knife in my other trouser pocket. And I cursed myself for not thinking the plan through thoroughly enough before embarking upon it. My hands went to the sides of my head. I felt my teeth clench, and I began to bend slightly at the waist then straighten up. Those who study autism spectrum disorders call this sort of behavior *self-stimulating* or *stimming*. Neither word is attractive, nor accurate. In this case, I was reacting to my frustration with the locked door and with myself, acting out physically and emotionally rather than rationally. I was very displeased with my actions, and I was glad no one was there to see me behaving that way.

But then there was. Epstein appeared in the door's narrow window and for the moment before I could contain myself, seemed reluctant to open the door. But he did so anyway. "It's okay, Samuel," he said. "The cops have found the preparation area, and there's no one there."

I was still catching my breath. "Show it to me," I said, and Epstein waited until I was through the door and in the corridor before hurrying down the hall. "What is your favorite Beatles song?" I asked him as we ran.

He must have been prepared by Lapides, because he had an answer ready. "'Rain'," he said.

Contemplative. Introverted. Questioning.

"You're a good man," I told Epstein. He smiled.

We reached the door marked GUEST PREPARATION, and Epstein pushed it open. Inside were a uniformed officer, a GSCI employee in coveralls, and Detective Lapides. "You got here very quickly," I said to the detective.

"It sounded urgent. But we didn't find anyone here."

I tried to picture the schematic of the facility in my mind. "There is another preparation area," I recalled aloud. "But this is the one where someone—probably Ackerman—brought Ms. Washburn."

"You're sure?" Lapides asked. I nodded.

Epstein looked horrified. "Then we're too late?"

I put my hand on Epstein's shoulder, a gesture that does not come naturally to me, but one which I know is intended as a signal of comfort. "No, Mr. Epstein. We are not too late. At least, I don't believe we are. Nothing of a surgical nature happened here. But we must widen the search for Ms. Washburn throughout the facility. She escaped her intended killer but is probably still being pursued, if for no other reason than that she knows who tried to decapitate her. Has anyone located Charlotte Selby or Commander Johnson?"

"Commander Johnson is being held under guard on the second floor," the uniformed officer, whose nametag read LONBORG, told me.

"For goodness' sake why?" I asked. "The commander was not involved in the conspiracy."

"We don't know who was and who wasn't," Lapides insisted. "What's going on? How do you know Washburn was even here, let alone that she escaped from someone trying to cut off her head?"

"We are wasting time," I said. "I'll tell you as we go. Let's make sure the other preparation area is not being used."

I led Epstein and Lapides through the door, leaving the uniformed officer and the institute employee, who had been sleeping at his console the whole time we were in the room. "It's relatively simple, after all the confusion," I said. "Charlotte Selby and Marshall Ackerman were trying to blackmail Laverne Masters into giving them millions of dollars for her daughter's remains, but they never had anything to trade for the money. They thought they could get by with threats and disappear before anyone realized what had happened. But Laverne forced the issue by refusing to pay until she saw evidence that Rita's cranium was in fact in the possession of the thieves, and time was short. They decided to substitute a similar-looking specimen, and Ms. Washburn is of the same general physical appearance as Ms. Masters-Powell, based on the photograph you provided, Mr. Epstein. So removing her head and freezing it in time to bring to the exchange was essential."

"How can you possibly tell all that?" Lapides asked as we squeezed into the small elevator. Epstein pushed the button marked 2, and the doors closed very slowly.

"I saw Ackerman and Charlotte in Ackerman's car right before he came to Questions Answered to hire me," I told him. "They were kissing. Ackerman and Charlotte were having an affair and wanted money to get away from Eleanor Ackerman and, probably, the institute."

"You get all that from them kissing in a car?" Lapides asked.

"That, plus the fact that Ackerman was getting his 'instructions,' as you did, detective, from someone inside the institute facility. And while Commander Johnson, Mrs. Johnson, Laverne and Arthur Masters, and all of us were present at one time or another when a communication from the thieves was supposedly received, Charlotte Selby was never in the room."

"She was, though," Lapides pointed out. "After I confiscated the cell phones, Charlotte came into the conference room to complain about it. She was there when the thieves sent their message agreeing to the exchange."

"That is something that I believe will be explained when Mr. Epstein's data on the wireless communications in the building is revealed in a few hours," I said. "But I know how it was done. Charlotte had the unregistered phone, the prepaid one, with her in addition to her usual cellular phone. Just before she walked into the conference room to complain about not having her cellular phone, she composed a text message to Ackerman. I saw her put her hand in her jeans pocket, and immediately after, Ackerman's cellular phone chirped."

The elevator doors finally opened. Epstein pointed to the left and said, "That's where the other preparation area is located. There are two officers inside already."

I started in that direction, and the other two men followed. "I'll look," I said, "but I'm willing to bet that the room is untouched. They were planning on using the one we've already seen."

Epstein looked puzzled. "Because there was a tray of instruments set up next to the operating table?" he asked.

"Very good, yes," I told him. "Clearly, Ackerman or one of his staff doctors—but I think it was Ackerman himself, to avoid having to tell anyone else of his plans—was interrupted by Ms. Washburn's escape before he could do what he'd planned."

We reached the door and walked inside, Lapides first, then myself, then Epstein. There were two officers inside, seemingly without a single task to perform. One sat behind a console, and the other stood, arms folded, leaning against the far wall.

Their nametags read JENKINS and PANG.

The room itself was identical to the last, the only missing elements being the evidence of Ms. Washburn's courageous escape. There were two operating areas: two tables set up parallel to each other under very strong lighting that could be adjusted to allow the surgeon views of specific body areas. There were also two wheeled carts that held many of the instruments that would be used in such a situation, as well as various computer monitoring equipment.

"I don't understand why you're so sure that Washburn managed to escape, or that she was even here," Lapides said.

"She was not *here*," I corrected him. "She was brought to the other preparation room and put on one of the operating tables. The stainless-steel surface of the table was unblemished except for three hairs at one end, the same length and color as Ms. Washburn's and, incidentally, very similar to that of Ms. Masters-Powell."

"So she was there," Lapides continued. "But an escape?"

"I would assume that Ms. Washburn was brought in unconscious, probably after having been transported in the rear seat or trunk of Ackerman's car," I explained. "But while Ackerman and whomever he had coerced into helping him—if anyone—prepared for the gruesome task ahead, Ms. Washburn must have regained her consciousness."

I pointed to the operating table. "Since every other patient ever brought into this room had no capacity to move, and since the surgery being done here was never going to be painful or cause a reaction, there has been no need for restraints on the operating tables before. They were not attached, see? But the one in the other room had improvised restraints, made of cloth from hospital linens or something of the sort, at each point where an arm or ankle might have been situated. They didn't expect Ms. Washburn to wake up, but there was no sense in taking chances."

"The hairs prove she was there," Epstein said. "The restraints prove they intended to ... do her harm. What proves her escape?"

"You didn't see the restraint on the right side of the table, at the patient's left arm?" I asked. Epstein shook his head; Lapides simply looked baffled. "The linen shackles were there to keep Ms. Washburn in place if necessary, but they weren't as firm or restrictive as normal Velcro or steel ones would be. So if she were able to conceal her consciousness from her captors, it would not be terribly difficult for Ms. Washburn to reach over to the wheeled cart next to the table and find one of the very sharp scalpels left there. One was clearly missing from the tray, and the restraint in question was sliced through. She must have untied the others herself."

Lapides and Epstein looked impressed; the two officers did not take much notice. Their job was to secure the room, and we were not perceived as a threat.

"There is nothing to see here," I said. "We need to find Ms. Washburn immediately. Gentlemen, separate. Detective, are your officers' communication links operating?"

He shook his head. "No. We've been checking in at regular intervals to the command center in the upstairs conference room," he told me. "Captain Harris should be there by now. Arthur Masters and his mother are there, and they're asking why we're not heading for the exchange. If we don't find something soon, we'll have to leave in about fifteen minutes."

"Then there's no time to spare," I said. "I'll go to the right. Epstein, you go to the left. I will meet you back here. Detective, perhaps one level up would be a good choice for you. But first, I think you should head back to the command center and try to get the captain to authorize the deactivation of the institute's security system so we can better communicate inside the building. Lives are at stake."

Lapides nodded. Epstein and I stepped out of the elevator, and the doors closed again. I nodded in his direction, and he acknowledged the gesture. In a motion picture, we would have both had firearms, but neither of us had anything in our hands at all. I am a second-degree black belt in tae kwon do; I had no knowledge of Epstein's defensive skills. I sincerely hoped that neither of us would have to test ourselves in that area.

My plan, improvised as it was, involved checking the doors in the corridor, each of which had a window that would allow for at least a partial view of the interior if the door was locked. It wasn't a very complex plan, but it would accomplish the necessary function successfully.

Time was clearly a pressing issue, but I could not rush through the task. Each door had to be opened slowly on the assumption that a hostile person might be inside the room, either hidden from view or behind the door, ready to take action. So my examination of the first three rooms, all of whose doors were unlocked, took seven minutes and eight seconds.

The next door was marked STORAGE, which meant it opened into a closet. The door was locked, which was only slightly odd; many facilities will lock their storage closets to prevent theft, and medical facilities almost always do, especially when the storage units house drugs or medical equipment that can be valuable. So I was prepared to walk by the closet and move on.

But then I saw there was a strip of light on the carpet in the corridor where I stood, coming from inside the room marked STORAGE.

There were numerous scenarios to explain this circumstance. The most likely one was that the last GSCI employee to use the closet had merely left the light on when he or she left and locked the door upon exiting. Another, more ominous, explanation was that one of the thieves or the murderer was behind the door, hiding from the police search of the facility. But such a person would be extremely foolish to leave the light burning and give him or herself away.

The third possibility was the one I hoped for, perhaps relying more on emotion than strong data. Quietly, but not so quietly that I would not be audible inside the closet, I said, "Ms. Washburn?"

For a very long moment, there was no response. It seemed like a very long moment, anyway. I did not count the seconds.

Then the doorknob turned, the door flew open into the hallway, and Ms. Washburn tumbled out, her arms spread. She embraced me, which made me especially aware of my arms and wonder what

I should be doing with them. They hung at my sides as Ms. Washburn held on.

"Samuel," she said. "I'm so glad it's you."

TWENTY-NINE

WE HAD VERY LITTLE time, but Ms. Washburn needed a moment to realize she was now safe. I put my hands on her upper arms and increased the pressure a bit, to let her know I was there and reassure her, and we stood that way for eleven seconds.

"Are you all right?" I asked her.

"Physically," she said. "I'm not so sure otherwise."

"You've been very brave," I told her. "Much braver than I would have been under the circumstances. How did you manage to get all four restraints cut before Ackerman saw you were free?"

I felt her arms tighten a bit at the memory, then Ms. Washburn ended the embrace and took a step back. She wiped a tear from her left eye. "I cut the left hand one first," she explained. "That was the closest. He still didn't know I had the scalpel at that point. So I could move the blade toward the right hand while he was preparing his computer program. Why he wanted a record of"—she shuddered—"what he was going to do is beyond me."

"He is a creature of habit, and that is the protocol," I explained. "It's a mindset I understand well."

"I untied the right wrist, which was faster than cutting it, but my luck ran out once my hands were free," she continued. "Ackerman turned his attention to me. I could just lie there pretending I was still unconscious and under restraint. When he reached for my hand to put in an IV, which I figure would have had something to put me all the way out, I sat up and put the scalpel to his throat. I made him release the two restraints on my ankles."

It was a staggering image; Ms. Washburn must have been terrified, and Ackerman frustrated beyond his capacity. "How did you get away from him?" I asked. "Surely he was right behind you when you left the room."

Ms. Washburn nodded; she seemed to have difficulty finding the words to speak. "I hit the door and ran," she said. "I could heard his footsteps behind me, and I knew he could probably run faster than I can. But for some reason, when he opened the door to the operating room, he must have turned right, thinking I was heading for the elevator. I turned left, just because it was a straight line out of the room, and I wanted to be away from there as soon as I … as soon as I …"

I did not look to see if she was weeping. "Come," I said, gesturing toward the elevator. "We have to meet Mr. Epstein and get out of here with you." I began walking in the direction I had come, and after a few strides, had a very alarming moment when I realized Ms. Washburn was not by my side. I turned back to see where she was.

She seemed rooted to the spot. She was looking at me but did not move. I could only assume the terror she had experienced was returning now that she no longer had to rely on her own courage to survive.

I looked at her a moment. Going back would only reinforce her resolve to stay where she was. I needed, I realized, to get her moving toward me. So I reached into my pocket and pulled out her cellular phone.

"I didn't lose it," I said. "I brought it to give back to you."

Ms. Washburn smiled then and ran to where I was standing. She took the phone from my hand, exhaled strongly, and nodded at me. "Thank you," she said. "I knew you wouldn't lose it." We walked to the elevator in stride.

Epstein was turning the corner just as we reached the elevator. "She wasn't ..." he began, then saw Ms. Washburn at my side. "Ms. Washburn, I presume," he said.

"Don't you start that stuff," she scolded him. "I'll let Samuel get away with it, but you call me Janet." This appeared to be some gesture of an amicable nature, because Epstein smiled when she said it and held out his hand, which Ms. Washburn took.

"Nice to meet you, Janet," he said.

I insisted we head directly to the command center on the uppermost level, and when we arrived there, we found Captain Harris, the Masterses, and Commander Johnson there. Arthur Masters seemed especially surprised to see Ms. Washburn with us, and positively grinned upon our entrance. He stood, but we walked past him and Ms. Washburn did not make eye contact with Arthur.

The captain immediately asked Epstein to go back to the security center and disconnect the circuitry jamming communications systems inside the facility. Epstein dropped his eyebrows in a determined expression and left the conference room.

"Are we sure Ackerman and Charlotte Selby are still on the premises?" I asked.

"We are sure about Ackerman, because there was visual confirmation of him in the building when our team arrived," the captain answered. "Once we surrounded the building, he couldn't have left without our seeing him. But Selby hasn't been spotted since we arrived, and we can't confirm her whereabouts at all."

I suggested that Ms. Washburn be given a police escort to her home, but she refused it, saying she was safer in the presence of the captain and the officers here than she would be outside the building. "After all, I was taken from in front of my own house earlier this morning," she said, "and I woke up on an operating table about to get my head cut off. I'd prefer not to risk that happening again. I'll wait until everyone is in custody, thanks." I felt it inappropriate to explain that since her head was no longer of any value to Ackerman, she was probably in no further danger, so I kept that observation to myself.

"Dr. Ackerman was acting alone?" Commander Johnson asked. He looked absolutely drained; he was sitting for the first time since I'd met him, and when not speaking, his eyes were fixed but not focused. He seemed confused or distraught; it was not possible for me to discern which.

"He was the only one I saw," Ms. Washburn answered, and the commander's head dropped down again. "I was walking from my car to my house, and Ackerman showed up on the sidewalk. He called my name, and I figured there must be some emergency, and he'd gotten my address off one of my business cards. I walked toward him. Then I felt a stab in my hip, and the next thing I knew, I was ..." She left the sentence unfinished.

"Ackerman was the only one Ms. Washburn saw, but he was not acting alone," I told the group. "He'd been receiving texts and phone calls from the supposed thieves, and we saw the messages. In addition, Ackerman came with us to the first planned exchange at Rutgers Village. Then he went directly to his home when we called with the news of the attack on his wife. But at that time, the video cameras you left behind, Captain Harris, taped someone picking up the cases Ackerman had left there. It could not have been Ackerman, since he was being driven to his home by one of your officers. So it's only logical to conclude that at least one other person was working with him."

Captain Harris nodded, then touched her shoulder-mounted communication link. She listened for a moment and turned toward me. "Mr. Epstein has managed to get us communications among the officers and inside the building," she reported. "He says that cell phone calls into and out of the institute will be possible in just a few minutes."

"That will be helpful," I said. "But we need to be prepared for the thieves to communicate with each other as well, if they are not together at the moment."

"It would help if we knew who besides Ackerman was involved," Captain Harris said. "You say Charlotte Selby was a conspirator, but your evidence is a little shaky. Do you think there were others?"

"Clearly, there were," I answered, trying very hard not to look at anyone else in the room. "Charlotte could not have been picking up the suitcases and attacking Mrs. Ackerman at the same time. There has to be at least one other person."

"Any ideas?"

"I prefer to keep my opinions to myself until there are verifiable data to back them up," I told her.

"It was Arthur Masters," Ms. Washburn said.

There was a stunned silence as everyone's attention turned toward Ms. Washburn. She walked from behind me, where she had been standing, toward Arthur, holding his gaze as she went.

"What?" Laverne Masters shouted. "That's absurd. What are you talking about?"

"You were left behind when we went to Rutgers Village," Ms. Washburn said to Arthur. She seemed to have removed everyone else in the room from her vision and was focusing only on him. "You were the only one who could have slipped out and gone to pick up the money. Commander Johnson would have been too conspicuous. Ackerman was with us. The person who picked up the suitcases was a man, so it wasn't Charlotte Selby and it wasn't Mrs. Johnson. You were the only one left."

Commander Johnson seemed like he gave some thought to protesting the implication that his wife could have possibly been involved, but he stayed silent.

Arthur stood slowly, with a very strange smile on his face. "That's ridiculous," he said. "I had no reason to be involved with this. I just want to end this crazy obsession with Rita's remains. Why would I try to extort money from myself?"

"None of the money in the suitcases was yours," I reminded him. "And when the agreement was made to pay the rest of the ransom, it was going to come from the company's funds, which are controlled by your mother. IDA is still a privately held company, so there was no board of directors to consult or stockholders whose money could not be used for that purpose; it was legal. That would have been one way to get access to millions you couldn't touch otherwise." I turned toward Ms. Washburn. "Excellent deduction," I told her.

Captain Harris's eyes narrowed. "It does fit the facts," she said.

I turned to Commander Johnson. "Commander," I said, "when you were here during the exchange of the briefcases at Rutgers Village, where was Mr. Masters?"

The commander seemed distracted, but he stood up as ever at attention to answer the question. "He said he was exhausted and went to one of the breakrooms where the standby medical staff have a cot to catch some sleep," he said.

"So he wasn't in your sight when the briefcases were recovered," I said.

"No, sir."

All eyes turned toward Arthur.

Laverne had taken a long amount of time to stand, but she was now on her feet and hobbling toward her son. "I won't listen to another word of this," she insisted. "Arthur. Tell them what that woman is saying is crazy."

"But before you do, consider this," I interrupted. "You and your mother drove here separately when you were called after the ransom demand was received. I noticed when Ms. Washburn and I drove up shortly afterward that your car was immaculate. But the area where the suitcases were left was all grass and dirt, and was quite wet. Would you like to go out into the parking lot and see how much mud is on your tires and the underside of your car, Arthur?"

Arthur looked his mother in the face and held her gaze. But he said nothing. He maintained the same eerie grin.

Ms. Washburn backed up and stood at my side. As she did, Captain Harris's cellular phone chirped. She reached into her pocket for it, read the screen, and showed it to me. SELBY IN CUSTODY. ON THE WAY UP. The text had come from Lapides.

"I gather Mr. Epstein has restored cellular communications in the building," I told Captain Harris.

She nodded toward the two uniformed officers at the back of the room. "Mr. Masters," she said. "You are being held for questioning in the extortion of seventeen million dollars from Laverne Masters and in the murder of Dr. Rebecca Springer. You are not being arrested, but we will have to insist you come to police headquarters to answer questions."

Laverne's mouth dropped open. "Arthur!" she implored him. "Tell these people how wrong they are!" She turned toward Captain Harris as the two officers flanked Arthur. They did not reach for handcuffs, but I saw the one whose nametag read CRAWFORD put his hand on his baton.

"I'll cooperate, captain," Arthur said. "But I will insist on having my attorney present before I discuss these matters. I will tell you now, however, that I had absolutely nothing to do with the murder. I haven't seen Dr. Springer in twenty years, since she was called Becky and used to hang around with my sister."

Laverne sat down hard on the nearest chair. "I'm shocked," she said. "Just shocked."

"Not nearly as shocked as you will be, Mother," her son said, a light chuckle in his voice.

THIRTY

CHARLOTTE SELBY WAS LED into the conference room, and while she was not visibly resisting the two officers who held her arms, she clearly was not cooperating with their efforts, either. They were exerting themselves.

Lapides walked behind them, looking pleased with himself. He carried an evidence bag whose contents were concealed in one hand. "We found her in the boiler room, of all places," he announced. Charlotte, her face mostly obscured by the hooded sweatshirt she was wearing, seemed to growl at him, and Lapides started just a bit before adding, "She hasn't said a word yet, but I've read her her rights. And she was carrying a prepaid cell phone."

"Good work, detective," Captain Harris told him.

I noticed Arthur Masters was looking especially amused at Charlotte's entrance, even as he himself was being flanked by two of North Brunswick's uniformed officers. He sat back down in his chair, crossed his legs, and laced his fingers behind his head. Laverne continued to stare at him, no doubt trying to convince herself that what she was seeing and hearing was simply a gigantic mistake, most likely on the part of the police.

"*Charlotte*," Arthur said. "How lovely to see you. *If* we could see you."

"Ms. Selby," Captain Harris said, "you've been advised of your rights. Do you understand them?" Charlotte did not respond except to drop her head a little lower, making her face that much more difficult to see.

I did not understand the family dynamic among the Masterses, but I found myself growing impatient with their coy gamesmanship. "Very well then, Ms. Masters-Powell," I said to Charlotte. "It is good to finally make your acquaintance."

Captain Harris and Lapides stared at me. Ms. Washburn gasped at my side. Laverne Masters turned her attention away from her son and looked at me, then at the woman wearing the hood over her face.

Arthur Masters looked, if I was reading his expression correctly, disappointed.

The woman in the hood let out a long sigh, then straightened her neck and shook the hood off her head, since the officers holding her arms and the handcuffs behind her back would not allow her to pull it off manually. She stared not at me, but at her mother.

Laverne Masters looked as astonished as I have ever seen a person look, and it was no wonder. She barely managed to breathe out, "Rita."

Captain Harris's mouth opened and closed twice, then she looked at me and said, "I don't understand."

"It's—" I stopped. I had been about to say *It's simple*, but the situation was anything but that. "It is Rita Masters-Powell we're seeing in this room," I told her. "There never was a Charlotte Selby before Rita 'died.' She simply took on a new identity for the purpose of getting some of her family's great wealth."

"They owed me," Rita hissed. "All those years married to Bill, living in squalor, and they wouldn't send a dime."

Laverne flailed her hands, looking a bit like I do when I find myself especially frustrated; she appeared to be stimming. "All this because we wouldn't send you money?" she asked. "You were the daughter of a very wealthy man, and you threw your life away with a busboy. We kept expecting you would come to your senses. And then you told Arthur you were getting a divorce."

"That was just about the time the story became interesting," I said. "Rita met Marshall Ackerman—was it through your high school friend Rebecca Springer?"

Rita nodded. "I ran into her at the mall, of all places," she said. "And she told me about this amazing place where she was working, even though she didn't think it was as wonderful as she'd been told in the beginning. And she introduced me to Marshall."

"That was the turning point," I told Captain Harris. "When Rita met Ackerman, she was in a marriage that she had long since given up on. Her mother was right—Bill Powell was a bore and possibly an alcoholic, but Rita was too proud to admit it. She found Ackerman the opposite of her husband. Why, Rita?"

Rita Masters-Powell laughed. "Are you serious? Marshall is everything Bill could never be. He's working to make people immortal.

Can you imagine that? To actually conquer death? Bill's working just to buy himself another bottle of bourbon."

"So they fell in love," Ms. Washburn said in a tone that indicated she was speaking mostly to herself.

"Exactly," I agreed. "And that gave Rita the impetus to divorce her husband. She came to her brother for financial help, didn't she, Arthur? And for some reason I do not understand, you turned her down."

"There was no *upside* for him," Rita sneered.

"Oh, it's not that simple," Arthur Masters told me. "Rita wanted money not just for her, but for this institute Ackerman was trying to run. Money for all the people-sicles downstairs in those freezer units. She tried to get me to invest the company's money in it, but I knew there was no benefit. Who believes that you can cut off their head and then wait until they develop the ability to put it on a robot body or something and live forever? It's ridiculous."

"It's *not* ridiculous!" Rita shouted, but no one answered her.

"But you offered Rita a second proposition, one that would make money for both of you and for Ackerman," I said, trying to continue the narrative.

I saw both Captain Harris and Lapides moving their heads from speaker to speaker as the drama played out, as if they were watching a tennis match. Commander Johnson, however, was absorbed in his BlackBerry.

That was unusual.

I was left with several options, but I was not sure whether it was better to call the commander out publicly or to surreptitiously discern what communication was being done while the rest of us attended to the Masters family and its strange situation. I saw Ms. Washburn was looking in my direction, so I initiated eye contact. She noticed immediately, and I signaled with my eyes toward the commander.

Ms. Washburn nodded, understanding my concern, and began to move very slowly toward his spot at the end of the table.

"I don't think it's appropriate for me to answer that," Arthur said.

"No, you're right, that's what he said," Rita piped up from across the room. "He said there was no sense just *giving* me money when he could make some of his own at the same time. He said it wasn't *sound business practice.*"

"How was it supposed to work?" I asked Rita. I already knew the answer to that question, but it was important to have her say so aloud in the presence of the police officers.

"See, I was divorcing Bill. That was so he'd have no claim on any money coming my way, and so that once I changed my name, I could marry Marshall." There were no legal records that Rita had ever changed her name; I'd checked that possibility while at Questions Answered earlier that morning. "Then I told my mother that I was dying, and my old 'friend' Rebecca Springer signed a death certificate in exchange for thirty thousand dollars, or roughly what my mother paid to have me 'preserved,' before the monthly maintenance charges began," Rita explained.

"For the first few months, it was simple—Arthur agreed to pay the institute the monthly rent on my head, and we split it fifty/fifty."

Ms. Washburn was moving slowly so as not to attract the attention of Commander Johnson, but she was almost within sight range of his BlackBerry screen now, and would be able to read it in a few seconds.

"What happened that changed the plan?" I asked.

Arthur looked away, suddenly finding the wall to his left extremely interesting.

"My brother changed," Rita said with a definite angry edge to her voice. "He got greedy. Decided the monthly rent wasn't enough."

"That wasn't all of it," Arthur said without looking at his sister.

Now it was Rita who severed eye contact with everyone else in the room. "There was one other thing," she said, more quietly than before. "Marshall needed some money because his wife wasn't going to be reasonable about a divorce."

"In other words, she wanted her fair share of his assets," Arthur replied. The grin came back to his face as he said it. "And that was going to be a pretty substantial sum, so he required a large infusion of cash."

Ms. Washburn was now looking over Commander Johnson's shoulder, but not leaning too far over, so the commander didn't notice.

"So that initiated the ransom plan. Whose idea was that?" I asked.

There was no time to answer, because Ms. Washburn gasped at what she saw on Commander Johnson's BlackBerry, and I turned to face them. The commander, alerted to the eyes over his shoulder, started noticeably and then put down the device, but it appeared to be too late for him to conceal what he'd been doing.

"What is it?" I asked Ms. Washburn.

"He's in touch with Marshall Ackerman," she replied, indicating the commander. "Ackerman's somewhere in the building, and the commander is trying to convince him to surrender."

"What?" Captain Harris was already rushing toward Commander Johnson. "Hand that over," she said, pointing to his BlackBerry.

The commander stood up, again at attention, and handed her the device. "I make no apologies," he said. "I am a loyal employee of Garden State Cryonics Institute."

"Where is Ackerman?" Lapides asked him.

"I'm not sure," Commander Johnson insisted. It was my opinion that no one in the room believed what he was saying.

"Let's get Ackerman to tell us where he is," I said. "Would you hand the BlackBerry to Ms. Washburn, captain?"

She did so, and Ms. Washburn activated the device. A text message appeared immediately from Ackerman: IS SOMETHING WRONG? WHY DON'T YOU ANSWER?

I decided to play the role of Commander Johnson in a reply. I requested Ms. Washburn to text, HAD TO PUT DOWN BLACKBERRY SO THEY WOULDN'T SEE. I CAN COME TO HELP YOU OUT OF THE BUILDING. WHERE ARE YOU?

Ms. Washburn sent the message as the commander protested, "That's a secure message! It's privileged information!"

"At ease, commander," Lapides said, putting a hand on the commander's shoulder. The commander sat down, looking angry.

It took only a moment for a reply to come from Ackerman: TOO DANGEROUS. THEY COULD FOLLOW YOU. JUST GET THE SECURITY SYSTEM OFFLINE, AS INSTRUCTED.

"You were going to turn off the security system so he could escape?" I asked.

"No," Ms. Washburn said before the commander could reply. "I read the texts. He was trying to get Ackerman to surrender to him, so he could get the credit for it. But Ackerman keeps trying to get him to help with an escape attempt."

She showed the message to Captain Harris, and then, as I suggested, typed in the reply, THEY ARE NOT WATCHING ME. MR. EPSTEIN BLOCKING SYSTEM TAMPERING. TELL ME WHERE YOU ARE. As I sent it, I heard a chirp from Ms. Washburn's cellular phone and saw her reach for it in her pocket.

A reply came almost instantaneously from Ackerman, and it did not speak well of my deception skills. WHO IS THIS? it asked.

"He knows it's not the commander," I told Captain Harris. "I'm afraid I lost our chance to find him."

"Not necessarily," Ms. Washburn said. "I just got a text on my phone from Jerry."

"Jerry?" Captain Harris asked. "Who's Jerry?"

"Mr. Epstein," I informed her. She continued to look puzzled. "The technical expert Detective Lapides requested."

Captain Harris nodded in recognition.

"He says he can see Ackerman from where he is," Ms. Washburn said. "He's on the lowest level of the building, right near the storage chamber where Dr. Springer died." Her cellular phone chirped again, and she read the text as Captain Harris spoke into her communications link, no doubt sending officers toward Ackerman's position. Ms. Washburn paled.

"There's a complication," she said. "Ackerman has taken a hostage."

I noticed Rita Masters-Powell smiling at the thought of her lover being so clever.

"A hostage!" I shouted, unintentionally. I had not anticipated that move on Ackerman's part. "One of the uniformed officers?" Ackerman taking a man with a gun would present a very serious difficulty indeed.

Ms. Washburn looked at me with very wide eyes. "No, Samuel. Dr. Ackerman has taken your mother."

I was running out of the conference room one second later.

THIRTY-ONE

Ms. Washburn was not far behind me, and Epstein, on his cellular phone, was giving us very specific instructions to the area in which Ackerman was holding my mother. I cannot recall whether I was breathing as we ran toward the stairwell.

"Tell Epstein to be ready to open the door to the stairs," I told Ms. Washburn as I ran. "The elevator is just too slow."

"He's already heading that way," she answered a moment later. Ms. Washburn was breathing heavily. I realized I was running very fast, but I could not wait for anyone. I wasn't even sure if Captain Harris or Lapides had followed us. I assumed they had, and that they had alerted any uniformed officers left in the building to converge on the area in question, just outside the storage chamber's outer door.

Epstein let us through the stairwell door only eighteen seconds later, Ms. Washburn puffing behind me. I heard another sound that

I could not immediately identify, which turned out to be my own breathing. I hadn't realized I was taking in so much air so rapidly.

"He's down there," Epstein said, pointing toward the corridor's bend. "There are already a couple of cops holding guns on him, but he's calling for you, Samuel."

On cue, I heard Ackerman shout, "Is that you, Hoenig? I've got your mother. Come out and see us."

I started in the direction of the voice, but Epstein grabbed my left arm to stop me. "Before you do, Samuel, you should know: He's got a scalpel to her throat."

Ms. Washburn caught her breath.

There was no advantage to running now. I had to banish from my head the idea that Mother could be killed, and that I would have had at least a small role in the events that would lead to her death. I had to focus more closely and specifically than I ever had before. I would walk around the corner and see the image that Epstein had prepared for me to see.

That was the plan.

But I felt my hands start to flap at my sides and my head begin to quiver. I made sounds that were involuntary and must have seemed more animal than human. My eyes rolled upward, and I saw only marginally what was in front of me. I dropped to my knees. My teeth clenched. My hands went to the sides of my head and pressed. I started to bend rhythmically at the waist, head tilted forward. I was completely incapacitated.

And then I saw Ms. Washburn lean over me and hold my face in her hands, the way teachers and doctors would do when I was learning about social skills and proper classroom behavior. She gently forced my gaze toward hers and she said, "Your mother needs you now. No one else. Just you. And you can do this. Show Ackerman that you are the better man."

There was something about her voice, just the sound of it, that reached the rational part of my brain. I stopped shaking and listened.

"Breathe," Ms. Washburn said.

I took in a breath. I let it out.

"That's good," Ms. Washburn said. "Keep doing that."

"You have to come to where I can see you," Ackerman called from around the corner. "You can stop me from killing your mother, but you have to be in my line of sight."

Anger started to overcome fear in my mind. But anger would not be any more useful. Anger also leads to quivering and incapacitation, what the teachers in my middle school used to call a *meltdown*.

"Use your brain," Ms. Washburn said. "That's your best weapon."

I stood up, remembering to breathe. I took Ms. Washburn's hands, and she looked surprised. "I'm sorry," I said. Her hands were remarkably soft.

"It's okay," she told me. "Any rational person would be upset under these circumstances. Now, let's go."

I held her hands for one more second. "Thank you," I said.

"Not yet."

I stood straight and walked, a bit stiffly, toward the corner. I tried to picture the worst thing I could see, so that what I did see would not be as bad. But I couldn't imagine something worse than this.

Ackerman was backed up, literally, against the door to the storage chamber. There were two police officers in uniform holding their weapons up, trained on Ackerman. But they could not get a clear shot because Ackerman was using something as a shield.

Mother.

And her first words when she saw me were, "I'm sorry, Samuel."

"You have nothing to be sorry for," I told her, trying to eliminate any quiver from my voice. "You've done nothing wrong."

"I was trying to help. I couldn't just wait in the car. I was looking for exits they could have used. And when I came inside, he found me. It's my fault."

Ackerman, looking quite frightened himself, stopped our conversation. "You can help her," he told me. "You can get your mother back completely unharmed."

"What is it I have to do to accomplish that?" I asked. "Your plan is uncovered. Your accomplices are in custody. We know that you killed Dr. Springer."

"Oh, no," Ackerman said. "That wasn't me. I had no beef against Rebecca. It was Rita who wanted her out of the way. 'No witnesses,' she said. She injected Rebecca with succinylcholine. We keep it there in case a patient is still alive and needs to be on a breathing apparatus. It temporarily paralyzes the muscles and makes it impossible to breathe, so the machine can do it for you. But without the machine, it looked like Rebecca had suffocated. Then Rita fired a gun into the storage chamber that was supposed to have held her head."

"That made it clear to everyone who looked that the receptacle was empty," I said. "Was it also Rita who tried to kill your wife, Dr. Ackerman?"

Once again, I knew the answer to the question: Rita Masters-Powell, seeing that the money was not coming to herself and Ackerman, had decided to eliminate the competition for Ackerman and blame it on the mythical thieves of her own fictitious bodily remains. Ackerman acknowledged that plan and added, "That's when I knew she was really crazy."

"*That's* when you knew?" Mother asked.

I was inching toward Ackerman, attempting to get close enough to engage him physically, or at least wrench Mother away. But he saw what I was doing and tightened his hold. Mother gasped a little, and her eyes widened.

"I'm not kidding, Hoenig," Ackerman said. "You have one chance to save her life, and that's to escort me out of this building and into my car, and to get the police to guarantee they won't track me. I need an hour; that's all. Now, that's reasonable, isn't it?"

"He's bluffing, Samuel," Mother said. "I dealt with tougher cookies than him in the sixties."

"Don't help, Mother," I said.

"Make your choice," Ackerman said. "I'm not going to stand like this forever."

"The police won't agree to it," I said. "I have no special influence with them. They'll send a hostage negotiator, who will promise you many accommodations until you let my mother go, and then they will shoot you. If you kill my mother, they will shoot you. Your only option is to surrender and hope that the state of New Jersey does not reinstitute the death penalty during your prison sentence, which I assume will be for life without parole."

Ackerman used his free hand to swipe the key card through the reader next to the door. I did not understand why getting into the next room and cornering himself more than he already had would advance his cause.

"This may not be helping, Samuel," Ms. Washburn hissed from behind me.

"You're wrong," Ackerman answered. "The cops think you're some kind of genius. You should have heard them all day: 'Samuel Hoenig figured it out; Samuel Hoenig would have made a great detective. Why did you fire Samuel Hoenig? Bring back Samuel Hoenig.' Blah, blah, blah."

So this was what ranting was like. It was my first time hearing it in a real-life situation. Of course he had fired me from the case; he was not the least bit interested in my discovering the truth, and I had exceeded his expectations. I had to go. The only reason he had called Questions Answered back after the ransom note was probably because Lapides and Laverne Masters had insisted on it.

"Voice recognition," the system's voice requested.

"Marshall Ackerman."

"I am unable to help," I assured him. "Let my mother go, and you will not be shot. That I can promise. Otherwise, you have very little hope."

"Say good-bye to your mother, Hoenig," Ackerman said. I saw his hand move.

I took no time at all to interpret that statement, and launched myself at Ackerman. But the hand I'd seen moving was not the right hand, which was holding the scalpel to Mother's neck, but the left, and it moved behind him.

301

His hand landed on the door handle. He pushed the door open with his back leg, and he and Mother stumbled into the storage chamber. I was only two seconds behind them.

Once inside, I saw the first stroke of good luck Mother had experienced so far in this ordeal—Ackerman had fallen backward into the room and skidded on the smooth floor in the chamber. He had instinctively thrown out his arms to cushion his fall, and in doing so, released Mother. Ackerman landed on the floor next to the nearest computer console. There was no one else in the room.

I took steps to ensure that would remain the case. While I would have welcomed the assistance of the police, I was concerned that any aggressive action against Ackerman at this point would send his fragile mental state into a much more dangerous stage. Even as I saw Captain Harris and Detective Lapides rushing the chamber door, I locked it from the inside and then turned to move on Ackerman.

It was too late to take physical action against him, however. Ackerman had regained his balance and stood in front of me. Mother, exhibiting her intelligence, had rolled away from him the second she was released, and now sat on the floor near the inner chamber door behind a front console, hidden from Ackerman's view. She was breathing heavily, and I worried about her heart.

From the corridor, I heard the police and Ms. Washburn call to me to unlock the door.

Ackerman still wielded the scalpel defensively, swiping it through the air and appearing to enjoy the sound it made.

"You really are trapped now, Ackerman," I said. "You've cornered yourself. You have no choice but to surrender now. You can kill me and still not be able to escape." I purposely did not mention Mother, as I was especially interested in having Ackerman forget she was in the room.

He did not appear to hear me, or at least did not process what I had said. "This isn't my fault, Hoenig," he said. "I didn't want to hurt anybody. I just wanted the money."

One thing that can be learned from motion pictures is that police negotiators and psychologists always try to establish a rapport with the subject. Fortunately for the ones in motion pictures, they are fictional and have writers inventing their dialogue. Also, very few of them have Asperger's Syndrome (perhaps this is the moment to point out that Adrian Monk of the television series *Monk* had Obsessive-Compulsive Disorder, not an autism spectrum condition), which brings a certain difficulty in creating an instant connection with a person one does not know well.

I searched my memory of social skills training for clues on how to make people want to like you. Agreeing with them on an issue is one way to do so, but I had always been taught that doing so when you really disagree is dishonest and will not be received well in the long term.

Right now, I did not have to worry about the long term.

"Of course you didn't want to hurt anyone," I said, resisting the urge to call him Marshall, which I thought would have been too obvious an indicator that I was not sincere. "Your plan was to get the money from Laverne Masters and her company. Then you'd leave your wife and go off to live with Rita." If I could inch toward him, perhaps I could kick his legs out from under him and subdue him once the scalpel was out of his hand.

But something I had said clearly was not what Ackerman wanted to hear. "No, no!" he shouted. "That's not what I wanted at all! Rita thought I was going to run off with her, but she's *crazy*. You know she tried to kill Eleanor?"

He was very confused at this point, and the only thing I could do was try to get him under control. Logic would not convince him to surrender to the police, who were still calling to me from the corridor. I saw Mother sitting near the inner door, and she seemed to be texting on her cellular phone, which I would have thought was strange if I had been focusing on anything but Ackerman.

"She came in to my *bedroom* and tried to shoot my *wife*," Ackerman went on. "We never planned a message threatening Eleanor; she was supposed to send a text threatening Laverne. But Rita saw the money wasn't coming right then, and she figured she'd just kill my *wife*! Can you imagine?"

I was very close to Ackerman now, but not so close he could use the scalpel on me. "Let's sit down and talk about it," I said. "I don't know about you, but my legs are very tired." Perhaps if I sat, he would take the example and follow me without thinking about it.

So I sat down at the nearest computer console, but Ackerman did not duplicate my move. He did, however, set the scalpel down on the console, and within one second, I reached out and took it in my hand. I exhaled. The danger had passed.

Unfortunately, I was in error. Ackerman had divested himself of the sharp blade in favor of the more offensive weapon he pulled from the pocket of his white lab coat, with *Dr. Marshall Ackerman* stitched on the left breast over the GSCI symbol.

A gun.

"She left this for me," he said. "Rita shot the receptacle marked for her own head, then shot at my wife with this gun, and then she left it in my desk. She wanted the police to think *I* had killed Rebecca. And all the time she said she loved me!"

It is possible that no one else would have asked the question at that point, but I felt obligated to do so: "Why did you use the scalpel when you had a gun?"

"I was going to put the gun back in Rita's bag when she was supposed to be Charlotte Selby," he said. "I didn't want to touch it and leave my fingerprints on the weapon. But she left me no choice. Just let me load it. And then I'm going to use it."

Mother looked up from her cellular phone, alarmed. I confess that I was not very confident at that moment, either. People say their minds "race" in such situations. I am not sure what that might mean, but I do know it was difficult for me to think usefully just then. Ackerman began loading the gun with bullets from his jacket pocket. I lunged for them, but he slapped the revolver closed and pointed it at me.

"As I said, killing me will not help your chances of escape," I reminded Ackerman.

He continued to point the gun but was not making eye contact with me. In retrospect, I am no longer sure he knew who was in the room with him.

"The first three bullets should start the process," he said.

The process? Clearly, Ackerman was not talking about shooting me. I began to reconsider my decision to lock the chamber door, and started to walk toward it, seeing Lapides and Captain Harris, but not Ms. Washburn, through the window.

Ackerman shouted at me, "Don't unlock that! Opening the door will spoil the effect!"

Since he seemed to have no objection to explaining his plans, I decided to ask directly. "What effect?" I said. "What is it you intend to do?"

Ackerman looked at me as if I must surely be a complete fool. Clearly, his intentions were obvious: "I'm going to shoot the big tanks." He gestured with the gun toward the inner chamber.

That was a terrifying thought. If he ruptured enough of the larger stores of liquid nitrogen, the oxygen in the inner and outer chambers would be depleted to the point that anyone inside—and possibly some of those in the corridor, although that was unlikely—would asphyxiate.

"But you'll die, too," I said.

Ackerman ignored me and walked to the inner chamber door. I looked toward the floor, but Mother was no longer there.

Then I saw some movement near the ceiling of the room. One of the tiles in the dropped ceiling, no doubt put in for cosmetic purposes when the room was being insulated for its special usage, began to slide back on its own.

"I think with three bullets, I can put holes in at least five tanks," Ackerman said, now seeming to talk to himself more than to me. "If I have time to reload, I could take out another five. That should be plenty."

An arm, which appeared to be in a blue police uniform, appeared through the opening created by the moved ceiling tile. The hand was holding a police baton. It let go, and the baton dropped to the floor, but I did not hear it hit the tile, which did not seem to make sense. I understood the gesture—Mother had been texting with someone in the corridor, who had sent a uniformed officer through air vents to the ceiling. The baton had been dropped because another gun would simply multiply the danger of a tank being punctured.

Now if I could only make it to the dropped baton before Ackerman noticed it, or started shooting.

"If you're going to commit suicide, just shoot yourself," I suggested to Ackerman. "Why kill innocent people with you and destroy all your work?"

Ackerman began to laugh. "Innocent people?" he asked. "Who is innocent here?"

I did not want to mention Mother, since she was no longer in sight. I hoped she was crawling around the room to unlock the door, but I did not see her in that area of the outer chamber.

"I believe that I am innocent," I said.

"You are irrelevant," Ackerman said. "Just stand back and enjoy the show." And he reached for the handle to open the inner chamber door.

That was my chance. I lunged forward and reached into Ackerman's right jacket pocket. He turned at the movement, but did not point the gun. He seemed to be taken completely by surprise, as if he had forgotten I was behind him. I got what I wanted out of his pocket—his key ring—and stood back as he leveled the gun at me.

"My keys?" Ackerman laughed. "Couldn't you see the gun in my hand?"

"I missed my mark," I lied to him. Taking the weapon from him would have been far too risky. I backed up a few steps, shying from the weapon in his hand. "I was trying to grab the gun and slipped."

"I told you," Ackerman said, misunderstanding my retreat, "I'm not going to shoot *you*." And he turned toward the inner chamber door again.

I dove in the other direction and got to the nearest security console quickly. Knowing exactly what I was doing, and exactly what it would mean, I took the security key from Ackerman's ring and plunged it into the alarm slot.

I turned it before he could open the door.

The hellish alarm, with its impossibly loud siren, flashing red lights, and overwhelming sense of danger, began immediately. I had done my best to cover my ears as soon as I turned the key, but the sound was much too powerful to block out with only my hands. I fell to my knees, which was probably fortunate, given that the gun went off when Ackerman turned to see what had happened, and I heard the bullet pass over my head as I fell.

Also, the door to the inner chamber locked automatically, as did all the doors in the section.

I couldn't hear Ackerman, but I saw his mouth form a common vulgarity. He started to reach into his pocket for his wallet, which no doubt held his key card, but it was inside the lab coat, which he had to unbutton. Ackerman appeared to be speaking directly to me, but I was unable to make out the words. I did my best to think of the action taking place in front of me, and not the nightmare scenario I had brought upon myself, but I knew I was once again bending at the waist with fear, and my hands occasionally came off my ears to flap at my sides, beyond my control.

In the midst of it, I was somehow aware of breaking glass behind me, and I saw Detective Lapides and Ms. Washburn rushing into the room. But I could not see Mother, and I was especially concerned when Ackerman shrugged, turned to the inner chamber, and broke the window glass with several blows from the butt of his gun. Then he aimed the revolver into the chamber, apparently intending to carry out his plan.

I might have been able to reach him in time, but I found myself incapable of movement. Lapides and one uniformed officer aimed pistols at Ackerman.

With my hands still on my ears, just seconds from screaming and falling to the floor in the fetal position, I shouted, "Don't shoot at him! If you hit the tanks, we could all die!"

Ackerman laughed and took aim, saying something I could not make out. But from behind him, on a section of the floor I could not have seen from my previous position, Mother rose to her feet holding the police baton that had been dropped from the ceiling. And without hesitation, she pounded Ackerman hard on the head, stunning him, and then on the hand, making him drop the gun. The uniformed officer dove for the revolver and grabbed it before Ackerman could react. Lapides held Ackerman's arms and quickly restrained him with handcuffs.

Behind me, Commander Johnson's boots, which I recognized, appeared at the security console. He must have reset the system and turned the key, because the siren stopped.

I heard myself breathing. I did not hear myself whimpering, which was an improvement. And standing over me, suddenly, was Ms. Washburn, holding out her hands to help me to my feet. Slowly, after composing myself, I stood.

Ackerman was being led away, sobbing. His head was not bleeding, but his hand was discolored and swollen.

Mother's face, with an expression I had never seen before, was intent on Ackerman as he was taken slowly from the room.

"That's what you get when you threaten my son," she said.

THIRTY-TWO

"THERE'S A LOT TO sort out," Detective Glendon Lapides said.

We were standing in the parking lot of Garden State Cryonics Institute, watching as Marshall Ackerman, Rita Masters-Powell, and Arthur Masters were helped, in handcuffs, into the back seats of three separate North Brunswick police vehicles. There would be a considerable amount of debriefing to be done at the police department's headquarters later in the day, but for now, Captain Harris had decided that Ms. Washburn, Mother, and I should be allowed to go home and rest. I doubted that would be possible in my case, but it was certainly going to be worth a try.

"What is it you don't understand, detective?" I asked. "You know that Ms. Masters-Powell killed Dr. Springer with an injection before making it look like a release of liquid nitrogen into an enclosed space had caused her to suffocate. She also tried to shoot Eleanor Ackerman, and probably would have continued to try if she had not heard the police or Ms. Washburn and myself outside. Arthur Masters was

311

behind the financial end of the ransom demands, and there was never a frozen cranium to hold hostage, so Marshall Ackerman planned to use Ms. Washburn's as a substitute. Arthur would 'verify' that the head's was Rita's. It's all rather simple in the final analysis."

Mother, standing to my right, shook her head and laughed. "Simple," she said.

Ms. Washburn, off a short distance with her hand to one ear, was speaking into her cellular phone. "I'm perfectly fine," she said with an edge in her voice. "I texted you that more than an hour ago. Don't worry. I'll be home soon." Her husband was no doubt urging her to leave as quickly as possible, and in all likelihood would encourage her to turn down any offer of further employment at Questions Answered. I would have to find a way to counter that strategy, as I had found Ms. Washburn indispensable while answering the most difficult questions ever asked of me.

"I don't get how you knew all that stuff," Lapides said. "How did you figure it all out? I never had a clue."

"Yes, you did," I told him. "The clues were everywhere. Mrs. Johnson inadvertently provided one when she set off the alarm during our 'demonstration.' She made sure the alarm system activated when we were in the chamber together, so I did not see that the receptacle supposedly set aside for Ms. Masters-Powell's cranium had never been frozen at all."

"How would you have seen that?" Mother asked. She is always interested in hearing about my process.

"We found out that only three of the fifteen receptacles in that room were actually frozen," Lapides said. "All the ones working were in the same section as the one that was supposed to have Rita's, and

312

they had really frozen that receptacle, too, just to make it look good. The others were displays, just to keep potential customers believing that the institute was a healthy, going concern."

"In addition, we had the video security footage of Dr. Springer doing a routine check on the supposed Masters-Powell receptacle *after* the theft had been reported," I explained. "She was doing what she always did because she had *always* known there was no cranium in the receptacle. She hadn't been told about the 'theft' yet."

Lapides shook his head. "A lot of the frozen receptacles were empty," he said. "What a waste."

"It is very likely that GSCI is on the verge of bankruptcy," I added. "But there was a great deal more physical evidence in the chamber that 'Charlotte' did not want me to examine. First, when we discovered Dr. Springer's body, she was not wearing a protective suit, as she would have under any normal circumstances. So it is reasonable to assume that she was forced into the chamber against her will, without the time it would have taken to put on the protective clothing."

Ms. Washburn ended her cellular phone conversation and joined us as the three police vehicles, with Captain Harris in the first, drove out of the parking lot and onto US Highway 1, heading south.

"Also," I continued, "the receptacle, supposedly kept under extremely cold temperatures in liquid nitrogen freeze, was on the floor behind her, and Dr. Springer was not wearing protective gloves or any other kind of covering on her hands. But they were not burned or scarred in any way. Either she had not handled the receptacle, which was unlikely since her fingerprints were found on it, or the more logical solution, the receptacle had been taken out of its frozen state long before. Because the conspirators knew they were going to stage the theft and wanted the receptacle at room temperature so they could position it properly after the 'shooting.' And the only reason that would happen was that there had never been any remains inside the receptacle, and no reason to keep it preserved at a low temperature."

"How does that lead to Charlotte being Rita?" Lapides wanted to know. "That was the thing that made the least sense."

"That was a complete stroke of luck," I told him. "Ms. Washburn had taken a short video of me in my office yesterday morning, as part of a question unrelated to this affair entirely. When I looked at it early this morning, I saw that Ackerman, about to come in and hire Questions Answered—supposedly to find the missing 'guest,' but really to cover for the fact that he wasn't calling the police—had driven up directly behind me and was visible in the video."

"He was?" Ms. Washburn asked. "I don't recall seeing him."

"You were focused on your subject, and you knew the background would be digitally eliminated for our project," I reminded her. With the suspects now removed, we began to walk back to Mother's car, so she could drive Ms. Washburn home and then continue on to our home. "When I noticed his car in the background, it was clear there was a woman in the passenger seat next to him. It was the woman we knew as Charlotte Selby. Once Epstein e-mailed me the photograph of Rita Masters-Powell, I compared the two, and the face in the video was the same as the one in the photograph. Only her hair color had changed from blond to brunette, probably as a rudimentary means of disguise."

"Or she ran out of hair dye," Ms. Washburn suggested drily.

"You knew that Arthur Masters was behind the extortion plot," Lapides said to Ms. Washburn. "How did you figure that?"

Ms. Washburn looked at the ground and said quietly, "I didn't like the way he looked at me."

"What?" Lapides asked.

"She said that Arthur had been adamant about paying the ransom while his mother resisted at all costs," I said. "The fact that 'Charlotte' always chose to leave the room when Laverne Masters was there, but not when Arthur was alone, was telling. As a 'citizen journalist,' Charlotte should have resisted being removed from the action, but when Laverne was coming, she volunteered to leave. That indicated that Rita did not want her mother to see she was still alive, but Arthur knew the truth."

Lapides blinked three times and stopped chewing gum for a moment. "She said all that?" he asked, indicated Ms. Washburn.

"Yes."

The detective looked impressed. Mother smiled at me knowingly, but I could not discern what that expression was meant to convey.

We stood there for twenty-three seconds, during which I ran the details of the question through my mind, to see if there was anything I had missed. The others seemed to be doing something similar, each lost in thought and not saying anything.

"How did you know it was Ackerman?" Lapides finally asked. "I suspected something was up with him, but he always seemed so pained when anything would threaten the institute. How did you know he was behind the scheme?"

I did not make eye contact. I know I should have, but the fact is that I was embarrassed. "I did not know about Ackerman until very late," I admitted. "Until he had me ejected from the building, just as I was beginning to piece the answers together, I had no suspicion. But even then, I thought I was reacting emotionally to being fired, that I was angry because he would not acknowledge that I was competent at my profession. I suspected something was amiss with him later, because of one moment.

"When we were supposedly dropping the ransom at Rutgers Village, Ackerman stopped at one point and took out his cellular phone. I initially thought he was merely checking the time in the dark, but I came to realize he was sending a text message to an ally, probably Rita, alerting her about the snipers Captain Harris had stationed nearby. Immediately, the captain received a text warning her about the snipers, and they were withdrawn."

"I thought they were watching us," Lapides said, "but Ackerman was one of them." He shook his head again.

"Actually, the video footage of Ackerman kissing Rita Masters-Powell was the evidence that made me realize just how deeply he was involved," I said with some embarrassment. "I should have seen it sooner, and perhaps I could have avoided a good deal of ... unpleasantness." I looked at Ms. Washburn, who shook her head slowly.

"It wasn't your fault, Samuel," she said. "Ackerman was unpredictable because he gave in to all the pressure. You couldn't possibly have known what he would do, or that it would involve me."

Her cellular phone rang again, and she opened it to answer the call when she saw the word *Home* on the screen. Clearly shaken, she walked a distance away and spoke in a tone that could not be heard from where we were standing.

"When it was clear that Laverne was not going to pay the money without considerable coaxing," I went on, "the message came—from Rita as it turned out—that Mrs. Ackerman's life would be in danger. Ackerman came out of the building as we were leaving to go to the exchange at Rutgers Village, and he was loudly, and rather animatedly, trying to find out where Charlotte Selby might be at that moment. He knew how unstable Rita was and truly worried for the fate of his wife."

"But he didn't do anything about it," Mother pointed out. "He didn't go to his wife, and he didn't tell the police to look out for Charlotte at his home. If he was so concerned…"

"Ackerman was torn," I said. "He wanted to believe he loved his wife, but he was having an affair with Rita. And when you sent a cruiser to his house, detective, I'm sure he thought his wife's safety was secured."

Lapides shook his head. "The whole business is beyond me. I'm glad you were here, Mr. Hoenig. Thank you for all your help."

"I was pleased to do so, detective," I told him. Perhaps the North Brunswick police might think to employ Questions Answered again sometime in the future, although I would prefer it involve a much less violent question.

Ms. Washburn scowled as she closed her phone sharply and walked back to Mother's car. "Can you please take me home, Vivian? My husband is being… let's just say I need to go home and discuss a few things."

"Of course, dear," Mother replied and unlocked the car with her radio frequency key fob. I nodded a good-bye to Detective Lapides and opened the passenger door. But Mother shook her head to indicate that I should let Ms. Washburn take my traditional seat. I did not understand the gesture but felt it was best to ask about it later, and did as Mother had suggested.

As I turned to open the rear door, I saw the entrance to GSCI open, and out walked Commander Johnson, flanked by two uniformed officers. Lapides had said the commander would be brought in for questioning in connection to his trying to help Ackerman escape. It was not clear if charges would be brought against him, but the police certainly wanted to find out how much the commander had known about the conspiracy, and if it was enough, perhaps a plea bargain could be arranged.

I stopped when I saw the commander, and he spotted me from the parked police cruiser in which he would ride to his questioning. Our eyes met for a moment. I was not sure if I should do or say anything. From this distance, conversation was surely impossible.

But the commander communicated in another way. He straightened up, as I'd seen him do many times in the past twenty-four hours, and then, in perfect military fashion, he presented me with a very well executed salute.

I knew from many motion pictures what I should do: I returned the salute, and the commander dropped his arm. Then each of us sat in the back seat of an automobile, and rode away.

THIRTY-THREE

I DID NOT SEE Ms. Washburn again for three days, and then it was only to help complete the Yankee Stadium answer and, she was very clear, to conclude our business together.

Mother, who had taken to coming into the office for part of each day "just to get out of the house" (but probably to make sure that I was not taking on any further dangerous questions), was quietly knitting in the rear of the storefront, near where the pizzeria kitchen once operated. She had greeted Ms. Washburn with an enthusiastic embrace when she had arrived, and smiled more as she knitted than I had seen her smile in quite some time.

"Here, we can extend this swing by just a frame or two, and the follow-through will appear to generate more power than it did before," Ms. Washburn pointed out. "That will make the idea of a home run into the stands more natural-looking. I can put Mark Teixiera's face over yours if you like."

"I am not sure that would look natural," I told her. "I do not have an athlete's physique."

I enjoyed working with her again. After the marathon ordeal at Garden State Cryonics Institute, I had missed having Ms. Washburn explain where I might have misunderstood a facial expression or misinterpreted a turn of phrase that I found unusual or illogical. I had become dependent on her very quickly, which was strange, and had found her absence oddly disturbing.

We completed the work in less time than I probably would have liked, and after I paid Ms. Washburn for her work, we started to discuss the GSCI question and its aftermath. I told Ms. Washburn that Lapides had called after we both had been thoroughly questioned by the police, to indicate that the prosecutor would bring homicide charges against Rita Masters-Powell alone, but extortion charges against Rita, Marshall Ackerman, and Arthur Masters. Rita and Ackerman would also face attempted homicide charges for their actions against Mrs. Ackerman, Ms. Washburn, Mother, and me.

The prosecutor had, as I expected, failed to charge Commander Alvin Johnson with any crime, but "had given it a lot of thought," Lapides reported, sounding disappointed. Instead, the commander and his wife had agreed to testify against Ackerman, Masters, and Masters-Powell.

He also said the medical examiner, now alerted to check for succinylcholine in Dr. Springer's system, had found the drug that had caused her to asphyxiate, and the injection site on her right hip as well.

Miles Monroe had finally called Lapides from his vacation in Australia. He confirmed that he had been discharged from GSCI without a sufficient explanation, and that there had never been any insinuations of maltreatment by the staff of any of the institute's guests. "I was wondering what that was all about," Lapides said he had remarked. "Now I know why I got the golden parachute."

"The whole thing seems like it was a long time ago," Ms. Washburn said as I handed her a bottle of green tea from the vending machine. I was drinking from a bottle of spring water. "It's almost like it happened to someone else, and I just heard about it or watched a report about it on TV."

"It happened," I assured her. "And you played no small part in it. Without you, I doubt the questions would have been answered completely."

Ms. Washburn raised an eyebrow in a gentle warning. "Don't butter me up, Samuel," she said. That raised a disturbing image in my mind, but I did not comment. "I promised my husband that I wouldn't come back to work here because it's too dangerous. And even though our marriage isn't necessarily in the best place right now, I'm going to stick to my promise."

"I would not want to cause any undue stress in your marriage or otherwise," I told her honestly. "I am merely trying to thank you for helping out so ably in the work you've already done."

She frowned, and that did not make sense to me. "That's it?" she asked. "You're not going to try to convince me?"

Mother's eyes looked up, but she did not stop her work.

"I do not understand," I told her. "I was under the impression you did not want me to try to convince you to stay."

"Samuel," she said, shaking her head, "you have a great deal to learn about women."

"You can say that again," Mother chimed in. She had warned me once again before Ms. Washburn had arrived that she was a married woman, to which I had replied that the reminder was unnecessary.

"None of this makes any sense," I said, my mind receiving more information than I could process at once. "So you *do* want me to talk you into working here again? Because I would very much like you to come back."

Ms. Washburn let out a long, slow laugh and sat back in her chair. "Oh, I don't know," she said. "I really will have to decide. I do want to work here, Samuel, but I don't want to complicate my marriage any further. Give me a few days to think about it."

"You may have as long as you like," I said. "The invitation remains open."

She nodded and took a sip of the green tea. "If I do come back—and remember I said *if*—you're going to have to get some diet soda in that machine," she said. "But Samuel, there's one thing I wanted to ask you."

That triggered something in the back of my mind, but I stayed on topic, keeping Ms. Washburn's conversational desire in mind. I nodded.

"What's *your* favorite Beatles song?" she asked.

I did not hesitate. "'Strawberry Fields Forever,'" I said. "Although it is one of many."

"Why that one?"

"Because no one else is in my tree." At her blank expression, I quoted the exact lines to her.

Ms. Washburn smiled. "I think there might be more people in your tree than you realize," she said quietly.

We sat for a while and drank our beverages. The silence was quite comfortable. But then, I returned to the point I'd just recalled. Ms. Washburn had not said anything for thirteen seconds, so I could assume a new topic would be acceptable.

"There is something about which I have been remiss," I said. "Ms. Washburn, when you came here that first morning, you had a question you wanted answered, and I never considered it. What was it that brought you here that day?"

Ms. Washburn blushed and waved a hand. "It's not important," she said. "It was just something silly that morning."

"Please," I urged her. "I would feel I had cheated you."

She moved her head from one side to another, looking around as if trying to find a spot to focus upon so she would not have to face Mother or me. "It was just … I was doing the *Times* crossword puzzle, and I got stuck on a clue."

I smiled. "And you wanted me to answer it for you. But you can look those up on the Internet, or call a number the *Times* prints next to the puzzle every day. Why didn't you do those things?"

Ms. Washburn still did not look at me. "That would be cheating," she said.

I decided not to point out that asking me was just as dishonest. "Very well. What was the clue?"

It took three minutes of persuasion, but Ms. Washburn was finally convinced that this would settle the business between us to everyone's satisfaction. "Fine," she said with a resigned tone. "It was an eleven-letter word, and the clue was, 'Those which prevail.'"

"Did you have any of the cross letters?" Mother asked.

"Yes. They were—"

"No need," I said, standing. I must have been smiling very broadly, because both Mother and Ms. Washburn grinned at me with identical looks of expectation.

"What?" they said at virtually the same moment.

"The answer. To 'those which prevail.' It's very apropos." I believe I might have chuckled.

"What is it?" Ms. Washburn demanded.

"COOLER HEADS," I said.

THE END

ABOUT THE AUTHOR

E. J. Copperman is the author of the Haunted Guesthouse series (Berkley Prime Crime) with more than 100,000 copies sold. Jeff Cohen has published two nonfiction books on Asperger's Syndrome, including *The Asperger Parent*.